TORN

A BILLIONAIRE ROMANCE SERIES

MICHELLE LOVE

HOT AND STEAMY ROMANCE

CONTENTS

BLURB

Older sister Cosima takes a vacation to The Maldives, the place her father grew up, and while she is there meets a handsome, charming stranger. Deciding to throw caution to the wind, she spends a few very sensual, very erotic days with him, both of them agreeing: no names, no strings, and no inhibitions. Cosima has always guarded her heart fiercely, so when she returns to the U.S., she is amazed to find herself thinking of her lover – and even more amazed when he shows up in New Orleans as the billionaire owner of the hotel she and her firm of architects are about to start work on. Arlo Forrester, though, doesn't seem all that surprised to see her...and soon Cosima realizes that he deliberately tracked her down despite their agreement. Not knowing whether to be irritated or delighted, Cosima finds herself falling for the property magnate. But when his ex-lover follows him to New Orleans, Cosima finds herself torn between a peaceful existence and a possibly dangerous love. Will she decide Arlo's love is worth the pain? And what will it cost her to find out?

1

TORN ASUNDER

A Billionaire, Bad Boy, Romance

∽

osima thanked the young boy who had brought her luggage to the villa, gave him a tip and then, at last alone, flopped down onto the bed and sighed. The flight from the U.S. had been long; she had flown through Paris and been delayed there for nearly twenty-four hours.

Now though, she kicked off her shoes and padded out onto the deck. The clear azure water of the Indian Ocean swirled beneath the villa, and the sun beat relentlessly down. Cosima leaned on the railing and looked out to the mainland; one of the many islands of The Maldives. She breathed in lungfuls of fresh air and felt herself relax. It had been a hard year. Her job at one of the most prestigious architectural firms in New York had drained her and then, of course, when her family had been threatened, she'd had to leave abruptly, change her name, her identity, and relocate to New Orleans.

She gazed out over the ocean. She always felt closer to her late father here, even more than when she was in Mumbai. She had been born in the city, but when her family was exiled, they had spent some time here before moving to London. Cosima planned to revisit all of her old haunts while she was here – her father had been the center of her and her sister's existence when they were young, and he had made the islands seem magical just with his presence. She was looking forward to reliving some of that feeling as she explored the islands.

'But not tonight,' she thought now, going inside to change into her two-piece. 'Tonight is just about relaxing.'

She slipped out of her cotton dress and into her bikini, stretching her long, lithe body into a yoga pose to get rid of the last vestiges of plane cramp. She shoved her long dark hair up into a bun and went out, diving off the deck in one graceful motion.

The feel of the water streaming past her limbs was heavenly; she swam breaststroke hard for a few minutes, feeling her muscles unclenching, then flipped onto her back and floated, letting the vitamin D from the sun sink into her pores. Her dark copper skin gleamed gold in the fiery sun, and Cosima felt the tension of the last few months slip away.

SHE HAD BEEN twelve when her father died, killed in a car bomb blast in London. She and her younger sister, Harper, had been with their mother that night. Monica Lascelles had been the 'It' girl of the 1960's, and had unashamedly romanced some of the most handsome, richest and eligible bachelors of the time. Even when she reached forty, she was still a stunning woman and still commanded six-figure sums for her pictures. She'd been all set to marry an English nobleman when, at a very exclusive private party, she'd caught the eye of the young Indian prince who was visiting on a diplomatic mission. Prince Arjun Malhotra was ten years younger, confident, and the most gorgeous man she'd ever seen, with his dark eyes, long lashes and boyish smile. Two weeks later, causing scandal both in India and the U.K., she'd married him in a registry office in Paris. Cosima was born a year later; Harpa two years after her older sister.

They spent their time between Mumbai, London and The Maldives, and although Cosima and Harpa lived a happy childhood, tensions in the families of their parents grew unbearable. Finally, after his father was murdered by his own bodyguards, Arjun was exiled from India on pain of death. He took his family and left forever, his heart breaking and eventually, Arjun divorced Monica after discovering she was sleeping with just about all of his friends. But for a few of the more extreme anti-royalty nuts, banishment was not enough. They hunted down and killed every member of the Malhotra family... which was when Arjun sent his children to New York to begin new lives under new identities. He was set to join them a few days later, but instead, he got into his chauffeured car one night and was blown to bits, along with his driver and a couple of innocent bystanders.

Cosima never got over it. Harpa, from whom they'd shielded the worst details, clung to her sister; their mother, ever the attention seeker, wailed and tore at her clothes in grief. Even then, Cosima could see her mother as a vapid narcissist as she did interview after interview, draped in the saris that Arjun had gifted to her, smoking exotic cigarettes. Waving her cigarette lighter around imperiously, she told her life story over and over, embellishing it just a little more every time and forgetting that she and Arjun had been divorced when he died.

The FBI had told them they would have to change their names and move somewhere no one would find them or they'd never be safe...but Monica wouldn't hear of it.

'They don't want us. If they did, they would have killed us at the same time as my darling Arjun.'

Cosima would roll her eyes. If Monica had actually been in love with Arjun the man and not Arjun the Prince, she might have had more sympathy, but Cosima knew for a fact her mother had had a string of affairs beginning after Harpa's birth. When Cosima was sixteen, she moved out and applied to the court for legal custody of Harpa and got it. So impressed was the judge who saw the serious young woman, already two years ahead in her education, dedicated to raising her sister. Cosima took the last of her trust fund and bought her and Harpa a small apartment in New York City. Her mother had bleated and whined but soon found that life without her daughters left her a lot of freedom to do whatever she wanted – and whomever she wanted.

Now, at twenty-eight, Cosima was a high flyer at her architecture firm, about to become a partner. They specialized in designing boutique hotels; Cosima had an exquisite eye for color and design and soon she was a name to be reckoned with in the industry. That she was also beautiful didn't go unnoticed, and soon the attention transcended the architecture world and she was being courted by major publications who wanted to interview her and make her a star. She had resisted, and one journalist had taken exception to her reticence and researched her background. They exposed her as a Malhotra heir, and the FBI moved quickly to move her and Harpa out of New York when she'd received a death threat.

Cosima floated in the warm water of the Indian Ocean and sighed. Harpa had been devastated to leave New York and her job as a stylist, and their relationship had suffered as a consequence. Cosima had persuaded a reluctant FBI not to take them out of the country; instead, they relocated to hot, sultry New Orleans. Cosima, thanks to a few wise investments, was taking some time out before deciding what to do next – she already had offers from some of the biggest firms in New Orleans. Harpa was back styling for, to her dismay, far less glamorous clients than in the Big Apple – and now they had new surnames too: Bedi. Cosima and Harpa Bedi. Cosima felt so disloyal to her father's memory and his name, but it couldn't be helped.

Cosima swam back to her villa, and stood under the shower, shampooing the salt from her hair, soaping her body until she felt clean and refreshed. She toyed with the idea of heading onto the island for supper, but she wasn't even hungry yet. The complimentary fruit basket stood on the table in the main room, and she picked from that, trying to decide where to go to eat. The small island was so compact that she could walk into the small town in less than five minutes. Glancing at her watch, she decided to catch up on some reading. But less than a half hour later, she had fallen asleep, with the book slipping to the deck and the sun beating down her.

ARLO FORRESTER TOOK two bites of his fish then sat back to people watch as he ate. He loved it here on this tiny island; somewhere he wouldn't be recognized or harassed. Solace, he thought, that's what this place was, a haven. He noticed a few young women glancing his way and smiled. That's one complication I don't need. Arlo Forrester was almost forty, never married, just out of a long, long-term relationship with Sabine Karlsson, the supermodel with whom he'd shared a bed and a life with for the last fifteen years. And still might have been had it not been for his ex-best friend, Cole...who had been sleeping with Sabine for the last five of those years. A random comment at a party had led Arlo to discover their secret and that was that. Arlo Forrester didn't do second chances. Ever.

So, after Sabine had tearfully moved out of his luxury penthouse, Arlo had decided: no more commitment. After all, with his dark good looks, long legs, and hard body, it wasn't as if he would go without sex for long. He had enough respect for a woman that he would explain his mindset to them before he took them to bed – but he found while most agreed beforehand, they would always, always think differently afterward. That wasn't arrogance, just his experience.

So, no commitment and from now, he'd be damned if he wasn't going to stick to that. I can even do without sex for a while, he said to himself now – I'll just hang out with my friends, with myself.

Although I might make an exception for her...Arlo sat up as a stunning woman walked into the restaurant. 'Stunning' was actually a gross understatement; the woman, who he guessed was in her mid-twenties, had dark skin, a body that was slender and yet curvy in all the right places, dark hair that reached past her waist and an air of independence that he found compelling.

The maître d' led her to the table two down from him, and she sat facing him. He could hear her chatting in perfect Dhivehi....well, it was perfect to his untrained ear at least. She was wearing a simple, dark gold dress, her feet bare, no jewelry, and no make-up. Christ, who needed make-up with skin like that, those huge dark eyes rimmed with the thickest, darkest lashes, that deep pink full mouth. His groin tightened as he watched her order a drink, then as the waiter left, pull a book out from her bag and began reading. He squinted to see what she was reading and grinned. Harry Potter. He liked that; he liked she didn't try to impress the people around her with a literary classic. She looked totally absorbed in the book too – he watched her smile and frown as she read and even start when the waiter brought her food, thanking him with a smile that made Arlo's stomach warm.

Damn... She looked up as if he'd said the word out loud and their gazes locked. A flush crept up her face, and she looked away. Arlo grinned as she looked flustered, and then studiously ignored him as she ate her food. He relented, giving her privacy, but kept her in the corner of his eye as he finished his own supper.

Forty minutes later he saw her call for the check and tip generously, gathering her book and her bag to leave. Hell, what now, Forrester...decide? Are you going to let her go? Arlo sighed. This....this wasn't what he needed right now. She was a complication, but goddamnit; she was the most exquisite creature he had ever seen. He rubbed his hands over his eyes. So much for self-control, man, when a pretty face can distract you just like...

'I'm going to the bar. If you want, you can join me, and I'll buy you whatever drink is your poison.'

He looked up, shocked. The woman stood at the side of his table, looking down at him. Oh hell, close up, she was even more enchanting, and worse, he could smell her perfume...a clean, heady scent that sent his blood rushing to his groin. She nodded briefly, smiled and walked off in the direction of the bar – the easy, relaxed gait almost a sashay...and dear lord, the dress was backless, showing a long expanse of café-au-lait skin.

Jeez...Arlo called for the check, hurriedly signing it and over-tipping. Be cool, man, keep her waiting for at least ten minutes...ha.

No way. Arlo followed the goddess into the bar as if she had him on a leash.

She sat down in a private booth and smiled as he sat opposite her.

'Hi.' Her accent was a sexy mix of American and Indian, and her smile...man, anybody could get lost by staring at her smile.

'Hello. I'm –'

'No names.' Still, she smiled. 'I figure we can do the whole getting to know each other thing. You tell me your life; I tell you mine. Or we can just get right to what would be inevitable.'

Arlo chuckled. 'You're confident.'

She inclined her head gracefully. 'But hopefully not arrogant. If you're not interested, that's absolutely fine, no hard feelings, let's have a drink and say goodbye.'

Arlo shook his head in disbelief. 'Beautiful...you're stealing my best lines.'

She laughed. 'I just don't do games.'

Arlo nodded. 'Me neither. I like your honesty, let me repay it by telling you that there is nothing in this world I'd like more than to accept your kind offer.'

'But?'

'But nothing. I think a night of fucking a woman as beautiful as you would be a gift from the gods. That you don't want names...'

'Or strings or commitment...'

'Or inhibitions?' He raised an eyebrow, amused, and a smile spread across her face as she kept her eyes locked on his.

'No inhibitions,' she said softly, and Arlo nodded, considering this for a moment. Then he stood and held out his hand.

'Screw the drinks.'

She took his hand and stood. 'Agreed.'

THEY WALKED BACK to her villa hand-in-hand, the sand soft beneath their feet, the lights from other villas beacons in the darkness. Inside, their kiss was tentative at first, then deepened as their lips moved against the other's, and Arlo's fingers went to the straps of her dress, pulling them down. Her dress slithered down her body and onto the floor. She wore only panties and her breasts, large and perfectly formed, fell heavily into his hands, the large brown aureole framing the delicate nipples. Cosima closed her eyes as he caressed them, dipping his head to take the nipples into his mouth in turn. God, she tasted so good and soon he was unable to stop himself, dropping to his knees and burying his face in her belly as he pulled her panties down slowly. His tongue traced patterns over her skin, around her navel and down until it lashed around her clit and he heard her gasp. Grinning, he gently parted her thighs to gain better access to her sex, which was already glistening with her arousal. She knotted her fingers in his hair as he pleasured her, and by the time he felt her legs trembling so badly she could barely stand, he knew she was his. He scooped her into his arms and onto the bed, tearing off his clothes, his cock pulsing and straining, ramrod straight against his belly. She smiled up at him as he sat back on his haunches and grabbed a condom from his pocket. As he rolled it onto him, he took in the sight of this beautiful woman beneath him, her soft curves so delicious, so tempting, that when he finally slid into her, he was so turned on that it became a fast, furious fuck, thrilling and intense.

Afterward, they both collapsed, breathless and laughed. Arlo turned his head to look at her, her face covered with a dewy sheen of breath. 'God, you're beautiful.'

She laughed. 'That's the orgasm talking but thank you.'

'Are you kidding, look at you...?' He ran his hand down over her belly. 'How long are you here for?'

'Five days,' she said, turning to gaze at him. 'You?'

'A week. Listen I know we said no names but...'

'Pseudonyms okay?'

'Good idea. I'm...Turner.' His grin was wickedly infectious, and she laughed.

'I am not being 'Hooch.' How about...Bill and Ted?'

It was his turn to chuckle. 'Next time I come, I'm not shouting either of those names.'

'Fair point. Well, then, I'm...Camille.'

He nodded. 'And I'm...Adam'

She rolled on top of him, her dark hair cascading around her face. 'Well then, hello Adam.'

He put his hands on either side of her face, studying every inch of it. 'Camille...will you spend the next few days with me?'

She smiled. 'As long as you promise we'll be naked and doing this for ninety-nine percent of the time.'

'I think I can accommodate that...' He grinned as she straddled him, taking his still hard cock in her hands and stroking it against her lower belly.

'Adam?'

'Yes, sweetheart?'

'What would you like me to do?' She grinned at his raised eyebrows. 'Anything...'

'Anything?'

She nodded, and he put his hands around her waist and lifted her onto his cock. 'Just ride me, beautiful...but let's take it slow. This time, I want to watch that gorgeous body of yours while we fuck.'

And he did, admiring the way the full breasts gently moved with the rhythm of her thrusts, the way her tight little cunt gripped his cock, increasing the friction on him, her soft moans, and the gentle curve of her belly. She kept her eyes locked onto his, intensity building as they rocked together. A cool breeze came off the water outside and cooled their hot bodies. He reached between her legs to rub her hardening clit, and she let out such a melodic, beautiful sigh of pleasure that he could feel his orgasm beginning to build.

This time, it was a mellow, drawn-out climax and he actually wished that he wasn't wearing a condom, that he could pump his seed deep into this goddesses being, mark her as his own, taste this honey skin forever.

As the night went on, they made love again and again, sometimes urgently – he took her against the wall of the villa, thrusting deep into her from behind; she sucked him until he came into her mouth, her fingernails digging into his buttocks. They had each other in every way and by the time they feel asleep, Arlo knew in his bones – he wouldn't be able to let her go...

COSIMA WALKED through the New Orleans airport in a haze. Since she and 'Adam' had said their goodbyes, she had felt a chasm of sadness inside her. She thought she'd be able to do it; turn off her feelings, just enjoy those few incredible, sensual days for what they were. The trouble was, her mysterious lover spoke to her in every way: mentally, emotionally and of course, physically.

Cosima had never been one to flaunt her beauty or be overtly sexual, but something at the restaurant that night when she'd caught his eye and he'd smiled – every cell in her body had been set aflame. A pulse beat frantically between her legs and she had, for once, thrown caution to the wind. And, man, did it pay off. The five sensual days and nights she'd spent with him had caused an awakening inside of her. She reveled in the confidence it had given her, welcomed the aches in her muscles from the exertions, felt washed with happiness as they laughed and loved together.

But now she had to face the fact that it was over, and she was both sad and happy. No one could take that away from her – and it had been just the two of them. No family crap, no relationship bullshit, just...'the good bits,' she grinned to herself. If only real relationships could be that wonderful.

She took a cab home to find the apartment empty. Harpa had been spending less and less time there, and Cosima would not have been surprised to come home to find her stuff gone. She spent most of the time at her boyfriend's place now. Cosima sighed. She hadn't liked Deacon the few times she had met him, but Harpa's whole countenance had dared her to say something negative so she'd kept her mouth shut. Harpa was an adult now; she could do what she wanted.

'Just like I did,' she said aloud and laughed. She wanted to take a shower but didn't want to wash him off her skin yet. They had made love for the last time just before she left for the airport, making the most of their last moments together.

'I'll never forget you,' he'd said, his kiss tender and loving, his eyes soft. God, what a gorgeous man, she sighed to herself. Funny, smart, and with just enough confidence to be attractive. His body – God, she could crawl over it for days – was tight and cut, broad shoulders, thickly muscled arms. He was tall too, towering over her five-four frame, making her feel so tiny and safe in his arms.

'Adam,' she said out loud, and not for the first time wondered what his real name was. No, that wasn't part of the deal, she told herself, but she couldn't help fantasizing that somehow, they could be together again. Her sex swelled at the thought of it, and so, she drew a bath and relaxed into it, thinking of him, letting his fingers drift down between her legs.

At midnight, she went to bed, suddenly exhausted. Tomorrow, she would start to get her life back on track. An interview at one of New Orleans' most prestigious architectural firms and the hope of a junior partnership – that's what she should be focusing on. She fell asleep just as she heard the front door open and Harpa creep back into her room.

IN THE MALDIVES, Arlo sat in the lounge sipping his drink and wishing he could pour the aged single blend scotch all over 'Camille''s incredible body and then lick it off. God, it had been less than twenty-four hours, but the void she had left in his life was palpable.

Which is why, now, he sat with his private detective, looking at photographs of her. 'You're sure this is her real name?'

The detective nodded. 'One hundred percent. She's the daughter of Arjun Malhotra but now lives in New Orleans. She's supposed to have a new identity, but I found her easily – hopefully the people who killed her father won't have such luck. Both of the sisters have had threats against them which is why the FBI stepped in.'

Arlo winced. He couldn't imagine anyone wanting to harm

Camille – or Cosima, as he now knew her name to be. Cosima– it suited her well. He stared down at her beautiful face, drinking it in.

'Boss? What do you want me to do next?'

'Nothing yet. I got this.'

HE THRUST his cock deep inside her, grinning as she cried out. It seemed he had become bigger, almost too big for her now and as he fucked her, she began to feel pain instead of pleasure. She glanced up at him, suddenly fearful. His smile was terrifying.

'Did you think you could escape us, Cosima?' His face turned from 'Adam' to the face of an enemy, and suddenly she felt her body rocked with agonizing pain. She looked down to see an impossibly big knife cutting deep into her abdomen, stab, stab, stab....

'COS! COS! WAKE UP...'

Cosima opened her eyes, gasping for air, to see her younger sister, her eyes large and scared, sitting on the side of the bed, her hands on Cosima's arms. Breathless, she sat up.

'You were having another nightmare,' Harpa said gently. Cosima sighed and leaned back against the headboard.

'God, sorry...was I screaming again?'

Harpa nodded. 'Something about 'Adam, please don't'.'

Cosima flushed. 'Yikes.'

'Who's Adam?'

Cosima didn't answer her sister straight away; she kicked off the comforter and headed to her bathroom to grab a cup of water. Jeez, damn nightmares. She tried to smile at Harpa as she sat back down on the bed. 'Just some guy I met in the Maldives.'

Harpa's eyes lit up. 'Please tell me you got laid.'

Cosima's blush deepened. 'Harpa Malhotra, really, the things you ask.' Then she could have cursed as Harpa's face shut down.

'It's Bedi, now, remember?'

Harpa got up and walked out of the room; it was the only the lateness of the hour that made her refrain from slamming the door, Cosima knew. Cosima sighed again. Me and my big mouth. Their new life and their new names were still contentious between the sisters; Cosima knew Harpa blamed her for outing them in New York. The FBI had wanted them to change their first names too, but Harpa put her foot down on that and Cosima too was glad to retain something of their own. She knew their father had picked out their names when they had been born, and it felt good to honor him by keeping them. In business, though, Cosima used initials now, Cosima Jasmine Bedi became C.J. Bedi, architect, and Harpa too anglicized her name to 'Harper'. But at home, they were still 'Cos' and 'Harp' to each other.

Now Cosima lay back down and tried to go back to sleep, willing the nightmares to stay away. Her interview tomorrow was important to them both; what little money she had from the trust fund was depleting fast, and with their father's estate tied up and inaccessible to them while their lives were in danger, they needed another source of income. Especially if Harpa moves out, she thought to herself. I can just about afford this place on my own if I get this job. Otherwise, a tiny studio away from the French Quarter would have to do. Cosima wrinkled her nose at the idea of it – she loved being here, amidst the crowds of tourists and the Quarter folk.

She eventually fell asleep just as dawn crept over the horizon; her last waking thought was thank God the interview isn't until the afternoon.

TWO MONTHS LATER...

TALMIDGE HUNT LOOKED up as Cosima knocked on his door and smiled. Since joining his firm two months ago, after an interview that for both of them had been like a meeting of the minds, Cosima had won over practically everyone in the firm and had settled in so quickly they couldn't remember a time she hadn't been there.

Now, as he beckoned her in, he beamed at her. 'Now my dear, I have some exciting news. Arlo Forrester's people are coming to see us tomorrow.'

Cosima, sitting down opposite her boss, looked blank, and Tal smiled. 'I forgot, you're a New Yorker. Forrester is a California-based company, boutique hotels mostly.'

Cosima grinned. 'California? Did you just make that up?' She pretended to count on her fingers. 'New York, India, New Orleans... nope, no, never heard of this 'California.''

Tal flicked a paper clip at her, chuckling. 'Funny girl. Now, seriously, they're coming to see us to discuss a hotel right here in New Orleans. This would be a huge boon to our practice should we land the account. So, what do you think?'

'I think it's great...Harry or Jennifer would be fantastic for that kind of thing.'

Tal laughed softly. 'Cosima...I'm asking if you would like to be the lead on it.'

Cosima was stunned. She blinked at Tal for a second, trying to gather her thoughts. 'Tal...I've only been here for two months and although I'm deeply flattered, I wouldn't want to step on anyone else's toes.'

Tal shook his head. 'You wouldn't be, I promise. Both Harry and Jenny specialize in manufacturing premises. You know that. And no one else has your eye for detail when it comes to décor and aesthetic. I'll be your second on this – show you there's life in the old dog yet.'

Cosima grinned. Tal was nearly eighty, though a shock of white hair and the cane he used were the only indicators of his great experience. His blue eyes were still strong, his mind razor-sharp, and when he brainstormed with his team, Cosima was enraptured.

'In that case, I would be honored,' she said. Then, realizing what she'd committed to, blew out her cheeks. 'Wow.'

Tal clapped his hands together, delighted. 'Good. They'll be here, I'm assuming mid-morning, so I thought we'd do introductions then take them to lunch. I'm thinking Arlo Forrester won't be one of the party but who knows? I'll get Mandy to book us a table at Arnaud's, show these surfer types some real Cajun cuisine.'

ARLO WISHED he hadn't picked up the phone that morning. Sabine, sobbing, was calling him, begging to see him - 'Just to talk, bebe, please.'

His mind full of Cosima Bedi's luscious thighs as it had been constantly for the last two months, he'd absentmindedly agreed, and now Sabine, all blonde hair and long legs, was sitting on his couch, a glass of straight vodka in her hand, begging him to give her another chance.

'I'm so sorry, bebe,' she said for the hundredth time. 'Cole and I were stupid, reckless, and wrong.'

'For five whole years,' Arlo said coolly, really not wanting the same argument all over again. He was tired and wanted to get to bed. Tomorrow he would see Cosima for the first time – and she had no idea. That thrilled him, and all he wanted was to get Sabine out of his apartment. Sabine, however, had other ideas.

'Bebe...please. Won't you think about trying again?'

Arlo ran his hands over his face, frustrated. 'Sabine...why would you even want to? It's not as if we were ever going to be a family. You never wanted kids, I do...it wasn't working for a long time. Look, I forgive you for straying, although I wish it hadn't been with my best friend, but I admit – I was absent from the relationship for a long time, and that's my bad.'

'But still – '

'But still nothing. If I thought the relationship was worth saving, maybe things would be different.'

He was sorry he'd framed his response so harshly when he saw her wince. He went to sit by her, held her hand. 'Sabine...I'm sorry. I'd like to be friends still if that's possible. But please know, it can never be more than that.'

Sabine studied his eyes for a long moment. 'Who is she?'

Arlo blinked. 'Who?'

Sabine smiled. 'There's someone else.'

Arlo got up and went to pour another drink. 'No.' Liar.

Sabine sighed. 'Well, you can do that, Arlo. You can lie to my face but remember, I tried to take the high ground.'

Arlo nearly spat out his drink, wiping his mouth and grinning widely. 'Did you really just say that? Sabine, let me make it clear. My life – and those who are or aren't in it – are no longer your concern.'

Sabine sniffed. 'I can see we're getting nowhere.'

'We're getting nowhere because we are nowhere, Sabine. I wish you every good thing, but I do not wish to reconcile. Thank you for the offer.'

She flushed at his tone, which he had to admit, was condescending. 'Sabine, I really do have to get back to work now, so if there's nothing else?'

LATER, he stared out at the dusk falling over San Francisco. As much as he loved this city, he needed to get away. From Sabine, from Cole... ah, screw it, he didn't need to get away; he just needed to be near her. Cosima. Her face haunted his days and nights, the memory of her skin on his. He had meant every word about the pact they'd made – he really did. Right up to the moment he had entered her, and it had felt so right, so perfect, all his plans to remain aloof and unattached had faltered. Yes, it had taken two months to get up the courage to set up the meeting with her firm, but it had been necessary to wait. If he'd showed up on her doorstep the minute he'd landed on U.S. soil, she might have freaked out, turned him away, and he hadn't been able to bear the thought of it. No – patience was the key. He would not harass her; he would simply be...present. Charming. He was confident she would be responsive, plus there was the matter of her and her sister's security. He'd read everything he could find on Prince Arjun Malhotra, from his beginnings as a young prince to the assassination of both the king and of the prince. There the trail ended – at least via a Google search. The only mention of the prince's daughters was a brief article, obviously written by the prince's enemies, saying that all of the prince's offspring were to be exterminated before the 'taint' of the Malhotra family was wiped out.

God. The thought of anyone laying a hand on Cosima made his blood boil. Suddenly he wished himself back to the island, back to when he could have asked her for her number, called off the whole what-happens-here-stays-here thing, begged her to be with him. You are the least playboy-like of any alleged playboy; he shook his head, grinning to himself. You seriously have no game, dude. None.

What would the readers of Forbes think if they knew this year's 'Most Eligible Billionaire' was a geeky romantic instead of a devil-may-care heartbreaker? He liked that image: the dashing rogue, the aloof property magnate – it helped him deal with some of his anxiety issues. Had his beloved older brother, Mason, still been alive, he would have laughed at the image Arlo projected – not in a cruel way, but just because he had known his little brother better than anyone. Mason had been a professor of the arts at an upscale private college before he died in a homophobic attack by one of his students. Arlo still felt that grief and, reading over Malhotra's assassination, he knew Cosima must feel the same. Another thing they had in common.

You'll drive yourself crazy thinking like that, he told himself and grinned wryly.

Tomorrow I'll be with you, my beautiful Cosima. From tomorrow, I'll try to let you know just how much you mean to me...

COSIMA WAS SUSPICIOUS. So far today – the most important day of her career to date – nothing had gone wrong. The shower had run at the right temperature; her power suit had stayed where she hung it, on the back of the bedroom door, and no dreadful fate had befallen it. There had even been little traffic as she drove into work and parked easily. She got out of the car and looked around, her eyes narrowed. 'Zombie apocalypse,' she decided and laughed. 'Zombie apocalypse' was her go-to excuse for everything these days – she blamed The Walking Dead – Harpa was obsessed with that show.

So she was ready when, at eleven-thirty, she saw the entourage from Forrester walk in. Two women and a man, not too scary, she thought to herself. Tal beckoned her over, and she walked into the boardroom with them all. They introduced themselves; Beth Richards, the deputy CEO, was a kind-faced, dark-haired middle-aged woman whose eyes were sharp with knowledge and humor; Savannah Mills, buyer, was sharply dressed and elegant; and Ben Sandoval was a tall Native American with an easy smile and quick wit. Ben was head of design. 'Arlo will meet us at the restaurant,' he said. 'He prefers to let us do the preliminary work ourselves.'

Tal nodded and indicated they should all sit. 'We're very happy to have you with us. Cosima will be your main liaison and architect for the new hotel...shall we start by telling you our initial thoughts?'

AN HOUR LATER, with her brain spinning with ideas, Cosima followed the party down to the waiting town car for the five-minute drive to the restaurant. It had been a long time since she'd been this excited about a work project; from what Forrester's people had told her, Forrester himself was open to any ideas. 'He wants something that will fit in with the aesthetic of New Orleans obviously but not be derivative. No voodoo dolls on the nightstand,' Beth had joked. Cosima, relaxing in their presence, had pretended to screw up a piece of paper at that, throwing it over her shoulder. Tal gave her an encouraging wink as they laughed.

AS THEY WALKED into Arnaud's, Cosima could relax. She loved this place, loved the food, and now that she felt at ease with these people, she felt a wave of confidence come over her. This really was it, her big break, the project she could showcase her talents on.

They ordered some wine, and she sipped it gratefully. They had been at the restaurant for only a few moments when Ben said, 'Ah, good, here he comes.'

Cosima looked up curiously and nearly squeaked with surprise. Oh my God...

It was him. The tall, glorious, handsome man in an exquisite, expensive suit; the slightly smirking man walking towards them was Adam. Or rather was Adam aka Arlo Forrester. He never took his eyes off her as he approached the table. Only when he was introduced to Tal, did he politely smile at Tal and shake the older man's hand. 'So good to meet you at last, I've heard wonderful things.'

Tal smiled. 'And talking of wonderful things – if you'll excuse me, dear – ' he grinned at a flustered Cosima, 'Mr. Forrester, please meet Cosima Bedi, your architect for this project.'

Arlo Forrester had the nerve to shake her hand like his cock had never been inside her, that his tongue hadn't driven her almost insane with pleasure. Suddenly she wanted to giggle.

'Cosima,' he said, his dark green eyes intense on hers, 'An absolute pleasure.'

Why did she feel naked when he looked at her like that? 'Mr. Forrester, I've heard so much about you.'

Arlo Forrester winked at her. He winked at her. She didn't know whether to laugh or freak out. She settled on a knowing smile. 'We were just about to order, Mr. Forrester.'

'Please, call me Arlo.' The twinkle in his eyes was too much.

Please, call me Arlo. Cosima turned a snort of laughter into a cough as they sat down. Somehow, Arlo managed to snag the seat next to her. 'So,' he said, 'what's good here?'

'The mahi-mahi is something special,' Tal said, completely oblivious to the turmoil raging inside his young associate. 'Cosima, didn't you say you'd had a spectacular meal in the Maldives, some sort of curry dish with mahi-mahi?'

Cosima nodded. 'I had a lot of delicious things while I was in the Maldives,' she said, with a serene smile.

Arlo cleared his throat and out of the corner of her eye, she could see him smirking.

Luckily, the others kept the conversation going, and Cosima was distracted by the arrival of their food. Arlo had ordered the same as she had, and they shared a conspiratorial look. God, he was so damn good looking; memories of their time together in her villa, on the beach, in her bed came flooding back. Arlo...Adam....now that she thought about it, Arlo suited him better.

She almost dropped her fork when she felt his cool fingertips drift up her inner thigh. He was talking to Tal and Beth, explaining something, gesturing with his fork, but his other hand was warm and soft against her thigh. God, how many weeks had she dreamed of his touch? She leaned forward to shield his arm from view and engaged Ben and Savannah in conversation. But all the while, she was aware of the soft, sensual brushing of his fingers against the soft flesh of her thighs. God, I want you, she thought, but two can play at that game, mister. She slid her hand onto his lap and cupped his cock, squeezing it gently, feeling him start a little. She smiled, not looking at him as he turned to gaze at her.

'So, you're the big honcho on this project? Good...I'll be taking care of this one myself so we'll be working closely together.' His green eyes were amused, and she grinned back.

'Um, boss? We didn't know you were going to be so closely...' Ben looked confused, exchanging looks with his two colleagues. Arlo smiled – remarkably controlled seeing as Cosima's hand was stroking his cock, which was diamond hard against the fabric of his pants.

'Well, now, I did say I wanted a project. I get bored sitting in my ivory tower sometimes, and this is perfect for me.' He turned to meet Cosima's gaze. 'And I'll be living in New Orleans for the duration of the project so I guess we'll be seeing a lot of each other.'

Cosima felt a jolt. God, why hadn't she seen this? This wasn't a happy coincidence....Arlo Forrester had found her. On purpose. He'd hunted her down, broken their agreement – how? Because he was a goddamned billionaire of course. Suddenly she felt sick. God, woman, how stupid are you? The man thinks you can be bought with a job offer – this was planned. She withdrew her hand and concentrated on finishing her meal. Arlo's hand stroked her thigh, drifted higher but she rammed her legs shut, causing him to jerk his hand free.

Later, at the office, they finalized all of the details and the Forrester entourage left. At the door, Arlo turned and looked at

Cosima. She nodded, stone-faced and frowning, and he left, his confusion obvious. Tal went back to his office and Cosima followed. 'Tal, can I talk to you a second?'

'Sure thing, Cos, have a seat.'

Cosima sat and chewed her lip for a second. 'Tal, I have to ask you a question.'

'Go ahead.'

'Why did you offer me this job? I mean, why hire me? I know I had a lot of good recommendations but even so...Jenny told me you put her through the ringer before she even got a second interview.'

Tal smiled. 'Cosima...what do you really want to know?'

She steeled herself. 'Did Arlo Forrester recommend me for this job? What I mean is: did he tell you he would give you this major project if you hired me?'

Tal frowned. 'Absolutely not. Cosima...you were hired because you were the best candidate. Yes, I put Jenny through the ringer because, although she was supremely talented, she needed fire in her belly. You already have that. Now, I take it from your question, you and Mr. Forrester are acquainted...and yet you made no indication of it at dinner. Either of you.'

Cosima flushed. 'Tal...whatever acquaintance we may have had is nothing to do with how I will handle this project, but now that you know, maybe it would be best to put someone else on it.'

Tal shook his head. 'No. I trust you, Cosima, I trust you to keep anything personal out of office hours. Apart from that, you're both adults.'

Cosima started to smile, noticing the gleam in Tal's eye. 'Talmidge Hunt...are you matchmaking?'

He laughed. 'Cosima, I'm old, I'm not dead. Nor blind, I saw the chemistry between the two of you.'

She shook her head, laughing, as she got up to leave, relieved that she'd got the job on her own merits. 'Whatever you say, boss. Look, I'm going to get started...anything else you want me to know?'

Tal was still grinning. 'Yes. I want the gossip, Cos. I want to live vicariously through you.'

She burst out laughing, looking at the old man fondly. 'Tal, you are the worst – and the best.'

She was the last to leave the office that evening, switching off the lights just after eight o'clock. As she walked out to her car, she was alarmed to see someone leaning against it. Then as she stopped and her eyes grew used to the low light, her heart started pounding but not from fear.

Arlo Forrester grinned at her as she approached him. 'Good evening, Miss Bedi. I think we have some unfinished business.'

SABINE KARLSSON STARED at Cole Trent in disbelief. 'Cole...what the fuck are you talking about?'

Cole ran a hand through his short red hair. 'Sabine...we never said we were exclusive. How could we be when you were still fucking Arlo right up to the moment he found out about us?'

Sabine got up and crossed to the window. 'What difference does that make? I was never going to marry Arlo...but, in less than three months, you decided you wanted to marry this other woman?'

Cole looked tired. 'Sabine...I love Lana. She knows all about you and me and has from the start.'

Sabine stared out over the bay. The fog was rolling in, obscuring her view of Alcatraz. Shit, she thought, everything's turning to shit. First Arlo, now this. She had counted on Cole being her fall back, the other billionaire on her string. But Cole's guilt over the affair, over betraying his oldest friend, had done it for them, she knew that. Still, he'd been the net to the tightrope she'd been walking for the last five years and now...

'So she gave you an ultimatum: her or me?'

'No.'

'Of course, she did. Is she knocked up?'

Cole gave a frustrated hiss. 'Believe it or not, not everyone operates on the same moral code as you, Sabine. No, she's not pregnant, nor did she give me an ultimatum. I love her. That is all.'

Sabine gazed at her reflection in the window. The clear glass gave her a much kinder, softer face than the one she saw in the mirror. Nearly forty and alone. Damn you, Cole. Damn you, Arlo. Damn you all.

She turned back to Cole with a chilly smile. 'Then I guess this is goodbye.'

Cole got up and walked to the door, turning back to her before opening it. 'Sabine...we had a good time, we did. But I'll never forgive myself for what I did to Arlo. In the end, both of us lost. I'm going to try to make up for that mistake for the rest of my life. I suggest you do the same.'

And he was gone. Sabine flipped her middle finger up at the closing door. 'Damn patronizing moralizing asshole.' Fuck. What now?

Then she smirked to herself and looked back out of the window, over the city she'd come to as a teenager from Stockholm, all those years ago. Well, Cole, I might just take that advice of yours. I might try to redeem myself, and as far as I can see, there's only one way to do that. Arlo Forrester.

Sabine smiled to herself. 'I'm going to get you back, baby.'

***

COSIMA SAT opposite Arlo in the small bar. The room was semi-crowded, but thankfully, the noise wasn't overwhelming. Cosima sipped the cocktail Arlo had ordered for her.

'That good?'

'Yes, thank you.'

Arlo grinned at her. 'So...hello.'

'Hi.' She gave him a half-smile. Arlo nodded, reading her expression.

'Sorry for blind-siding you but...I had to see you.'

Cosima drew in a deep breath. 'So you hunted me down? That's not what we agreed.'

Arlo nodded, his smile fading. 'I know, and I'm sorry. I wouldn't use the word 'hunted,' more 'searched for.'

Cosima nodded, her expression tight. Arlo sighed. 'Look, Cosima...I did my due diligence. I know your story. Believe me, I took every precaution to protect the information I found, to protect you.'

'Arlo...why didn't you come to me directly? Why get involved with my work? I guess I'm wondering if you think you were doing me a favor by hiring my firm. That smacks of control and I'm really not up for that. My life is already regulated enough by other people...my sister, my mother, the FBI. My work is mine, do you understand?'

Arlo nodded. 'I do, and I have no answer for that other than I thought it would be a good way to contact you. I thought turning up at your door might scare you.'

Cosima stared out of the window at the crowds of people milling around the Quarter. 'Was I easy to find?'

Arlo smiled. 'No. I covered the tracks too, so you'll be even less visible. Like I said, I know your story.'

'And yet I know so little about yours,' she sighed and rubbed her eyes. 'Look, Arlo, the time we spent in the Maldives was incredible, but if we're going to work together, we can't just pick up where we left off. I take my job very seriously.'

'Good,' Arlo sat back, 'Because I'm serious about wanting the best for this new hotel. Cosima, your reputation precedes you; your artistic flair, your commitment.'

She studied him. 'Then...'

'Then we'll be colleagues, and friends. For now. Eventually, you'll be mine, Cosima Bedi. I fully intend on marrying you.'

She gave disbelieving snort. 'Oh really?'

'Absolutely. I knew the moment I touched you, the moment I ran my fingers over that glorious, soft skin of yours, kissed those rosebud lips.'

Cosima felt her body react to his words, a burning longing for him, but she pushed those feelings down.

'Mr. Forrester...I don't know what you're used to, but here in the twenty-first century, women aren't so easily acquired. Just because we fucked,' she spat the words to illustrate her annoyance, 'it does not give you the right to lay claim to me.'

'I'm doing nothing of the sort. I would never coerce you into something you didn't want; that idea is abhorrent to me. I just know, with every cell in my body, that we belong together. I'll wait, Cosima. Forever if necessary.'

She was staring at him now. 'You don't know me.' Her voice was a whisper.

Arlo inclined his head in agreement. 'No, I don't know all of you. And maybe I'll be proved wrong – but I don't think so. I spent fifteen years with a woman who, it turns out, I didn't know at all. I learned more about what it means to love someone in five days with you than I ever did with her.'

Cosima couldn't help but smile at that, and Arlo chuckled. 'I know what you're thinking. Pretty words.'

She shook her head. 'No, I was thinking that's the nicest thing anyone has ever said to me.'

'I'm glad.'

'But we live in the real world, Arlo. I mean it about my job; I love it, I earned it, I worked my butt off to get here. If you know anything about my family history, then you know that I got here the hard way.'

'I do know that, and as I said, I'll wait. While you're working with me on the hotel, nothing should happen. But when it's over...'

Cosima, her cheeks a deep scarlet – God, she wanted to touch him so badly – nodded. 'When it's over, we'll see.'

HE WALKED her back to her car. 'I guess I'll see you in the morning.'

She nodded. 'I guess so.' He gazed down at her, stroking her cheeks with his fingers.

'Cosima...' He was going to kiss her, and she couldn't bear it knowing that if he did, all her words would mean nothing and she would beg him to screw her right here, right now.

No – she was being adult and professional about this – but, damn, if the scent of his cologne wasn't driving her crazy. She fumbled behind her and opened her car door. 'Well, goodnight.'

Arlo smiled. 'Goodnight Cosima.'

DRIVING HOME, she glanced in the rearview mirror, checking behind her to see if she was followed – it had become second nature since they'd gone into hiding, but now she wasn't looking for potential assassins. Now she was looking for him.

And was disappointed that the road behind her was empty.

WHEN SHE GOT HOME, Harpa was sitting on the couch painting her toenails. She looked up and grinned, and Cosima was relieved that her sister seemed to be in good mood. She had been so angry lately, about everyone and everything. A delicious smell permeated from the small kitchen, spicy, rich.

'Hey, sis. Before I forget, Handsome Jack called. He needs to see us tomorrow. I said you'd call him back and arrange a time because I'm free all day, but I didn't know what your schedule was. You hungry?'

'Starved.' And she was, all of a sudden. 'Let me change first – what did you make?'

Harpa was a fantastic cook, especially when it came to Indian food. 'Prawn and cod biryani with paratha nan,' she said, 'And I made way too much as usual.'

Cosima grinned. 'Good, bet you I can finish the lot.'

Harpa laughed. 'I'll take that bet; you always think you can eat more than you actually do.'

Cosima went into her bedroom to change, and as she changed into her sweats, she called Jack Hampton, their FBI liaison. Harpa had a huge crush on the man – hence the 'Handsome Jack' comment – but Cosima couldn't see it. He was tall, blonde, rangy and was an efficient and friendly liaison. He worked tirelessly to protect the two Bedi women, and when they were forced to leave New York, his intervention and friendship had made the change more bearable than it would have been.

'Hampton.'

'Hey dude, it's Cosima.'

His tone changed from professional to warm in a second. 'Hey you, how's things in the Big Easy?'

'Sweaty, sultry and wonderful. How's the Big Apple?'

'Sweaty, sultry and morose. Or that might be just me,' he chuckled. 'Look, I need to come down and check in with you – I know it's short notice, but my schedule got cleared for tomorrow, so I thought maybe...?'

Cosima chewed her lip. 'I do have to work, but maybe I can skip off early. Do you want to come to the apartment and we'll feed you? I know how little the FBI pays you.'

He laughed at her joke. One thing she knew about Jack Hampton was that he came from old New England money, had eschewed the family banking business and went to Quantico in the hope of making people's lives better. It was one of the reasons he was more of a friend to them than a protector, and Cosima trusted him implicitly.

'That sounds good...hell, I'm already drooling at the thought.'

'You should be here now; Harpa's made a curry that I'm about to demolish.'

Jack groaned. 'Torturer. Look, good, I'll fly down tomorrow and be at your place by...'

'Eight? Is that too late?'

'Not at all,' he said, 'I'll be staying a couple of days.'

'Good, see you then.'

HARPA WAS RIGHT – Cosima got through two plates of the curry then, giving up, groaned, placing her hands on her belly. 'God, so good, Harp. Tell me again why you're not a professional chef?'

Harpa colored. 'Funny you should ask that...'

Cosima's eyebrows shot up. 'Huh? What's going on?'

Harpa shifted nervously in her seat. 'Cos...since we've been here,

I've not been able to pick up the kind of clientele I need for the styling business.'

It was Cosima's turn to look uncomfortable. 'I know, and I'm sorry about that. It doesn't seem fair that I get to have my dream job and you...'

'That's just it. I don't think it is my dream job. I've been thinking it over more and more, and I've talked to Deacon...I'm going back to college, Cos. To become a chef, a professional chef.'

For a beat, Cosima was stunned. Then she grinned widely and leapt up to hug her sister. 'Harp, that's fantastic.'

She felt her sister relax in her arms. 'Really, you don't mind?'

'Of course not – why would you think that?'

'Because it's a big change and because we'll see each other even less than we do now?'

Cosima didn't understand. 'Huh? Why?'

Harpa sucked in a deep lungful of air. 'Because the college is in Seattle.'

'WELL, WHERE IS HE?'

Sabine tapped her long fingernails on the glass table, her cell phone pressed to her ear. Margaret, Arlo's fiercely loyal PA was telling her that Arlo was out of town.

'I'm afraid I cannot tell you where, Ms. Karlsson.'

Margaret had always disliked her, but Arlo would never fire the woman because she was rude to Sabine. 'She's practically my mom,' he told Sabine, 'I've known her all my life.'

Now, Sabine narrowed her eyes. Margaret knew damn well where Arlo was. 'Tell him to call me,' she hissed and ended the call. Fuck it, she thought, I wanted to get this done, tell him I wasn't going anywhere, that I love him too much to take no for an answer.

She sat thinking about what to do next, pondering blackmail or trying to steal Arlo's schedule from Margaret – a nearly impossible feat, but Sabine still had some friends within the company. Sam, that I.T. guy who never stopped gawping at her whenever he was fixing something in Arlo's office. She was sure she could get to him – whatever it took. Sabine was a mastermind at turning her feelings off – hell, she'd done it for years with the various men in her life. Except Arlo. Arlo she had genuinely loved. Cole too, to a lesser degree, but then she'd only begun the affair to get Arlo's attention.

Yes, that's what she'd do – get Sam to hack into Margaret's online scheduler...Sabine grinned to herself and went to grab a shower.

I'll find you, Arlo Forrester, and show you just what you're missing.

COSIMA FELT a nervous thrill go through her when Arlo showed up at the office the next morning. 'I thought we'd look at some sites,' he said nonchalantly, and Tal had nodded eagerly.

'Good idea...you both go check out the ones we ring-fenced, Cosima, I'm sure three would be a crowd.' Tal couldn't hide his grin.

Cosima shot her chuckling boss a death stare as she followed Arlo out to his Mercedes. Arlo was polite and courteous in the office, but when he started the car, he gave her a wicked grin. 'Time to show me what you're made of, Bedi.'

She couldn't help returning his smile. 'You better be ready, Forrester, I have a whole stack of potential sites and places up for sale.' She waved a thick stack of papers.

They drove to each site, Cosima giving him the pros and cons of each. The first few were empty lots. 'I'm sure you don't need me to tell you that although your initial outlay may be more if you build from the ground up, you get to build exactly what you want.'

Arlo nodded. 'Right...that's where I'm conflicted. I took a look through the papers you're holding – Tal emailed the details last night. If you'd offered me an empty site this time, yesterday, I would have gone with it. But there was this one place in the Quarter...'

'The old 'LaBelle'? I know, right, it's fantastic,' Cosima was delighted he'd seen the same potential in the old broke-down hotel that she'd seen. 'Damn, Arlo, do you even realize the potential in that place? And it has that NOLA aesthetic you were talking about yesterday. I know it looks a mess, but there's so much we could salvage there…keep the shabby chic about it, really infuse it with…' She stopped suddenly and laughed. 'Sorry, I got carried away.'

Arlo grinned. 'Not at all. I was thinking the same thing myself. Listen, let's blow off these other sites and go there now – I want to see it for myself.'

Cosima grinned. 'Then hang a left here, sport.'

Arlo steered the car deftly through the traffic until they reached the outside of the LaBelle. It was an old building, one of the oldest in the Quarter, standing only seven floors high but almost a block wide. Cosima dug out her cell phone. 'The realtor is only a few blocks away, and he knows we're coming today. Shouldn't be a problem to get him here.'

It wasn't – he was there in ten minutes - and soon they were being led through the hotel, Cosima noting all the old features and fittings that could be salvaged, getting more and more enthused as they walked through. She looked at Arlo, waiting for his reaction. He nodded, looking around in silence for a few moments. Cosima, impatient, shifted from foot to foot. Finally, Arlo turned to the realtor. 'How much? For everything?'

The realtor told him, followed by another silence while Arlo considered. Cosima, her heart thumping, watched him.

'You've got a deal…and I'll throw in another two hundred grand if we can close escrow by Friday.'

The realtor's eyes bugged out; he and Cosima exchanged a stunned look. 'Well, I'll see what we can do.'

Arlo smiled at him. 'Make it happen, would you please? My… colleague and I are keen to start work on it.' And he gave Cosima such a lust-filled, wanton look that she felt naked and hot under his stare. The realtor, clearly nonplussed, excused himself and went to make some calls.

'I can't believe you did that. I can't believe you just bought the place, just like that.' Cosima shook her head in wonderment. 'What convinced you?'

'You,' he said simply. 'The look in your eyes when you talk to me about wainscoting and staircases and hand-crafted metalwork. The sheer joy of turning this old wreck into something spectacular, Cosima. I haven't felt that in years and today, you bring me here, and I find it again. Thank you.'

Cosima swallowed. Arlo's expression was nothing but genuine; he wasn't playing her, trying to suck up, trying for anything but the truth. 'Thank you, that's...'

She couldn't finish because Arlo stepped forward and took her face in his hands, pressing his lips to hers. The kiss was so sweet it made her head swim, but gently, after a beat, she placed her hands on his chest and pushed him away. 'Arlo...'

He grinned unashamedly. 'Just a celebratory kiss. No strings.'

Laughing, she shook her head. 'You are the worst.'

The realtor came back in, beaming. 'Mr. Forrester, I have good news. I can do one better than Friday. How would you like to be the proud owner of this hotel by Thursday?'

SHE AGREED to go out to lunch with him, but clearly young Sam was expecting far more before he'd hand over the information. No problem, Sabine smiled to herself, as she led him to her hotel room. Sam looked like he could hardly believe it as she unzipped his pants and reached for his cock. He tried to kiss her but she turned her head away. 'I don't kiss, Sam. I'll suck your cock, and you can fuck me in whichever way you want, but I don't kiss.'

She could tell he'd stopped listening at 'suck your cock.' She sank gracefully to her knees and took him into her mouth, rolling her tongue around the sensitive tip, feeling it twitch and thicken as she tasted him.

When he was hard, she stripped off, pushing him back on the bed, and straddled him. He was young, early twenties, but his cock was impressive and with a sigh, she impaled herself on it, riding him, thrusting hard onto him. His hands were on her waist, or cupping her small breasts, and she murmured encouraging words to him. Of course, he came too quickly, and she'd had to pretend to come, afterward excusing herself to the bathroom to finish herself, muffling her moan with a hand towel.

Strolling naked back to the bedroom, she smiled down at him. 'So what have you got for me?'

Sam grinned and reached for his bag. 'Printouts. Mr. Forrester's schedule for the next three months. Looks like he's going to be out of town.'

Sabine took the printouts, frowning. She scanned through them. 'New Orleans?' She kept looking, flicking through the papers again and again. Then she looked at Sam, her gray eyes cold. 'What the fuck is in New Orleans?'

ALL DAY he'd been trying to resist touching her tawny skin. Then, in the old hotel, with the scent of her skin driving him crazy, he hadn't been able to hold back, grabbing her and kissing her. She had kissed back too, before pushing him away.

It didn't matter. Just in that brief moment when Arlo's lips had molded so naturally to Cosima's, he'd been taken back to the little villa on the water in the Maldives, her body twined around his, his cock buried deep inside her.

Arlo looked over at her as he drove them back to the office. Her dark hair had escaped the clip she'd used to put it up into a chignon, the faint blush of her cheeks reminding him of her afterglow, the breathless undulation of her body under his. God, the need for him to make love to her again was beginning to hurt and...

'I still can't believe you bought the place, just like that,' Cosima said, chuckling. 'The heady delight of being a billionaire.'

He smiled at her. 'Surely your family is well off? I know your father's assets were seized, but your mother...'

'Put her entire earnings up her nose or injected into her forehead,' Cosima interrupted, and he was surprised at the bitterness in her voice. She gave him a half-smile. 'It doesn't matter; Harpa and I have never needed her money, we do just fine. Money had never been an ambition for me.'

'I respect that.'

'Says the billionaire.' But she was chuckling, and he joined in.

'Hey, look, that's just the result of my work, not the goal I was aiming for.'

'What was?'

Arlo shrugged. 'I just wanted to design beautiful buildings. Somewhere along the way, the practical side kicked in, and the company ended up going where the market dictated. Soon, we were mass-building hotels that were impersonal, functional and profitable. Now I want something different. I was recently shown how being spontaneous could bring great fulfillment.' He slid her a sideways look and saw she was blushing.

After a moment, Cosima put her hand on his arm. 'Arlo, I want you to know, whatever our situation is now, those few days in the Maldives were the best of my life. Truly. I've never had that connection with someone. Ever.'

AFTER HE'D DROPPED her back at the office, he went to his hotel and checked in with Margaret. His secretary reeled off a list of calls he'd gotten then told him Sabine had been calling.

'Lord, that woman doesn't know the meaning of 'he's not interested.''

Arlo grinned. Margaret had never liked Sabine. 'Thanks for putting up with her nonsense.'

'No problem, dear, as long as I have permission to go full Mrs. Landingham on her.'

Arlo laughed. Margaret was a huge fan of The West Wing. 'If only I were like President Bartlet, I'd be happily married to Stockard Channing, and she would hand Sabine her ass.'

'Yes, she would,' Margaret laughed. 'Speaking of happily married...'

'Oh yes?'

'Cole Trent is getting married. Just thought you ought to know.'

Arlo was stunned, but he gathered himself. 'How'd you know?'

'He came by to see me.' Unlike Sabine, Margaret had been genuinely upset by Cole's betrayal; she had, after all, seen both the boys through puberty working for their fathers, then through college, and had been as much of a part of their businesses as either of them.

Arlo sighed. 'I don't know what to say to that. Look, if you speak to him, pass along my congratulations.'

Margaret's voice softened. 'I will, dear. I'm hoping the idea of getting married rubs off on you.'

Arlo laughed. 'I'm working on it, Margie.'

'Don't call me that.' But she chuckled. 'Call me if you need anything, dear.'

'Okay, Maggie.'

'Demon child.'

Arlo hung up the phone feeling remarkably happy. Margaret always had that effect, being as she was his de-facto mother and had been since his own mother had died. Arlo was almost forty and yet Margaret, with her joie-de-vivre still intact at nearly eighty, made him feel a like teenager.

Talking about feeling good…he flicked through his photos on his phone to the one he wanted. He had taken it surreptitiously; Cosima was asleep in a lounge chair, her dark skin a perfect foreground to the crystal blue ocean around them. They had said no names, no strings – he reckoned that probably meant no photos too, but right at that moment, Cosima in a white bikini, her breasts golden and ripe, and her belly gently rising and falling with her breath as she slept…God, she was a goddess, and I'm her willing slave…damn. He respected her decision to focus on work, and he wouldn't do anything to jeopardize her career, but for him, it was a foregone conclusion.

They would be together, and he couldn't wait for that day to come.

HARPA OPENED the door and grinned. 'Hey, Handsome Jack, come on in.'

Jack Hampton rolled his eyes at her. 'Harpa, I hope you checked it was me before you opened the door?'

'Yeah, yeah, Grumpus, come on in,' She tugged him into the apartment, and he waved a hello at Cosima, who was watching the scene with amusement.

'Hey, Jack, I hope you're hungry. Harpa has made what I can only describe as a planet load of food.'

Harpa flipped her sister the finger, grinning. 'Didn't hear you complaining when you wanted to try it all.'

Cosima took Jack's coat while Harpa grabbed them cold beers from the refrigerator. 'How's New York?'

'Still there, despite their grief at you leaving,' Jack winked at her, and she beamed. Harpa wasn't subtle when it came to her crushes. Cosima poked her sister.

'Serve already; I'm starving.'

The food was magnificent, and as they ate, Harpa told Jack about wanting to move to Seattle. Jack looked at Cosima.

'You going with her?'

Cosima shook her head, smiling at Harpa. 'This is Harp's thing. My place is here.'

Especially now. All afternoon, all evening, she hadn't been able to get that kiss out of her head. She'd nearly forgotten all of her rules and gone back to his hotel with him, even wished herself there now, naked and climbing on that incredible body of his, feeling his huge cock pushing deep inside of her...

'Cos? Jack asked you a question.'

Cosima blinked and brought herself back to the present. Jack looked amused. 'You looked absorbed in something.'

'Just work,' she smiled, and picked her fork up, 'So to what do we owe the pleasure of your company, Jack?'

Jack's expression became somber and just like that the atmosphere in the room changed. Cosima and Harpa exchanged a worried look. 'What? What is it this time?' Cosima felt a fist clench in her chest.

Jack sighed. 'We have intelligence of another possible threat. To you, Cosima. We don't know if it's tied to your father but we got a call to say someone had been looking into you, Cos. Some detective from San Francisco.'

Cosima's face paled. Arlo. That's how he found her. On one hand, she felt relieved it wasn't some random death threat; on the other, she knew she had to tell Jack about Arlo. She shoved her rice around on her plate for a moment.

'I don't think that's anything...to worry about,' she started slowly, looking away from both Jack and Harpa's curious gazes, 'I think it was to do with work. My...client is Arlo Forrester.'

'The property magnate?'

She nodded. 'He's based in San Francisco. He, um, head-hunted me after we met a few months back. I assume the detective was to find out who I worked for, because when I met him, I was between jobs.'

Jack nodded, his eyes still fixed on her blushing face. 'Work?'

'Yes.'

'Okay then, well, if we find out anything else about the private dick, we'll let you know. Good to know it isn't anything more...challenging.'

Harpa, who had been watching her sister carefully, smiled. 'That's good news, because how many potential murderers does a girl need? What are they going to do, re-kill us?'

'No-one's going to kill you, Harpa. I won't permit it.'

Cosima tried to smile. 'Well, let's forget all of that and just enjoy this amazing food, shall we? Harpa, tell us some more about this college course.'

LATER, when they had said goodbye to Jack, Cosima started to clear the dishes, shoving the copious leftovers into their refrigerator. She studiously ignored Harpa who was standing, leaning against the doorjamb with her arms cross and watching her.

After a few moments, Harpa could bear it no longer.

'So,' she began, pulling out a chair and sitting down, 'I figured out that the only time you were between jobs was a couple of months ago...and most of that time, you were in the Maldives.'

Cosima shrugged but said nothing, rinsing out a washcloth in the sink. Harpa studied her sister. 'You fucked Arlo Forrester?'

Cosima sighed, giving up. 'Yes.'

Harpa gaped. 'No, really?'

Cosima threw her hands up. 'Harpa – what do you want me to say? I had a holiday fling with the man. It was wonderful. I came home. The end.'

'Except he's looking for you,' Harpa was grinning, 'Dude...Arlo Forrester is hot.'

Cosima nodded. 'And here. He found me, Harp. And I'm working for him now, so our relationship is just professional from now on. Why are you looking at me like that?'

Harpa was smiling. 'Because it's so unlike you. You don't do casual hookups, you never have. And you've been unreasonably cheerful since you got back like you...'

'Like you what?'

Harpa burst out laughing. 'Like you got laid properly for the first time in your life.'

Cosima snorted with laughter. 'Well, that's not far off the mark. But, hey, look, it's over now so let's just drop it.'

'Except it's not. He's here, and you're going to be working with him, mmm, getting close, working late...' Harpa got up and put her arms around her sister. 'New Orleans is hot even in the fall, and you'll get all sweaty and say 'Gosh, Mr. Forrester, I do believe I'm feeling faint, I might just have to open my blouse."

Cosima was giggling now as Harpa continued her skit. 'And then he says 'Say, Missy, let me just help you out with that...' Her voice had dropped significantly, and she strode around the kitchen like a Neanderthal. Cosima wiped her eyes.

'Yes, because that's the way it works.'

Harpa, exhausting herself, finally dropped into a chair. 'Seriously, though, Cos...do you like this guy?'

Cosima nodded. 'I do. But, at the moment, my career comes first.

When we've completed this project, who knows? We'll probably be sick of the sight of one another.'

Harpa grinned then yawned widely, setting off Cosima. 'Yup. Bedtime.'

Cosima was just getting into bed when Harpa stuck her head around the door. She smiled at her sister.

'Cos, I just wanted to say...I'm really happy that you had that, the fling or whatever it was. For months I was worried – check that, years – that you were missing out. On life. On love. You were always so serious, Cos, and since you came back from the Indian Ocean, there's been something new in your eyes.'

Cosima was touched. 'What's that?'

Harpa smiled softly. 'Joy. Night, Cos.'

'Night, Boo.'

Cosima switched her lamp off and lay back in bed. She thought about what Harpa had said, thought about that kiss this afternoon some more. You're right, Harpa, I did feel joy. I feel joy whenever he is near me. Cosima smiled to herself. She was looking forward to working on the LaBelle Project – and part of her was looking forward to it finishing. She hoped Arlo Forrester meant what he said.

She hoped he would wait for her.

'You're wrong.'

'I am not wrong; you're just a jackass.'

'That's Mr. Jackass, sweetcheeks.'

Cosima couldn't stop laughing. It had been a month, and the hotel was in a state of complete disarray. Contractors knocking walls down, electricians and joiners working everywhere. Arlo had been impressed with how quickly Cosima had organized everything. 'You sure you don't want to appoint a project manager?'

She shook her head. 'I'm a control freak, and since you didn't need me to, you know, build a hotel, I'm good.'

'Well, I'm impressed but not surprised.'

She grinned. 'Wait until you have a dumb idea and I have to talk you out of it.'

Which was what was happening now. Cosima wiped her eyes and put her hand on his. 'Arlo...you cannot put a fireman's pole on the penthouse.'

He was smiling that wicked smile of his. 'Why not? Who's to say what I can or can't do in my home?'

That stopped her. 'What?' Her eyes were wide with surprise.

'I fully intend to make the penthouse my permanent home here in New Orleans.'

Cosima was stunned. 'You're staying here?'

Arlo picked up his glass of scotch and sipped it before answering. 'I told you I would wait...'

They were in the bar of the Le Richelieu. It was late evening; both of them had worked since very early that morning and now Cosima, light-headed from not eating lunch, put down her cocktail.

'Arlo...'

'Cosima, let's just stop. Stop pretending to be just friends. Don't get me wrong; I'm glad we are friends because I could never contemplate spending my life with someone who wasn't my best friend. But this is driving me crazy.'

He got up and moved his chair next to hers, cupping her face in his palm. 'I want you, Cosima; I want you in my bed, in my life. You're already in my heart. I won't let it affect your career; I swear to God, I won't.'

He leaned in and pressed his lips against hers. 'I will wait, I promise if that's what you want. Just say the word and I'll stop.' His eyes dropped to her mouth, then her throat then up again, holding her gaze as he kissed her again, not caring if the rest of the bar's patrons saw them. Cosima kissed him back, the longing inside her overwhelming her. She adored this man, his kiss, his face, his hands, his humor...everything. And she didn't want to wait any longer. Arlo broke away and looked at her.

'Well?'

She gazed back, the fire inside her obvious. 'Don't stop.'

IN THE ELEVATOR to his room, Arlo had her against the wall, kissing her fiercely, his hands on her body. Cosima, breathless, dug her fingernails into the huge muscles of his back. 'Tell me what you're going to do to me,' she gasped as his hand slipped under her dress and between her legs. She pressed her sex onto his fingers, and he growled.

'I'm going to fuck you all night long, Cosima Bedi. I'm going to nail you to the fucking bed, my cock filling you until you scream. I'm going to taste every part of you, your breasts, your belly, your delicious cunt....'

As the elevator reached his floor, they ran, laughing, hand-in-hand to his door. 'God, Cosima, just wait until I get you inside...'

She grinned as he fumbled with the key card as he opened the door; he bowed extravagantly and waved her in. He followed her in and almost collided with her as she had stopped dead. Frowning, he stepped around her...and saw what she was staring at.

Sabine. Naked. On his bed. She smiled lasciviously.

'Hello darling,' she purred and very slowly, very deliberately, spread her long, long legs as wide as she could.

HARPA WAS TALKING to Deacon when she heard the apartment door close. She glanced over at the clock. Eleven p.m. 'Deac, I gotta go, I need to tell Cos what we've discussed.'

She tugged on her robe and went to find her sister. Confused, she searched Cosima's room, the living room, the kitchen. Finally, she heard the shower running and peeked around the bathroom door. Cosima was sitting – fully dressed – in the bathtub, the shower running above her, soaking her.

'What on earth are you doing?' Harpa frowned. Cosima wouldn't look at her, and as she approached, she saw her sister was crying.

'Cos, what's the matter?' She cranked the shower off and grabbed a towel, throwing it across Cosima's shoulders.

'Nothing, it's nothing,' but Cosima sobbed harder. Harpa let her cry herself out. When she shuddered to a stop, Harpa helped her out of the tub.

'Why were you in the shower?'

Cosima, still gulping, shook her head. 'I don't know. I've just seen people do it in the movies.'

Harpa couldn't help the giggle that escaped her. 'Doofus. Come on, let's get you out of those clothes.'

She helped Cosima into dry clothes, toweling her sister's hair dry. When Cosima was tucked into bed, Harpa sat on the edge. 'Come on, spill it.'

Cosima groaned. 'It doesn't even matter.'

Harpa fixed her with a stare and Cosima shrugged. 'I went back to his room,' she blushed furiously, 'and there was this gorgeous – and I mean, drop-dead gorgeous, woman there. Blonde, leggy, naked. On his bed. And she was good enough to show him – and me – what he was missing.'

Harpa made a disgusted noise. 'And what did Arlo do?'

Cosima sighed. 'He yelled. A lot. I could hear him still yelling when I ran.'

'You ran?'

'I did.'

Harpa chewed her lip for a moment. 'In the circumstances, I think I would have done the same thing. Is she still there?'

'How do I know?'

'He didn't follow you?'

Cosima shook her head and her eyes filled with tears. Harpa hugged her. 'I bet he tried to call you, did he call?'

Cosima flopped back on the pillows. 'I don't know; I can't find my phone.'

Harpa got up and went searching for Cosima's purse. She came back waving her phone. 'It's dead. Grab your charger.'

She plugged it into the outlet and flicked it on. She smiled triumphantly. 'Fifteen missed calls and your voicemail is full.'

Cosima took the phone but hesitated. 'What if it's not worth getting involved, Harp?'

Harpa rolled her eyes and grabbed the phone, dialing the voicemail. 'Joy,' was all she said and handed the phone back to Cosima.

Cosima stared at her sister for a long moment then nodded. 'Joy,' she said softly. Harpa got up and left her alone. Padding silently back to her own room, she found herself wishing and hoping that Arlo Forrester wouldn't break her sister's heart.

ARLO DROPPED his head into his hands. He'd been trying to call Cosima for the last hour, ever since he'd finally gotten Sabine out of his hotel room. The shock he'd felt at seeing her there, blatantly, revoltingly sexual in her temerity. He caught a glimpse of Cosima's pale, horrified face before she had darted past him and one thought hit him: I've lost her.

Torn between going after Cosima and getting rid of Sabine, he'd chosen the later.

'What the fuck are you doing?' He'd yelled, his temper a volcanic thing, anger making him not care what anyone else thought. 'Get the fuck out of my room, Sabine.'

She'd smiled, cat-like, and closed her legs. 'So that's the new girl, is it? She seemes very different to me, isn't she? Flighty.'

Arlo saw Sabine's clothes on a chair, picked them up and threw them at her. 'Get dressed, get out. Now.'

She smirked but pulled on her dress, not bothering with her underwear. 'I don't know why you're getting so upset; isn't ex-sex still a thing?' She came up to him and curled her body around his, looking up at him from beneath long blonde lashes. 'Would she do to you what I always did? Make you crazy? Make you moan?'

Arlo looked down at her, his eyes cold. 'Cosima is everything to me. She does what you never could; she makes me feel loved, feel more than just someone with a bottomless wallet. She makes me feel like a man. Is that what you want to hear, Sabine?'

Sabine winced a little but turned away so he couldn't see her face. 'Cosima. Stupid name. What is she, Mexican?'

'Indian and it's a beautiful name for a beautiful woman. Now, for the last time, get out of my room, and my life. It's over, Sabine, done, finished.'

She stared at him then, and he could see the hurt, the spite in her eyes. 'Did you ever love me?'

His mouth set in a straight line. 'I didn't know what love was until I met Cosima. So, I guess that means no.'

Sabine turned and walked out of the room, slamming the door, and Arlo locked it behind her. God damn it. He grabbed his phone and called Cosima. Voicemail.

'Cosima, I can't begin to apologize. Please know I had no idea Sabine would be here, and I'm disgusted with her. I've thrown her out – look, please, Cos, call me and let's talk. I don't even know where you live so I can't follow you and beg for your forgiveness. Tonight was supposed to be magical. I'm crazy about you, Cos, please, call me.'

Over the next hour, he called again and again to radio silence from Cosima. Eventually, he gave up and sat on the bed, wondering what the hell to do next.

Which is when his phone rang.

ARLO WALKED to the LaBelle the next morning, wanting to get some air and clear his head before he saw Cosima. They had talked long into the night, and he was sure he had managed to convince her that Sabine had been an unwelcome guest, but still, he wanted to take her in his arms and make sure she knew that she was the only woman for him.

His heart faltered when he saw her. A pale blue summer dress on that heavenly body, her hair scooped up into a messy bun, she was studying some paperwork at the reception when he arrived. The hotel was a mess but there she was, like a beautiful oasis of calm in the center of it.

'Cosima,' he said, and she looked up and smiled. Cursing silently as he saw the dark circles under her lovely eyes, he strode to her and took her in his arms.

'It's so good to see you,' he said, tilting his chin up with his finger. He kissed her thoroughly, ignoring the amused glances of the workmen around them. Cosima sighed, as they eventually broke apart.

'That's a nice way to be greeted,' she said softly and smiled. He stroked her face with his thumbs.

'Tonight,' he said, 'there will be no interruptions.'

Cosima nodded. 'Harpa is staying over at her boyfriend's apartment tonight, so...'

Arlo smiled. 'I get to see the Bedi bed?'

She laughed. 'More than see it, Mr. Forrester...'

He made a low growling sound in his throat which made her smile. 'I can't wait.'

Cosima checked her watch. 'Well, if we get done by lunchtime...' She smiled up at him, and he grinned.

'Then let's get to work.'

As it turned out, they were kept busy all day and by the time they finally left for her apartment, it was after eight and dusk had fallen. Arlo followed Cosima's car back to her street and met her at the steps to her apartment. She took his hand and led him up, and as she unlocked it, his excitement grew to almost fever pitch. Inside, he took her in his arms and kissed her with such passion that soon they were stripping each other's clothes off and tumbling to the floor.

'Don't wait,' she begged him and he slipped his hand between her sex to find her already wet for him. She grinned up at him. 'I've been thinking about this all day.'

He laughed and buried his face in her neck. 'Me too, beautiful.'

She freed his cock from his pants and wrapped her legs around him. 'Please, Arlo, I need you inside me.'

His cock was diamond-hard and ready, and as he entered her, they both sighed with the release of the months-long wait. He sank into her, hitching her legs higher so he could plunge deep into her. His hands were on her face, his eyes locked on hers as they moved together.

'Cosima Bedi,' he was breathless, all his blood on fire from the feel of her, 'I am so in love with you...'

Cosima's eyes filled with tears and as she gasped and moved beneath him, her hands clawing at his back, she moaned, 'I love you, Arlo...'

Arlo began to thrust hard, Cosima urging him on until her back arched, her head dropped back, and she cried out as she came, her hands on his chest. Arlo felt his cock respond, and he groaned as his hot semen pumped deep inside her. They collapsed together on the floor, dragging lungfuls of oxygen in. Arlo grinned down at her.

'Thank God for that,' and she laughed.

'I know...god, why did I want to wait again?'

Arlo pressed his lips to hers, savoring the taste of her. 'No, I get why...and we have to make sure that this, us, doesn't interfere with your career. But I won't be able to stop this now, you understand? I need you, I love you. I've never been so sure of anything in my life more than we are meant to be together.'

She nodded, a single tear dropping down her face. 'I love you so much. When I left you in the Maldives, I thought my heart wouldn't take it, and yet we had agreed, and I knew the rules. But I never stopped thinking about you, not once.'

Arlo smiled and trailed the back of his fingers down her cheek. 'I'll never get over the way you approached me. So confident, so sure. God, what a turn on.'

She giggled shyly. 'If you only knew how unlike me that was, but I saw you and something in me shifted. Just from that one look we shared. I knew.'

They kissed again then Arlo scrambled to his feet and lifted her up. 'Show me to your chamber, your highness.'

She grinned and took his hand, leading him into her bedroom. Arlo looked around. It was a riot of colors, Indian fabrics at the window, on the dresser and the nightstand. Her scent, jasmine and spice, permeated the room, sending his senses reeling with pleasure. He ran his hands down her body, cupping her breasts and splaying his fingers over her belly; Cosima shivered with pleasure as he stroked her. She led him to her bed and lay down, opening her arms to him.

'Come here, Arlo, love me...'

And they began again where they had left off.

SABINE KARLSSON SAT outside Cosima's apartment, in the car she'd rented in which she'd followed Arlo from his hotel that morning. She looked up at the warmly lit window, thinking she could see their shadows, kissing, screwing. The thought of Arlo fucking that little whore...Sabine gritted her teeth. She would find out who she was and destroy her – how dare she think she could take what belonged to Sabine? She was Sabine Karlsson, for fuck's sake, supermodel. She scribbled down the address and started the car.

I won't let you be happy without me, Arlo, not ever. I'll do anything I need to do to ruin your life...anything.

COSIMA AND ARLO walked to the LaBelle the next morning, hand-in-hand. Arlo grinned at her. 'Last night – and this morning – was incredible.'

She smiled. 'My body should feel exhausted...instead, I just feel exhilarated.'

Arlo nodded. 'Me too. Look,' he stopped her, 'I'm not saying we should rush things, but I want us to start planning our future. Would you consider sharing the penthouse with me, when it's finished?'

Cosima studied him, considering. If anyone else had asked her to move in with him this quickly, she would have laughed in their faces but with Arlo, it just seemed natural. And anyway, she reasoned, the hotel wouldn't be finished for months.

'Yes,' she said simply, 'I will definitely think about it. Harpa will be in Seattle by then and...well...waking up with you every day sounds perfect.'

Arlo was pleased. 'Good. Wow.' He suddenly grabbed her and spun her around, making her giggle furiously. 'We're moving in together.'

He spun her until she protested and set her down, steadying her when she wobbled. 'God, Arlo Forrester, I said I'd think about it,' she laughed breathlessly, 'You are a lunatic.' She put a hand on her chest, catching her breath. She patted his arm. 'Come on, let's get to work.'

NEITHER OF THEM saw the blacked out car across the street and the occupants who were watching them. The driver turned to the man in the back seat.

'You sure that's her?'

'One hundred percent. Damn, I'd forgotten how beautiful she was.'

The driver smirked. 'Does that make a difference?'

The other smiled. 'No. It just means I'll get even more enjoyment out of it when I kill her.'

'How will you do it?'

The man smiled, watching as Cosima laughed at something her companion was saying. She made his groin tighten with desire, but the thought of her dead under his knife was even more exhilarating. 'Slowly,' he said, 'Slowly and painfully.'

AFTER THE SABINE DEBACLE, Arlo had changed hotels and now, when they made their way to it, Cosima was confident that nothing could ruin their evening together. His hotel room was as luxurious as she could have imagined. Not so much a room as an entire apartment, she thought, looking around with obvious pleasure. Arlo watched her with amused eyes.

'You can't turn off the artist's eye, can you?'

He was pouring her a flute of champagne, and she took it gratefully. Her hands were trembling, and he steadied them with his own, the fire his touch ignited in her was searing. She tilted her head up, and he caught her mouth with his, kissing her softly, tenderly. When they broke apart, he smiled down at her.

'Hello again,' he murmured and slid his hands around her waist. Cosima wobbled then relaxed into his embrace.

Arlo took the still full champagne flute from her hand and scooped her up into his arms. She started to protest, but he just smiled. 'Cosima – my belle Camille – there's no way that we're doing anything else at this moment but going to bed. I need your skin on mine, your sweet lips against my own, and my cock buried deep inside your tight, heavenly cunt.'

His coarseness made her sex pulse and dampen, and she didn't protest as he stripped her. 'Christ, look at just how beautiful you are,' he growled, pushing her legs up to her chest and burying his face in her sex. Cosima moaned as his tongue found her clit, already so ready for him, swelling and pulsing under his touch. He drove her to madness with his tongue then slowly moved up her body, kissing and tasting her skin.

'Cosima, my lovely girl, I want you to see how beautiful you are...'

He left her on the bed, bereft at his going, but pulled the dresser over so that the mirror faced the bed. Cosima could see her own body stretched out, golden in the dim light. It was slightly surreal, the dust on the mirror giving an otherworldly appearance to their bodies. Arlo stripped, and she admired the broad shoulders, the deep vee of his hips, his large cock, curving upwards as he fisted the root of it, pumping it even harder.

'I could look at you for days,' he said, and she smiled.

'Right back at ya, handsome.' She loved that they could fool around and laugh when they had sex, that it wasn't a solemn occasion but a joyful one. He grinned back at her then dropped to all fours over her body, his hands braced either side of her head.

'I want you to realize how beautiful you are...' he lifted her leg so her sex was exposed. 'Look at you, look at your sweet little cunt, Cosima.'

Gazing into the mirror at herself, seeing him stroke her clit, feeling herself get damp with longing.

'Do you want my cock now, Cosima?'

She nodded and grinned; he shifted so he could slide, oh so slowly, into her. She watched as his cock sank deep into her sex, felt the stretch of her vaginal muscles accommodating him. They watched as he slid in and out of her, Cosima almost losing her mind with pleasure as he fingered her clit at the same time. She came violently, again and again, and as Arlo neared his own climax, he whispered, 'I want to come on your belly.'

She nodded, her eyes alive with arousal as he pulled out and with a shuddering groan, pumped creamy white semen onto her skin. 'God, Cosima...Cosima...'

She pulled him into her arms as he finished and kissed him, wrapping her legs around him. 'Let's not move from this place ever.'

'Good idea.'

THEY LAY in silence for a few minutes just gazing at each other. Arlo stroked her face and Cosima smiled.

'You know, one thing we need to discuss is, I think you need to meet Jack.'

Arlo frowned. 'Who's Jack?'

'My imaginary friend. He travels with me everywhere. He's here now,' Cosima tried not to giggle at Arlo's expression but failed. 'No, seriously, he's our FBI liaison. He needs to know about us, about what we plan. He kind of already knows that you are I are...um... acquainted. They found out about your detective.'

Arlo nodded. 'Makes sense. I hope I haven't caused any difficulties for you by seeking you out.'

Cosima wriggled into his arms happily. 'Nothing that wasn't totally worth it. But he will need to know if we move in together. Sadly, there are still some of my father's enemies who want Harpa and me dead.'

Arlo winced. 'God, I can't imagine living that way. How do you do it?'

She shrugged. 'We've never really known anything different – at least not for the past few years. You get used to it. Moving from city to city has helped, although it's stressful, and relationships are difficult. When the call comes, you have to go, right then, no time for good-byes. Those are the extreme cases, the ones where our lives have been in imminent danger. New York was really the only time that happened.'

'Last year?'

She nodded. 'The FBI has been great. Why they should want to protect us is beyond me, but there you go. At least they've been able to narrow down the parties involved. Most of my dad's enemies have either died or simply don't care anymore, but there are a couple of offspring that have been radicalized. What's weird is...I grew up with at least one of them - Naveen. We played together as kids, and I had the biggest crush on him, and now he wants to kill me. I'll never understand that kind of mindset.'

She sounded sad, and her eyes glistened with tears. 'It's Harpa I feel the most bad for. I'm scared someone will get to her; she's such an extrovert, so the opposite of me that she rubs against any restriction, and she takes risks. If anything happened to her...'

'Hey, hey,' he brushed the tears from her cheeks with his thumbs. 'I promise you, Cosima, I won't let anything happen to you or Harpa. I can have protection arranged this instant – protection that will be unobtrusive but comprehensive. Harpa will never have to know they are there. I was going to talk to you about that, anyway – and now you've mentioned this Jack person, yeah, I need to meet him. Not,' he added, hurriedly, 'that I want to give the impression that I'm in control of your life. Entirely your choice...but I will do everything to protect you, Cosima. I love you.'

She smiled. 'As I love you. Man,' she rolled on her back and laughed, and Arlo enjoyed the way her full breasts danced as her chest moved. 'This is all such a fairytale, isn't it? You're so perfect...it's a little annoying.'

He grinned. 'Sorry, ma'am.'

'You should be. Now come over here and fuck me good.'

'Dirty girl.'

'You bet.'

SABINE HAD CASHED out some of her savings and hired a private detective to find out what he could about Arlo's new love. When he gave her his report, she couldn't believe it. She read through his findings and looked up at him.

'She's a goddamned princess?'

Her detective, Hal, nodded. 'Exiled but yeah. Looker, her sister too. Pity about their situation.'

Sabine read and reread the section of the paper that caught her eye. 'Threat of assassination, hey?'

'Yup. Nasty stuff too, which is why the FBI moved them around every few years. My guy at the FBI says someone got too close to the older girl last year; that's why they had to move and change their name.'

'So...if they were exposed, they'd be killed?'

The man nodded. He didn't like the woman in front of him; she creeped him out with her blank stare and icy beauty. But she paid well, and at least he got to follow the two Malhotra girls who were both very easy on the eyes.

'What do you want me to do next?'

Sabine smiled. 'Nothing. Thank you, this has been useful, but I'll take it from here.'

WHEN HE'D GONE, she sat back, considering. Well, now this was interesting – so much more interesting than just a love rival. She weighed her options. One: she could kill the girl herself, frame her enemies and swoop in to console a grieving Arlo. She wrinkled her nose. Too risky, and she didn't trust herself not to chicken out at the last moment then everything would be ruined. No, it was better to lead the killers to the girl, then act horrified and offer to help Arlo track them down when she was murdered. That was option two, and she liked it a whole lot more. But it left her unsatisfied. She wanted the girl – Cosima – to feel fear, to know the consequences of stealing Sabine's man from her. Prolong the agony, like a Chinese water torture.

'Drip, drip, drip,' she said to herself now, laughing. She would torment her, make her paranoid, feel the fear, and when the time was right, she would expose her and lead the killers to her. She could see it now: Arlo bent over the bloody corpse of his Indian princess, her body riddled with bullet holes, Arlo screaming his grief then Sabine herself, gently taking him away as the police came.

Yes. That was perfect. That was just. The girl dead and Arlo once again in Sabine's arms.

'Where you belong, my love,' she whispered, 'Where you belong.'

COSIMA CALLED JACK, and he agreed to fly down to New Orleans the following day to meet with her. She didn't talk about Arlo on the phone, just told Jack that both the sisters were planning major changes in their lives, and they needed to discuss them with him.

She left the LaBelle early that day, kissing Arlo goodbye and checking in at the office. There was someone else she needed to talk to too.

Tal was in his office, and he smiled delightedly when she knocked at his door. 'Well, hello stranger. You've been out on site so much we've hardly seen you.'

She grinned. 'I know, and I'm sorry. Look, Tal, I have to talk to you about something.'

He indicated the seat across his desk, and she sat. 'Want a drink?'

'Yes, please.'

He poured them out some sloe gin. 'From Mrs. Beavers, a client. It's magnificent.'

Cosima sipped the drink then choked. 'Jeez, strong enough.'

Tal grinned. 'Now what have you got to tell me? Not that I can't guess. It's written all over your face.'

Cosima blushed. 'Well, yes, okay. Arlo Forrester and I are involved; we're dating if you can call it that. We're talking about moving in together when the LaBelle is finished, and I wanted you to know that we have kept our relationship purely professional during working hours.' She felt nervous all of a sudden. 'Tal, I would never disrespect you or the company's reputation by acting like a love-sick teenager. There was one kissing incident that may have been witnessed by a contractor.' She shifted in her seat, looking sheepish.

Tal smiled. 'Look, Cosima, you're doing an incredible job. And really, it's not the biggest surprise; I've seen the chemistry between the pair of you. And besides, if it weren't for your acquaintance, we might never have had this opportunity. Relax, dear, it's fine.'

She nodded, satisfied. 'Good, I'm glad. Look, I have to skip out early today to meet my FBI guy.' She had told Tal at the beginning about her situation, and now he nodded.

'Good. Hope you get on okay.'

COSIMA DROVE HOME, lightness in her heart. For the first time since they left New York – and not counting those heady days in the Indian Ocean – she felt everything in her life was right. Harpa was happy – albeit with Deacon who Cosima was trying to like for Harpa's sake – and planning her future in an occupation which Cosima thought would serve her sister's talents better than styling. Her own job was a place of teamwork, encouragement and fraternity, and her love life... she couldn't believe how utterly consumed she was with love for Arlo. Even now, all she could think of was his voice, his dark eyes, his wicked smile, the way he would kiss her throat, stroke her belly, his cock thrusting inside her...concentrate, she told herself with a grin, a fender bender would not be conducive to a happily ever after.

She was still smiling when she got back to the apartment, but as she climbed the stairs, she heard a voice call her name. She turned to see a tall blonde woman staring at her. Cosima's eyes narrowed. 'Yes?' She said politely.

The woman half-smiled. 'You probably don't recognize me with my clothes on.'

Fuck. Sabine. Cosima reluctantly walked back down the stairs. 'No, I didn't.' She injected just the right amount of ice in her voice to make the other woman hold her hands up.

'Seriously, I came to apologize. I had no idea you were with Arlo – that he was even seeing anyone. We were together for fifteen years, and I screwed it up. And I keep screwing it up, obviously. Please forgive me.'

Cosima studied her. 'How did you find out where I live?'

Sabine had the grace to look sheepish. 'I followed Arlo one day. I am sorry for that, for the intrusion, for that night at the hotel, but I'm not sorry for getting the opportunity to apologize. I feel bad.'

Cosima looked at the other woman and believed her. 'It's okay, it's all in the past. Hopefully we can all move on.'

'Yes. Look, it's up to you, but I'd rather you didn't tell Arlo about this. I hope one day we can all be friends should we cross paths. This wouldn't help, I don't think.'

Cosima nodded. 'Okay. Well, goodbye, Sabine...and good luck.'

'Thank you.'

Cosima started to walk back up the stairs.

'Cosima?'

She turned. Sabine was smiling again, and this time, there was a hint of mockery about it. 'Make sure, Cosima, make sure he treats you like a princess.'

With a shocked gasp, Cosima stared after her as she got into her car and drove off.

'ARE YOU OKAY?'

Cosima had been quiet since Arlo arrived, preparing the food for the meal. She smiled and nodded. 'Of course, sorry, I'm just trying to remember this recipe.'

Arlo was satisfied with this. There was an array of colorful vegetables on her kitchen counter and the scent of jasmine rice hung in the air. 'Can I help?'

Cosima grinned. 'How do you feel about preparing the garlic? You can use the press so you don't have to touch it.'

'No worries.'

She watched as he expertly peeled the garlic bulb then squeezed them through the press, mixing them into a paste. 'Want me to add the spices to this?'

Cosima's eyebrows shot up. 'You can cook? Why, Mr. Forrester, you are a dark horse. Yes, please.'

Together they constructed the curry, Arlo frying off the spice paste with onions, Cosima preparing the chicken and vegetables. They moved in tandem, working together on the meal as easily as they did working on the hotel.

Arlo grinned at her as the curry bubbled gently on the stove. 'Our first home-made meal together.'

She nodded. 'You're a great sous-chef.'

'Why, thank you. Can't wait until we can do this in our own home.' He wrapped his arms around her, kissing her. She tasted of coriander and cumin. 'God, I love you. You and your curry.'

She grinned. 'You haven't tasted it yet, and I warn you, Harpa is a much, much better cook.'

'When am I going to meet this master chef?' He took the wine bottle she offered him and opened it.

Cosima considered. 'Soon, I hope. Maybe, after everything's cleared with Jack.'

'Hmm. Not sure I like the idea of my relationship having to be approved by 'Jack,' but as long as you're safe, I'll live with it.'

The doorbell rang. 'Speak of the devil.' She went to the door and greeted Jack. Arlo wiped his hands on a dishcloth and shook the man's hand. The two men sized each other up. Cosima rolled her eyes at them.

'So, Arlo Forrester, meet Jack Hampton. You're both rich and cute. The end.'

They burst out laughing as Cosima deflected the awkwardness. She ushered them into the kitchen. 'Supper's nearly ready. It's curry again,' she said, apologetically, to Jack. 'We always seem to feed you the same thing, I'm sorry.'

'Hey, don't apologize. I live for your curries. So, let's get the awkward stuff out of the way before we eat. Arlo, when Cosima called and told me that she was in a new relationship, I did what I had to do in that situation and checked you out. Sorry for the intrusion but I'm sure, given the circumstances, you understand.'

'I do, and it's no problem. I have nothing to hide.'

Jack smiled. 'Indeed you don't – at least not you, yourself. I do have a couple of questions, no biggie, but I'd appreciate if you would answer them.' He took out his notepad.

Arlo nodded, seeing Cosima glance at him nervously. He put his hand over hers. 'Like I said, nothing's too much trouble if it helps protect Cos.'

Jack nodded. 'Good.' He shot a look at Cosima, and Arlo saw his face soften. 'Don't worry, Cosima, it's just the finer details. Arlo, you were in a relationship previously, yes?'

Arlo nodded, and Cosima sighed. 'The delectable Sabine,' she said, rolling her eyes. Jack looked surprised.

'You've met her?'

'All of her,' Cosima said with meaning, then grinned at Arlo. He winked at her, glad she could look back on that awful evening with humor.

'Sabine was still married when you began seeing each other?'

Arlo nodded. 'Yes, but she was separated. I never knew her husband.'

Jack looked at his notes. 'Her husband was Sanjit Khan, a wealthy businessman from Mumbai.'

Arlo shrugged. 'Honestly, she rarely mentioned him, and his name passed me by. I got the impression it wasn't a happy union.'

'Did you know he was Sabine's third husband?'

Arlo was shocked. 'No. I had no idea.'

Jack nodded. 'The reason I ask is this: Khan has some links – albeit not directly – to the group who overthrew Cosima and Harpa's grandfather. Now, we don't think it's an issue, but you never know. If it seems like I ask inappropriate questions, please know, it's only to protect Cos and Harpa.'

Arlo nodded, but something was bugging him about the man's attitude. He couldn't figure out what, though, so he pushed it to the back of his mind. 'Did you have any more questions?'

Jack looked through his notebook. 'Your cousin, Hunter? He did some time for arson?'

Arlo's face shut down. 'He was a kid, and he was messed up. He got clean and is now a stand-up guy. How did you find out about that? He's over twenty-four; those records should have been expunged by now.'

Jack gave him a wintry smile. 'There is no information we can't find out, Mr. Forrester.'

Cosima, sensing the tension between the two men, cleared her throat and smiled at them both. 'Food's ready if you've finished.'

Jack smiled at her. 'Of course, I'm sorry. To both of you, it's never a pleasure to be questioned.'

Arlo helped Cosima bring the food to the table and they ate, chatting casually. Jack told them the arrangements he was making so Harpa could move to Seattle for catering college.

'It's going to be weird, not living with Harpa,' Cosima said, a tiny quiver in her voice. 'I can't remember a time...anyway. It'll be a new thing for both of us.'

'At least she'll have Deacon, so you know she won't be alone.' Jack dug into the curry with enthusiasm. Arlo noticed Cosima had stopped eating.

'Deacon is going with Harpa?'

Jack looked up. 'You didn't know?'

Cosima shook her head and looked down at her food. She seemed to be struggling with something but then she shrugged. 'I guess, if that what she wants, it's okay.'

Jack patted her hand. 'He checks out, Cos. He's cleared.'

She nodded then looked at Arlo. He gave her a smile, and she nodded. 'Yeah. I want her to be happy and if he makes her happy... then I guess I'm okay with that.'

'Good. Now, why don't you tell me some more about this hotel you're renovating?'

LATER, when Jack had gone, Arlo cleared the dishes, insisting on Cosima taking it easy. She sat in a kitchen chair, sipping the remains of her wine, deep in thought. Arlo loaded the dishwasher and switched it on. As he wiped down the kitchen surfaces, he kept glancing at her. 'It really bothers you about Deacon, doesn't it?'

Cosima gave him a sheepish smile. 'It does and it shouldn't, I know. Deacon hasn't done anything but...did you ever just get a gut instinct about someone? That's something was off?'

Arlo wiped his hands and sat down. 'Funny you should say that.'

Cosima looked confused. 'Huh?'

Arlo smiled and touched her face. 'You really don't know, do you?'

'Know what?'

'Jack Hampton.'

She shook her head, bemused. 'What about him?'

Arlo picked up her hand and kissed her fingers. 'Cosima, darling, that man is in love with you.'

THEY'D FOLLOWED the blonde after she spoke to Cosima on the street, and now he was sitting beside her in her hotel bar. He ordered a scotch then sat sipping it, waiting. He knew women like her, and he knew that sooner or later, she would check him out, see the wealth radiating off of him, and move in for the kill. He'd fuck her, lead her on, pump her for information, and use her. When she became a problem, he'd deal with that too.

It took less than an hour, and now he was in her room, stripping her as she told him she didn't kiss. She'd do anything else but not kiss. He smiled and agreed; neither did he, he told her. She had a spectacular body, tall, lean; her tits were small but perky. She sucked his cock until he thought he might explode, then he fucked her hard in the bed, on the floor, against the wall.

When she was asleep, he went through her bag, finding any information he could. Her name, her California driver's license. He texted the information to his associate who came back to him quickly: she's Arlo Forrester's ex-girlfriend, Sabine Karlsson.

He smiled. So that was it – she was checking out the opposition. Arlo Forrester was fucking Cosima, and this woman wasn't happy about it. He was starting to change his mind about the blonde in his bed. She might prove useful – and maybe she would even want what he wanted so badly...

...FOR COSIMA MALHOTRA BEDI, the sweet, beautiful lover of Arlo Forrester, to die...

END OF PART One

2

TORN APART

A Billionaire, Bad Boy, Romance

〜

e have to talk.

In Harper Bedi's experience, those words were never followed by good news. Which is why she was sitting in a coffee shop waiting for her boyfriend of four months, Deacon McCoy, feeling sick to her stomach. He'd been radio-silent for a few days; then this morning, the text message.

Can you meet me at Lou's, 11 a.m.? We have to talk.

Her heart was thumping unpleasantly, and her palms were damp. Inside, she knew what was about to happen - Deacon was breaking up with her. *Fuck – why now?*

She'd only just talked Cosima around on Deacon coming to Seattle with her; her older sister, blissfully in love with Arlo Forrester, had never liked Deacon but last night, they sat up and talked for hours about how Harpa felt about the man. Cosima had finally told her that as long as Harpa was happy, she'd accept it.

Harpa had woken up so excited, so optimistic, that she'd tried to call Deacon right away – only for the call to go to voicemail...again. His text message came about five minutes later. *We have to talk.*

Harpa looked up as the door opened and Deacon, his face blank of expression, walked in. He nodded at her then indicated he would grab a coffee before joining her. While she waited, Harpa felt awkward, embarrassed – even tearful. *Do not cry; do not give him the satisfaction.*

Deacon sat down, a steaming mug of coffee in front of him. Harpa tried to smile. 'Hi, babe...I missed you these last few days.'

He looked away from her gaze and now fear began to make her heart beat faster. 'What is it, Deacon? What's the matter?'

He looked back at her, his eyes cold. 'I don't want this anymore.'

She was confused. 'What? The coffee? Okay then, we'll go some-place else, I...' her voice trailed off as she saw his jaw clench.

'Not the coffee. Us. You and me. I don't want this anymore.'

Even though she had been half expecting it, all the breath was pushed from her lungs, his words a sucker punch to her gut. She started to tremble and grabbed the coffee in front of her with both hands.

'I don't understand,' she tried to speak steadily, 'what's changed?' She wanted to scream, to sob, to beg, but she kept it all inside. Deacon was silent, just watching her reaction. For a moment they sat in silence. Finally, she exploded.

'Say something! I don't understand what you're talking about, I thought we were...'

'I can't do it. I can't move to Seattle with you, I...'

Harpa's face was wet with tears, but she stared at him coldly. 'What? What is it? Are you fucking someone else?'

'No. Not anymore.'

Not anymore. Wrecking ball to the chest. 'Not...'anymore'? You've been cheating on me?'

Deacon nodded. 'And for that I'm sorry. Truly.'

Harpa was silent for a moment. 'I forgive you. Every relationship goes through things like this....we can make it work, Deacon, please.'

'No, we can't.'

'Why not?'

'Harpa...'

'Just tell me!' She was trembling now. 'Just tell me why.'

There was a long silence then Deacon sighed, looked her straight in the eye and told her simply. 'I don't love you anymore.'

His words, spoken softly, calmly, felt like a death to her. She stared at him for a moment then got up and stumbled out of the coffee-house, oblivious to the stares of the other customers. Tears were pouring down her face, her breath coming in short, painful gasps. She staggered to the edge of the sidewalk and threw up. At any moment, she expected to feel his hand on her back, comforting, helping, begging for forgiveness. It never came.

Cosima Bedi smiled up at her lover as he gathered her to him and thrust his cock deep inside her. She gave a low moan of pleasure that made him smile and his cock thicken and swell. Her velvety vagina enveloped him as he moved, her legs around his waist, her soft lips against his. The feel of her skin on his was intoxicating to Arlo Forrester, and as they made love, the early morning sun falling over their bodies, he wished they could stay in the moment forever.

Afterward, they showered together...a task made longer by the fact he had to have her again, pushing her up against the cool tile and thrusting deep inside her from behind.

Now, as they ate breakfast, he linked his fingers with hers. 'Cosima...do you know how happy you make me?'

She grinned. 'Hopefully as happy as you make me, Mr. Forrester. Listen, I have a couple of meetings back at the office this morning; can you do without me for a couple of hours?'

'Absolutely not,' but he grinned, 'but I suppose if it's work...'

'Ha ha,' she kissed him, 'I'll be with you by lunchtime.'

After he had dropped Cosima at her office, Arlo continued on to the LaBelle, the hotel he and Cosima were renovating together. He liked to think of it like that – their hotel – in that they had chosen the project together rather than he had hired her firm to help design and build it. He was actually glad she wasn't with him this morning though because he had a meeting with the local councilmen to discuss changing the name of the hotel; his preferred sign writer was ready to go ahead once he had permission. He wanted it to be a surprise for Cosima; one she would love, one that would show her how much he loved her.

Arlo wasn't used to feeling like this, so utterly wiped out with love. He had always been controlled, sensible, measured in everything in his life – since his brother Mason had died, he was always careful not to let anyone too close, so as not to have that terror of losing them. He'd almost managed it – Margaret, his beloved assistant, and de facto mother was an exception – but everyone else got close enough...then he would put up barriers. He knew he had with Sabine – and that's why he bore some of the responsibility for her affair with Cole. But now, he felt wide open, laid bare by the beautiful woman who spent the nights in his arms.

His meeting went well with the councilmen, and he gave the go-ahead for the signs to be made. He was just looking over some blueprints when he heard his name being called. He turned to see Jack Hampton walking towards him, his smile friendly. 'Hey Jack, I didn't know you were still in town?'

The other man nodded. 'Harpa's move to Seattle needs to be arranged and seeing as she wasn't at dinner last night, I thought I'd drop in and see if Cos knows when Harpa will be free.'

Oh, really? Arlo kept his expression mutual. 'Wouldn't it be easier to call Harpa directly?'

Jack smiled as if he knew what Arlo was thinking. 'It would, and I've tried, but it just keeps going to voicemail. I get a little uncomfortable when I can't reach one or both of the girls.'

Women, not girls. Why did this dude irritate him so much? Arlo gave him a half-smile and nodded. 'I see.'

Jack looked around. 'This place sure is something...' Indeed, the interior of the hotel was beginning to take shape. Arlo nodded, pleased despite himself.

'Cosima's touch. She has the best eye I've ever seen.'

Jack nodded. 'She's always been a star, that one. Even when she was younger, she was always doing something creative...really knows color and how to use it. Amazing imagination. Hey, I don't suppose you could give me a tour?'

Arlo hesitated then shrugged. 'Sure, why not?'

He handed Jack a hard hat and motioned for him to follow him. 'We found the basic structure is sound and that a lot of the features could be salvaged for reuse. To a developer, that's money in the bank.'

Jack nodded. 'Got it. My understanding was that you were going to build from the ground up, and that's why you hired Cosima's firm.'

'That was the original plan; but then both Cos and me,' he smiled a little, 'well, we fell in love with this place. I bought it on the spot.'

'Spontaneous. I hear it's catching.'

Arlo stopped and smiled at him. 'Is there something you want to ask me, Agent Hampton?'

Jack made a show of looking confused. 'No, man, I'm just saying. I've known Cos for years, and she's always been organized, reliable and solid. Then you come along and ...' He made an 'explosion' gesture with his hands. Arlo conserved his words.

'Believe it or not, Jack, I'm just as astonished as you. Like Cos, I was all business, all the time. Maybe we're just like two chemical elements, benign on their own but put them together and boom.'

Jack nodded. 'That's what concerns me, man. Look, I'm happy for both of you, I am, but my job is to protect these girls, and I know you can provide round-the-clock security, I know that. My experience, though, is that if two parties are actively protecting someone, the ball often gets dropped because of miscommunication. I'm just asking – don't shut me out.'

Arlo nodded, listening to the man and feeling a little better about his involvement in Cosima's life. 'I understand that, and I agree. Look, I do not want to step on anyone's toes here – as long as Cos and I are given our privacy, I have no problem with anything you do. I want her safe.'

'That's all I want too, man.'

Arlo stuck his hand out, and Jack shook it. 'Deal.'

Jack smiled. 'Good. Now, show me around the rest of the Pleasuredome.'

HARPA WAS CURLED up napping on the couch when Cosima got in that night, and she leaned down and stroked her sister's hair. She frowned when she saw the deep shadows under her eyes.

'Harp? You okay, honey?'

Harpa opened her eyes, took one look at her sister and burst into tears. Cosima wrapped her arms around her sister and let her cry herself out. Finally, when Harpa had calmed herself, she told Cosima about Deacon.

'He just came right out with it. *I don't love you anymore.* There was no regret, no sadness in his eyes. He just looked desperate to get out of there.'

'*Asshole,*' Cosima spat out, gritting her teeth. 'I'm so sorry, Harp, I really am.' She hugged her sister fiercely. Harpa leaned against her and sighed.

'Sorry for blubbing.'

'Don't be silly.'

Harpa closed her eyes. 'God, I'm so angry, Cos.' She sat up and wiped her face on her sleeve. 'He was cheating. He admitted it to my face.'

'What the fuck?' Cos was enraged. 'That rat bastard, I'll kill him...' She was up, and Harpa had to yank her back to the couch.

'Dude, calm down. If anyone's going to kick his ass, it'll be me. But just now, I need sister alone time and a lot of junk food.'

Cosima looked a little guilty, and Harpa groaned. 'You're not going out, are you? I need you,' she said in a wheedling voice then grinned suddenly. 'Wow, I'm not passive-aggressive at all, am I?'

Cosima smiled. 'To answer your question, no, I'm not going out, but Arlo *is* coming here. He wants to meet you finally. But I can call him and postpone; you clearly need me more.'

Harpa shook her head. 'No, don't do that, I want to meet him too. Just don't be too smitten in front of me; I don't think I could take that.'

'I promise.'

Harpa sighed and then got up. 'I need to take a shower then I'll cook something.'

Cosima shook her head. 'No, don't worry about it, we'll just order in tonight.'

'You sure?'

'Yes, now go grab a shower; I need to take one too.'

Just as Harpa was leaving the room, Cosima called her back. 'What about Seattle?'

Harpa half-smiled. 'I'm still going to Seattle, Cos. No man's going to stop me from my dreams.'

An hour later, Harpa opened the door to Arlo Forrester. The two of them sized each other up.

'Well,' said Harpa, sticking her hand on her hip and trying not to grin. God, he was *gorgeous* – *lucky, lucky Cos* – but she'd be damned if she'd let *him* know that. 'I suppose you'll do.'

Arlo grinned widely. 'I'm pleased that her Majesty is satisfied.' He bowed extravagantly, and she giggled, standing back to let him in. He was dressed casually, vintage t-shirt and jeans, his hair short and dark, his dark eyes twinkling at her. Friendly. Warm. That was the impression she got.

'So, it's good to finally meet you, Harpa, and I'm sure all the terrible stories Cosima had told me about you aren't true.'

Harpa grinned and swatted at him. 'I can tell you're trouble. Cos! Your fuckbuddy's here!'

Arlo choked with laughter. Harpa led him into the kitchen. 'Want a beer?'

'Sure, thanks.'

They sat down at the kitchen table. 'Hey,' Harpa took a swig of beer, 'I had some leftovers of that curry you helped make. Pretty good. For an amateur.'

Arlo smiled. 'Glad you think so – maybe when you're a five Michelin-starred chef, you can tutor me and help me perfect it.'

Harpa flung her hair back. 'I'll be too busy cooking for kings and queens.' But she grinned at him. 'So...you and my sister...is it all revoltingly mushy and stuff?'

'Completely revolting.'

'Excellent. Hey...' She looked up as Cosima came in, her dark hair still slightly damp from the shower. She watched her sister's eyes light up when she saw Arlo; saw the tender way the man stood and kissed her, stroking her face, gazing at her. *So much love,* Harpa thought and felt a pang of both sadness and relief. Deacon had never looked at her like that...*so it couldn't have been love, could it?* She pushed her feelings aside and went to get Cosima a drink. She excused herself and went to the bathroom and could hear Cosima talking in low tones to Arlo.

'Don't mention Deacon, the fucker just broke up with her.'

'Ah man, poor kid. From what you told me, she could do better. Let's just cheer her up tonight, hey?'

Harpa felt warmth in her chest for her sister's boyfriend. *What a good guy he was*...Harpa went to the bathroom, washed her hands and face and sat down on the edge of the bath. Her mind felt muddled, blurry. She had been right when she told her sister she was still going to Seattle – her place at catering college was set, her funding was in place, her dorm room booked. Jack had gone ahead to set things up and in less than a week, she would be boarding a plane to fly to the Emerald City and begin her new life. Alone now. She tested her heart and found that it was not as smashed as she thought it would be. Definitely repairable.

She looked in the mirror and smiled. *A new life,* she thought, *one of my own making.*

A new life...

.   .   .

COSIMA WRAPPED a blanket over her sister's sleeping frame and put the note beside her.

Gone to Arlo's hotel so we don't wake you. Call if you need anything. Love you xxx

Arlo was waiting by the door as she crept out and smiled as she took his hand. 'She's adorable,' he said as they walked down the stairs. 'I could beat that dude's ass for dumping her like that.'

Cosima nodded grimly. 'Join the queue. Still, at least she seemed cheerful, and I'm glad she's still going to Seattle.'

They were in the car when he nodded to a black sedan parked across the street. 'That's my guys,' he said softly, studying her for her reaction. 'I cleared it with Jack, and he's cool with it. There will be six guys, two every eight-hour shift. They won't get too close, but they'll be vigilant. Same for you when you're not with me...in fact,' and he looked a little sheepish, 'they were there outside your office this morning. Hope you don't mind.'

Cosima considered. 'Well, I certainly didn't notice them, so my answer is no, I don't mind. As long as nobody else is affected by them.'

Arlo leaned over and kissed her, grinning. 'I honestly don't care who is affected if it means you're safe.'

She cupped her face in her hand. 'Arlo Forrester...you need to drive back to your hotel right now because I've got something for you...'

He gave a growl and started to the car, making her giggle. Halfway back to his hotel, he suddenly pulled off of the route and drove out of the city. She looked at him curiously, not worried but a little surprise.

He grinned over at her. 'Just an idea...'

He drove out to a secluded lake where the light pollution from the city was low enough they could see the Milky Way. Arlo put the convertible's top down, and they gazed up at the stars.

'Why'd you bring me out here – not that I'm complaining, but, you know...sexy times?'

She grinned over at him, and he laughed, turning to face her. 'Because, Miss Bedi, I want to see your beautiful, sumptuous curves in the moonlight. I want to fuck you under the stars. I want to make you come so hard that they'll hear you scream in Alabama.'

Cosima was grinning lasciviously at him. 'You are a dark horse, Mr. Forrester...outdoor sex?'

'We did plenty of it in the Maldives.'

'Yes, we did.'

He kissed her slowly, deeply, then leaned his forehead against hers. 'Do me a favor, and just sit still for a moment.'

He got out of the car and she watched him pop the trunk and pull out a blanket. 'Someone planned ahead.'

He grinned but said nothing, opening her door and scooping her into his arms. He walked a little way then set her down as he laid the blanket on the grass. He took her in his arms and kissed her again until her head swam, then laid her down onto the blanket, covering her body with his. He stroked the hair away from her face. 'You look gorgeous in the moonlight as well as the daytime,' he said, 'I can't take my eyes off you, Cosima Bedi.'

She grinned and stretched her body out, arching her back up to meet him. 'Best you open your present then.'

He smiled and sat up. She was wearing a dark maroon wrap dress, set off by a delicate gold chain, a tiny yellow diamond at her throat. He pulled open the belt of the dress, and then slowly peeled back the fabric. Under the dress, she was naked, and as his eyes widened in surprise, she laughed, and her curves undulated with her movement.

'You are breath-taking,' Arlo said with a catch in his voice. Cosima smiled and slowly spread her legs for him. Arlo groaned and buried his face in her sex, his mouth greedy for her and her dark copper flesh, her scarlet labia swelling, and her cunt dampening for him. His tongue found her clit and she made a small noise of pleasure as he felt it harden under his tongue. He teased and tasted until she was shuddering and crying out his name, his long, strong fingers clamping onto her buttocks as she writhed beneath him. As she came, she arched her back, almost sobbing with pleasure, and he ran his tongue up her belly, around her navel, and onto her nipples, sucking on them until she was half-crazed. Finally, he took her mouth as she reached down to free his rock-hard cock from his underwear. He hitched her legs around his waist, but she shook her head, smiling. 'Not yet,' she whispered, 'Let's prolong it – I want to taste you.'

Arlo grinned, and as she made her way down his body, he rolled onto his back and sighed as her hot, wet mouth enveloped his cock, her hands massaging his sac, the root of him as she licked and tickled the sensitive tip with her tongue. He stroked her hair gently as she sucked him, letting himself experiencing all the incredible sensations she was giving him. When he was almost coming, he asked her if she wanted him to pull out but she shook her head, and he came, shooting into her mouth, her fingers on his hips as she drank him down. *God, this woman*...he needed to bury himself in her...*now*. He deftly flipped her onto her back and pushed her legs apart, not caring if he was rough; the excitement in Cosima's eyes willing him on. He grabbed the discarded belt from her dress, and bound her wrists together, pulling them above her head. Cosima groaned, 'Tighter... tighter...' and to his delight, she seemed even more turned on. His cock, almost ready to explode and so engorged with desire and blood, stood ramrod straight against his belly, and he teased her opening with it, making her give an impatient squeak.

'You want to beg me, beautiful?'

She nodded. 'Please...'

'Say the words...'

'Fuck me, Arlo, please...'

'Louder.'

'Fuck me! Fuck me now, please Arlo, now...'

And he rammed his cock deep into her cunt, pressing her legs apart, driving his whole weight into her; Cosima screamed his name, begging him to please, fucker harder, until they both came, crying out the other's name, Arlo's cock pumping hot, thick semen deep inside her.

·   ·   ·

AFTERWARD, they lay on the blanket and stared up at the universe. Well, Cosima did; Arlo, proped up on his elbow, was looking at *her*, the lush curves of her. He couldn't help compare her softly rounded body with Sabine's sharp edges. Where Cosima curved, Sabine jutted; where Sabine was concave, Cosima gently curved out, lush and ripe.

She glanced at him studying her and smiled. 'You like what you see?'

He bent his head to kiss her. 'It's the most beautiful sight in the universe.'

'Flatterer,' but she put her hand on his face. 'I love you.'

He turned his head to kiss her palm, then her wrist. 'You are my life, Cosima.' He noticed her wrists were a little red from the belt he'd tied them with. He trailed his lips across the welt then smiled at her. 'Did you like being bound, my love?'

'Yes, I did...funny, I'd never even considered it before you but, yeah, I could explore that further...if you want.' Cosima grinned shyly at him, and he shook his head, bemused.

'How'd I get so lucky as to meet you?'

She giggled as he tickled her, and then sighed happily as he caressed her body, stroking his hand down over her belly then pressing his lips to her skin. 'You are delicious, Miss Bedi.' He covered her body with his, his cock getting hard again. He stroked his hand down over her shaved pubic mound – really, everything about her body was soft and velvety. He slipped a finger inside her, feeling her wet and slick from his cum. She ground her sex against his hand.

'I want to ride you, big boy,' she grinned as he lay down and she straddled him, her hands on his thick cock, pulling and stroking it until it was rock-hard. Arlo spread the lips of her labia wide and she slowly lowered herself onto him, moaning softly as he filled her. They rocked gently, eyes locked. Arlo's hands roamed gently over her breasts and belly until finally, they both came with a shuddering, mellow orgasm that left them both blissed out and relaxed.

Arlo drove them back to his hotel, and they made love once more before falling asleep exhausted, their limbs tangled, and their lips against the other's.

Sabine Karlsson was in another hotel across the city, also fucking, this evening's lover above her, thrusting hard – almost too hard. Sabine winced a couple of times.

'Too rough, ma cherie?'

She smiled and shook her head. 'No, not at all.'

After he'd come, she slipped off the bed and padded to the bathroom. She heard the Frenchman zip up his pants then the door to the room close. *Good* – she hated it when she had to go through the whole '*Look, this has been fun but...*' part. It was better when they just understood it was a fuck, not true love.

She showered quickly then slipped into her shorts and t-shirt, switching on the t.v. and grabbing her iPad. She checked her email – she had Google alerts on both Arlo and his little Indian princess. Nothing new today. She also looked for an email from her new... acquaintance. He had told her his name was Naveen and that he was from California. She had no reason to disbelieve him – except she did. The accent for one thing. Naveen was hiding something.

Not that she cared. Unlike the poor Frenchman who had just left, Sabine wanted more from Naveen. He had been an incredible lover – almost as good a lover as Arlo – and after two nights, he had bid her 'farewell...but not, I hope, goodbye.'

That simple sentence had her hanging on every buzz of her phone for his call like some damn lovesick teenager. She'd tried to Google him, but a simple search of 'Naveen, California' didn't really cut it. She threw the iPad aside in frustration. She hated being at a man's beck and call. Back in Sweden, with her family, she'd been the only girl in a family of three brothers – all of whom treated her like she was their personal slave. When she left at sixteen, she vowed 'never again.' Her glacial beauty – and willingness to fuck anybody to get ahead – meant that she rose to the top of the modeling world easily. She hadn't made any friends on the way up – indeed, she was one of the most reviled amongst her fellow models – but she couldn't have cared less. When her star finally began to wane, there had been Arlo. Arlo, who had been the most handsome, richest, and charming of them all. God, she had loved him desperately – so much she'd walked away from a huge job for a major design house – one that would set her up for life. The design house wanted an 'older model' – read over twenty-five – to be their brand spokesmodel for the next twenty years; to go from young to middle-aged with the brand to bring in all age ranges. She was to be the first, the standard-bearer for this new type of campaign, and she would have earned a quarter of a billion over twenty years. But it meant staying in New York full-time, and Arlo was a West Coast man.

He'd told her to do the job – that it would set her up for life – but she couldn't bear to leave him. Well, that was *mostly* the reason. The other reason was she was scared. Scared that her fellow models would laugh at her, having her aging process documented and displayed for the world to see. The bitching campaign had already begun, so she cut her losses and told the brand 'thank you but it's time to focus on my family.' She could have sworn Jessica, the leading editor, looked relieved. But she'd walked away with grace and less than twenty-four hours later, the brand announced the Merry Widow, Monica Lascelles, as their figurehead. So far Monica, ten years Sabine's senior and an even bigger bitch than Sabine, had earned just shy of five hundred million and she, Sabine, was scraping by on the last of Arlo's goodwill. It galled her that it had been Monica; the two of them had never gotten along. Sabine was jealous of the older woman's terrible beauty, dark eyes, dark hair, a body with breakneck curves and a mind devoid of morals. Sabine rather admired that about her.

Curious, she took up her iPad again and searched 'Monica Lascelles,' checking out what else her rival had been up to the intervening years. She'd married an English Lord – one who she had dumped years before but who still held a candle for her – and had cut back on the modeling. Sabine snorted. Monica was nearly sixty now, and Sabine knew the jobs for women that age were few and far between. But then again, with the massive fashion house contract and a rich husband, she didn't need to work. She certainly didn't cut down on the partying. The society pages were full of the woman and her 'friends.' Monica was still stunning, Sabine had to admit, and then something struck her. A photograph of Monica when she was younger...there was something familiar. Sabine stared at it, trying to make the connection. Then it came to her.

'No way,' she murmured and went back to the search engine. *Monica Lascelles children,* she typed in and pressed enter. She read down the information page. Two children by her late husband... Arjun Malhotra. No names or genders of the children. That was strange. She clicked on the images tab, but no pictures with Monica and her children existed on the web. That was weird. Sabine got up and went to get her bag, grabbed some of the photos her detective had taken of Arlo and his new paramour. She placed the picture of Cosima alongside the images of Monica, her eyes flicking between the two. '*Fucking A,*' she hissed, shaking her head. The resemblance was unmistakable.

Arlo's new lover was Monica Lascelles' daughter.

COSIMA WATCHED Harpa packing the last of her books into a box and sighed. 'Are you sure you don't want me to come help you settle in?'

Harpa smiled at her older sister. 'No, Momma Bear, I'll be fine. The less fuss there is, the easier it'll be.'

Cosima nodded. 'Got it. Damn, this day came around so quickly.' Her voice wobbled, and Harpa hugged her, chuckling.

'I'm a plane ride away, Cos, less than a day. I'll call you every other day if you like, or at least text. I promise. Now, let's go enjoy our sister time.'

Harpa's flight left at noon the following day, so this evening was all about them spending quality time together. 'I warn you,' Cosima told her now, 'I was home all day cooking, so I hope you're hungry.'

'From the amazing smell, I guessed as much,' Harpa smiled, 'And I've brought treats too.' She went to grab a large paper sack she'd left near the door. She pulled out a large green bottle. 'Fizz for us, chocolates, potato chips...even some Indian sweets from this deli I found.'

She waved the box of sweets under Cosima's nose, grinning, knowing her sister couldn't resist the delicious cakes. Cosima swooned. 'Gimme.'

Harpa whipped them away from her. 'Not until you show me the goodies.'

Cosima laughed and hauled her into the kitchen. She laid out their feast: naan bread, curries, sag aloo, tarka dahl – and French fries. They sat and talked while they ate, reminiscing on the time they'd spent in the apartment.

'It's strange; we've only been here a few months, but it feels so much longer. So much has happened here.'

Harpa smiled. 'You fell in love.'

'You like Arlo, don't you?'

'Very much, sis, very much. I wouldn't have felt like I could leave you unless you had him here to protect you. Not that you can't look after yourself,' she added in a hurry, but Cosima nodded.

'Wouldn't it be nice to just not have that hanging over us all the time? To be able to be truly free of our past?'

Harpa rolled her eyes. 'Goes without saying but I don't think it'll ever happen. Do you worry about it all the time?'

Cosima considered. 'Most of the time I try to forget it. Most of the time, it would be very hard to get to me...I worry about your safety more than my own.'

Harpa squeezed her arm. 'Don't worry. What with Jack and now Arlo's fleet of bodyguards, I'll be fine.'

Cosima was silent for a minute. 'I'm not sure Arlo is a big fan of Jack's.'

Harpa was surprised. 'Really? Why?'

Cosima looked uncomfortable, her face scarlet. 'He thinks Jack's in love with me.'

Harpa shrugged. 'He is. Has been for years. But you knew that, right?'

Cosima stared at her sister and slowly shook her head. 'I had no idea.'

Harpa laughed. 'Dude...how the hell did you manage to get Arlo? Did you think it happened magically? Look in the mirror.'

'I propositioned Arlo, not the other way around.'

'You did? Cosima Bedi, I never knew you had it in you...' Harpa was impressed, and Cosima chuckled.

'Do you blame me?'

'Hell, no. Arlo's a catch but then, so are you, Cos. I wish you'd realize that more.'

Cosima, embarrassed, changed the subject. 'Well, what about you? Will you be looking for someone new in Seattle?'

Harpa snorted. 'No way. I'm done with men at least until I've graduated and found a new job.' She yawned suddenly, and Cosima grinned.

'Unless you want to feel like a zombie on the plane tomorrow, I suggest you get some sleep. I'll clean up in here.'

Harpa nodded, pulling herself up. 'Are you going over to Arlo's tonight?'

'No. I'm staying here tonight. Get some sleep, I love you.'

'Love you too.'

HARPA GOT into bed and lay back on the pillows, listening to Cosima clear the plates in the kitchen. 'My last night here,' she murmured and sighed. She was looking forward to starting her new life tomorrow.

IT SEEMED to Naveen that the Malhotra sisters were now surrounded with top-level protection. The FBI and now Forrester's private security service had the two women's safety locked down, and he would find it very hard to get close enough to them. Time to reconsider his plans...

Harpa, the younger sister – as far as he was concerned, she didn't really figure into it. If he could kill her too it would be a bonus, but for the moment, all his focus was on Cosima. She haunted his dreams and his waking thoughts, and now it had become more than fulfilling his family's wish for her death; it had become his obsession. He wanted her...badly. He wanted to fuck that glorious body of hers before he ended her life, slowly, painfully, torturing her until she begged for his knife. Then he would stab her in the belly, watch her bleed out...god, it made him hard just thinking about it. But Arlo Forrester would not easily let harm come to her.

Which was why Sabine Karlsson was so useful, so pliable. He knew he had left her wanting more, that she would obsess over him. Leave her dangling for a few days then call her, fuck her, and see just how useful she could be. If he'd got the measure of her the last time, it was that she didn't like to lose, that she was sociopathic enough that he could tell her what he wanted, and she would help him make it happen. Cosima's murder would be front page news – and now he had someone to frame for it...

Harpa and Jack stepped out into the Seattle sunshine. He turned to grin at her. 'Here we are, at last.'

Harpa grinned although inside she felt sick with nerves. It was happening, she was here, a country away from the only family she knew, and it was time to strike out on her own. She had originally planned to stay in the college dorm, but Jack had persuaded her against it for security reasons.

Jack drove the rental car to her new apartment block, and as they walked in, Harpa noticed a black sedan parked across the street. The driver nodded at her, and she smiled. Arlo's security team. It made her feel good, feel safe, knowing they were there, and it was a link back to her sister – who no doubt had the matching pair at home. *Thank God,* Harpa thought now as they rode the elevator to her floor, *because for a while now I've had this feeling that I can't shake. That something might happen. That someone might hurt Cosima, that she isn't safe.* Which was ridiculous, she reasoned, her sister was safer now than ever. But still, it nagged at her.

'Hey, space cadet, we're here.' Jack nudged her as the elevator doors opened and they stepped out. Her door was the closest to the elevator – convenient for late night food runs, she smiled. Jack unlocked the apartment door and went in; his men had already swept it before they arrived but always on the lookout, Jack palmed his pistol and darted from room to room. Harpa ignored him and went straight to the large window in the living room. The view was incredible...Harpa turned to Jack as he was tucking his pistol away.

'Dude...tell me again how you found this apartment – and how the hell it's so cheap?'

Jack had the grace to smile sheepishly. 'Probably something you should talk to your sister's boyfriend about.'

Harpa's mouth fell open. Arlo had found this apartment? For *her*? She felt tears prick her eyes, and when Jack pointed out a huge fruit basket on the kitchen counter, she found a note from her benefactor.

Hey Harpa,

I hope you don't think this is overstepping the mark, but I wanted both you and Cos to feel you could be safe in Seattle alone – ish. The place is yours for as long as you want – rent free. Live, love, enjoy – please. I know you want to make it on your own, and there's nothing I admire more – just think of this as a gift from a brother to a sister. It's not charity, it's a helping hand.

So please, enjoy,

All best,

Arlo x

Harpa felt a tear escape at his generosity. 'God...' she groaned, 'How bummed am I Cosima got to meet him first?'

She was sorry she said that when Jack looked away from her, and she went to hug him. 'Sorry, dude.'

Jack smiled at her brightly. 'About what? Come on, let's give you the tour then I'll take you for something to eat.'

In the end, they didn't go out but ordered pizza, and it wasn't until it arrived that Harpa found that the kitchen had been fully stocked, the refrigerator and freezer stuffed full of fresh produce and meats. A full spice rack sat on the counter. Harpa shook her head. 'I'm sure I just walked into a dream. Fairy godfather.'

Jack snorted with laughter then checked the time. 'Listen, kiddo, I have to eat and run, I'm afraid. I'm getting the red-eye back to New York tonight.'

COSIMA WAS ARRANGING invoices into alphabetical order when Arlo found her. The office behind the reception of the hotel had been finished for a while, and Cosima used that as her base, only occasionally wondering if the men working above would come through the ceiling.

Arlo stood at the door and watched her. On her desk were six neat piles of paperwork and, Arlo noted with amusement, her office supplies were also neatly placed. 'Are you really that bored?'

Cosima looked up and grinned. 'It's true, I'm struggling to find things to do – the contractors are all running on time, within budget, they all know what they have to do.' She sighed. 'Yup, I'm bored, and that's something I never thought I would say in this job.'

Arlo chuckled and came to the desk to pull her to her feet. 'Hmm, how can I make you un-bored?'

'Un-bored is not a word.'

'Is too. Miss Bedi, I recognize this dress.'

She was wearing the same wrap dress she had on when they had driven out to the lake and made love under the stars. He hooked a finger into the belt and pulled. She grinned.

'Ha ha, foiled. I double knotted it,' she giggled as he groaned and buried his face in her neck.

'You honestly think that would stop me, Cosima,' he nibbled her earlobe, and she shivered with pleasure.

'No...but there's no lock on that door yet...'

He met her gaze. 'So?'

Her eyes widened. 'Exhibitionist.'

He grinned wickedly. 'Come here.' He led her over to the door and made her face it, her stomach against the hard wood. He pulled his tie from his neck and tied her hands behind her. Cosima, her breath quickening, gasped a little as he pushed her skirt up, and tugged her panties down. His fingers found her sex and began to stroke and excite. With her ear pressed to the door, she could hear the workmen outside talking, and as their voices got closer, Arlo increased the pressure on her clit before suddenly thrusting his cock into her from behind, the friction on her cunt delicious and delirious. Cosima sighed, her head falling back to rest on his shoulder. Arlo kissed her as he plunged deeper inside her. 'Cos...?'

His question was said in a curious way as if asking permission and suddenly she knew what he wanted. 'Do it,' she whispered, 'I trust you.'

He tilted her chin up so he could kiss her mouth deeply, then used his hands to gently part her buttocks. He eased himself out of her vagina, and then pushed gently into her ass. Cosima gasped and shuddered at the quick pain. Outside she could hear the men talking and laughing, but then as the pressure increased, she heard nothing but her own ragged breathing, Arlo's excited breaths as he fucked her, his hand still rubbing her clit. Cosima came quickly, such was the overwhelming feeling of him, and she cried out a little, hearing the men outside stop talking. For a moment they both froze, then Cosima got the giggles which made Arlo laugh. He pulled out and they tidied themselves up. Cosima's legs felt strange as she walked back to her desk.

Arlo, his face flushed, grinned at her. 'Well, that was thrilling... what say we do that in every room in this hotel?'

Cosima laughed. 'You are a nymphomaniac, you know that?' She kissed him, sliding her arms around his waist. 'But, yes, absolutely.'

He kissed her thoroughly then regretfully let her go. 'I have bad news, though; I have to go back to Frisco for a couple of days.'

Cosima pouted. 'Boo. Why do you have to go?'

'Shareholders meeting. Just know that I will be bored out of my skull without you.'

'Good.'

LATER, at home, after Arlo had left for the airport, Cosima took a long soak in the tub then padded around her echoingly empty apartment. Harpa's leaving had been more of a wrench than Cosima had admitted and now, without even Arlo here, she felt lonelier than she had done in years. *Stop being so self-pitying,* she said to herself and resolved to pull it together. She went to the kitchen to seek out food but couldn't be bothered to cook, so she grabbed a box of cereal and ate straight from it.

She went into the living room and sat in the window seat to gaze out at the night; something that drove Jack crazy from a security point of view but she loved to watch people as they drifted through the Quarter on their way to clubs and bars and music venues. She had turned all the lights out in her room and sat a little back so she could watch while being unseen. It had been raining and the lights of the Quarter reflected in the water on the road creating an ethereal scene below her window. She leaned her forehead against the cool glass. She had thought it impossible to love a city more than New York, but New Orleans had captured her heart so completely that she couldn't ever have imagined leaving it.

She got up and went to bed, leaving her window open to let the cool night breeze wash over her hot, tired body, and fell asleep almost immediately.

Outside, the man who had been watching her from the street below flicked out his cigarette and walked away.

HARPA CLEANED the last of the kitchen counter down and dumped the dirty water in the sink. She had been working part-time at this restaurant for a month now, and she loved every single, hot, sweaty, stressful, exhausting minute of it. The head chef, a coarse but brilliant Englishman called Stanley – 'Or call me Stan, love, I don't give a shit, I ain't posh' – had taken her on but told her 'Everyone starts out as a pot washer in my kitchen. You'll get your chance to learn, I just want to see you earn your keep.'

So she did just that, without one complaint, putting in even longer hours than necessary to show the bluff Briton that she was committed. She knew she had impressed him because two weeks in, he'd taken her aside and shown her some of his signature dishes, watching her try to emulate them. She'd watched him taste each one with nervous trepidation, then he'd give her feedback, constructive criticism, and praise where it was earned. When she perfected something, he would just taste it, and a big smile would tell her everything she needed to know.

Harpa glanced at the clock. Just after one a.m. *God*, and she had a nine a.m. class, too. She yawned expansively then grinned. Nights like this she was glad of the constant presence and therefore convenient 'cab' potential of Arlo's security team. They must be bored out of their minds, she thought now, grabbing her coat. Sitting around all day. She grabbed the foil-covered tray of leftovers she had saved for them – tonight she knew it would be Tony and Sean who would be in the car. They were her favorites – not as po-faced professional as the others, and both were nearer her age and had a sense of humor.

'Evening, boys,' she said now as she clambered into the back seat.

'Evening, Princess,' Sean beamed at her from the front passenger seat. 'What you got for us tonight?'

'Beef Wellington, sautéed potatoes and green beans.' She waved the tray to let them smell it, and they both drooled. 'Hey look, why don't you just come up to the apartment and eat tonight?' Too late, she remembered her nine a.m. class. Sean grinned at her.

'That's good of you, but we need to keep our distance – part of our contract, we stay a certain distance away unless you need us....for cab rides and the like.'

Harpa chuckled, relieved. 'Well, okay then. You may need to stop at a bodega, get some plastic cutlery then.'

On the ride home, she checked her phone. A text message from Cosima: *I miss you, Bubba, when can I come visit?* Harpa grinned. *Anytime you want, Cos, you're always welcome, I miss you too. How's my sugar daddy?*

At home, she showered quickly then fell into bed, exhausted but exhilarated.

ARLO NODDED to the foreman at LaBelle. 'Hey, have you seen Cosima?'

The workman, Al, smiled. 'Miss Bedi wanted to look at the penthouse; we're almost done up there so she grabbed a hard hat and went up about ten minutes ago.'

Arlo thanked him and took the stairs up to the penthouse. The apartment was spacious and rang with emptiness; it still needed decorating and furnishing, but Arlo couldn't help but be excited. This was to be his and Cosima's home – if she hadn't changed her mind. She'd been quiet these last few days, and he had been concerned that she was starting to regret telling him yes to living with him so soon.

He found Cosima in the living room, gazing out of one of the large windows. He slid his arms around her waist, feeling her start as she felt him behind her. 'Hey, beautiful.'

She turned in his arms and kissed him. 'Hey, yourself. Just taking in the view.'

She smiled, but he could see the sadness in her eyes. He stroked her cheek. 'What is it, Cos? Talk to me.'

She sighed. 'I'm sorry I've been quiet, it's just...it's the anniversary of my father's murder today.'

Arlo was appalled. 'God, Cosima, I'm so sorry. How long has it been?'

'Sixteen years,' she shook her head sadly. 'Every year I keep waiting for the pain of it to lessen, and it never does.'

He pulled her close and tightened his arms around her. 'I wish I could say I can't imagine, but sadly I can.'

'Your brother?'

He nodded. He had told her about Mason at the beginning of their relationship. 'We both of us know what violence can do. You don't talk about your dad a lot.'

Cosima shook her head. 'I can't form the words to tell you how much he meant to me, to Harpa. He was everything.'

'I'm so sorry, baby. Do you have anything you like to do on the anniversary?'

She shook her head. 'Harpa and I usually just have a meal in his honor, toast his memory, and thank him for everything he did. But now Harpa's in Seattle...'

'Would you let me be her proxy? We could have a quiet meal in my hotel – room service?'

Cosima smiled. 'I'd love to spend the evening with you, but I'll cook, if you don't mind, it's a tradition...my father loved Indian cuisine and even more if it was homemade.'

'Sounds perfect – if I can help you cook.'

'It's a deal.' She smiled then looked around the empty penthouse. 'This place will be mind-blowing when it's finished. Still sure you wanna share?' She grinned at him, and he laughed.

'Hell yes, you think I'd let you off that easy? Come on, let's get planning décor and furnishings; the quicker it's done, the quicker I get to wake up with you in *our* home.'

HARPA READ the message from Cosima as she was driven to work.

Thinking of you today, Harp, and of Dad. I love you both so much. C.

Harpa smiled, feeling tears prick her eyes. It was definitely strange to be away from her sister today. She quickly sent a reply then stuck her phone away. She was nervous because today one of her dishes was going to be on the restaurant's menu. She'd cooked it for everyone as a one-month anniversary treat for making her feel so welcome, and they'd eaten it after service one night. Everyone had fallen in love with it, especially Stanley, and he'd told her if she just perfected it a little more, then he would try it out on the customers. She couldn't quite believe it, and today was the day. What made it more nerve-wracking was that one of Seattle's most prominent restaurant critics had booked a table at the lunchtime sitting. Stanley, grinning, had told her that gleefully, and she had swatted away his teasing. 'As if this wasn't scary enough!'

Her two bodyguards today were the oldest and most remote pair, but she was grateful for that today – she didn't want to talk, just go through every step of her preparation for the dish – of course, there may not be any orders for it, but she hoped...

Stanley was already at the restaurant when she walked in, and with a smile saw he had done a great deal of prep for her. 'Don't get used to it,' he told her, smirking. 'Tthis is a one-time deal even if your meal does make it onto the main menu.'

Harpa hugged him. 'Stan...god, thank you. Man, I'm so nervous.'

'Don't be,' he threw her apron at her. 'Just do what you do, step by step, don't panic, and you'll be fine.'

And she was. Following his advice, she soon switched into chef mode, slicing and peeling, making the spice paste for the base, prepping the chicken breasts, making heavenly scented jasmine rice.

By the time service started, she had everything organized and was waiting to see if anyone ordered her dish. Stan and some of her other colleagues teased her every time she jumped to see what orders had come in. Finally, Stan waved a piece of paper. 'Seven orders, chicken dhansak, tables three and seven.'

Harpa swung into gear, and less than a quarter hour later, she called 'Service, please' as the steaming curry dishes were placed on the pass. She didn't have time to mull over what the reaction would be as Stan called out for more orders and she leaped into action.

Over thirty orders for her dish came in over the lunchtime service, and Harpa was running on pure adrenaline. She was clearing her station when Wendy, one of the waitresses, came in.

'It smells like heaven in the restaurant,' she told them, 'As soon as we took one of Harpa's curries out, the patrons made like meerkats and asked what that gorgeous smell was. You killed it, Harp.' She grinned at a stunned and red-faced Harpa. Harpa looked at Stan who nodded, his pride obvious.

'You did good, kid. They're asking for you out front.'

Harpa blinked at him, not understanding, and laughing, he pushed her out into the restaurant. 'Ladies, gents, thank you for your comments...and as requested, your chef for today, Harpa Bedi.'

The patrons applauded her, and although she was touched, she still could have disappeared through the floor. Instead, she walked to each table and accepted their praise and thanked them. She could see Stan nodding approvingly out of the corner of her eye. At the last table sat a middle-aged, well-fed man with spectacles on the end of his nose. He reminded Harpa of a younger, chubbier Dumbledore. His dining companion was a striking black man with such a beautiful face Harpa thought she might get lost in his smile. His older companion gave her praise and a couple of pointers on style.

'But on the whole, a very welcome addition to this place,' he smiled benevolently at her, and Harpa suddenly realized who he was. The restaurant critic. She shook his hand.

'Thank you, Mr. Sheridan; it's a pleasure to meet you.'

'Yes, I imagine it would be,' the man said with a self-deprecating laugh. Harpa liked him immediately. 'Miss Bedi, my companion here was even more impressed than I – may I introduce Mikah Ray?'

His companion stood – *God, he was tall* – and shook Harpa's hand, his dark eyes merry and flirtatious. 'That dish was incredible, my congratulations.'

'Thank you, Mr. Ray...are you a food critic too?'

Both men laughed. 'No, I'm afraid I'm just a lowly art dealer.'

Sheridan Farr made a scoffing noise in his throat. 'Yes, very lowly. How much did you bring in last year?'

Mikah Ray was still gazing at Harpa, who couldn't look away. All sorts of strange butterfly feelings were whirling around inside her as she took in the smooth skin of his handsome face, half covered with a beard, the faint crinkling at the corners of his eyes. A pulse started beating between her thighs, and she had to look away from that gorgeous face that perfectly shaped mouth...

She missed what Mikah Ray had answered to his friend, so when they laughed, she smiled uneasily. 'Okay, well, thank you both again, and I'm glad you enjoyed the dish. Hope to see you again.'

Sheridan smiled at her. 'Thank you, dear.'

Mikah took her hand and kissed the back of it. 'Oh, you will see me again, I promise.'

She escaped back to the kitchen, her heart beating wildly, and joined her friends and colleagues in clearing the kitchen. Harpa was working like an automaton, though, torn between thinking about her success and Mikah Ray's smile, the feel of his lips against her skin.

'Hey, doofus, you've just cleaned that bit six times,' Wendy was nudging her. Harpa grinned at her. Of all the staff, and with the exception of Stan, Wendy was the person she had bonded with most; a fun-loving blonde in her mid-thirties, Wendy flirted with everyone and was the best at what she did, but when she went home at night, she was the single mother of three gorgeous kids. She was happy about her status quo, telling Harpa, 'I've never felt the need to be married or coupled-up. The kids' fathers are all friends, all show up for them whenever they want. I count myself pretty lucky.'

Now, she passed Harpa a folded napkin, grinning. 'Go get yours,' she whispered then walked off, cackling to herself. Harpa knew before she even opened the napkin who it was from. Her face warmed, and that pulse between her legs began again, more frantically.

Drinks tonight? The Cupola House, 8 p.m. If yes, call or text me. If no, peace be with you. Mikah Ray

Underneath he'd scrawled his number. Harpa ran her finger over the number and then, before she could talk herself out of it, she texted him.

Yes. Looking forward to it. Harpa Bedi.

She debated putting a smiley face then decided against it. Too kiddish. Something told her that although he looked a lot of fun, there was nothing but pure adult virile male about Mikah Ray.

She was looking forward to finding out.

.   .   .

CosimA HAD SKIPPED out of work early to go to the Crescent City farmer's market to get some fresh produce for their meal that evening. She had decided their meal would be a mix of Indian and American to honor both of their loved ones, so when she spotted a vendor selling traditional Creole food she couldn't resist. Walking slowly through the market, she got lost in the fresh produce and didn't notice when the man started to follow her.

She stopped at a seafood stall and ordered some shrimp and lobster for the curry. As she was paying for it, there was a commotion behind her and as she turned she saw Arlo's security guards barreling towards her shouting, their faces angry and panicked. Then she saw him. Her heart stopped. He was running toward her, his eyes fixed on her and in his hand, she saw a flash of silver. In an instant, she raised her arm as he bore down on her and in the second it took her bodyguards to tackle the man, she felt a searing pain across the flesh of her forearm. She dropped her bags, clutching at the wound, blood pouring from her arm. She panted for breath, from the pain and the shock of the attack as one of her guards pinned her attacker to her ground, and the other, Steve, came to help her. He put a steadying arm around her and then checked her wound and winced. In a flash, she was back in the car and being driven to the hospital. Her head whirled, not from the blood – she wasn't squeamish – but just from the speed of it all. Steve had wrapped his jacket around her arm, but she eased it off now to check. It was a nasty cut, deep into the skin below her elbow and now that the adrenaline was leaving her, it was starting to hurt. She wrapped it up again as they raced across the city and she could hear Steve talking to someone – Arlo? – on the telephone.

'Yeah...yeah, she's fine, just a small cut but I'm taking her to the E.R. now to get stitched up. Okay. Okay. See you there.'

'Was that Arlo?'

'Yes, ma'am. He's going to meet us there.'

Cosima leaned back in the seat, feeling dizzy. Her clothes were spattered with blood, and she felt lightheaded and woozy. She saw Steve looking in the rearview mirror at her.

'Stay awake if you can, ma'am. Keep pressure on the wound.'

In no time, she was being led into the emergency room and into a cubicle. The doctor came and looked at her wound. 'Pretty clean but deep, that's why you've lost some blood. How do you feel?'

Cosima nodded just as a worried-looking Arlo arrived. 'I feel okay, just a bit sore.' Arlo came and put his arm around her, kissed her forehead. He looked pale and scared.

'Sweetheart...what happened?'

She told him, and he looked angry. He rounded on Steve, who looked like he was expecting that reaction, firing questions at the man.

'Arlo...Steve and Roger saved my life,' Cosima couldn't bear any more harsh words or violence. 'They did their jobs exactly the way we wanted them to. No one could have seen that coming.' Cosima winced as the doctor injected anesthetic into her injured arm.

'Lay back, Miss Bedi, we'll get this fixed up. I would recommend you stay overnight...well, it's up to you,' he added when she shook her head vehemently.

'No, doctor, I'd rather not. I don't want any of our lives disrupted by this...foolishness.'

The doctor looked unhappy. 'Well, okay, but I beg you, don't overexert yourself.'

'I promise.'

'I'll be back in a few minutes to sew you up.'

After he'd gone, Steve cleared his throat. 'I'll be outside.'

Cosima called out after him. 'Thank you, Steve. I mean it, thank you.'

Steve smiled and nodded. 'Anytime, ma'am.' Arlo, still stony-faced, hesitated then held his hand out to him.

'Thank you, Steve. I mean it, sorry about before.'

Steve smiled. 'No problem, Mr. Forrester. Feel better soon, ma'am.'

'Thank you.'

Arlo waited until he'd left, then put his arms around Cosima. He buried his face in her neck, and she realized he was trembling. She put her good arm around him and held him tightly. When he looked up, she was shocked to see he had tears in his eyes. He studied her for a long time as if drinking in every one of her features.

'When my brother died,' he began, his voice low and rough, 'I had to go identify his body. Because of a mix-up at the coroner's office, he hadn't been prepared or cleaned since the murder. He'd been stabbed in the chest, neck and face. He didn't look like my brother anymore. When I heard you'd been attacked, that he had a knife...*God,* Cos, I could have screamed. Thank God you're okay.'

She kissed away his tears. 'I am, I really am.'

The doctor came back and attended to her arm. Afterward, Cosima got up from the bed, and Arlo walked her back to his car. She saw Steve and Roger parked behind them and waved. They both signaled back.

Inside the car, Arlo looked at her. 'Where to? Shall we go back to my place for tonight, order room service? We can do our thing tomorrow night if you like?'

She nodded, suddenly exhausted. 'Okay, that sounds like a good idea. Can we stop at my place for a change of clothes?'

IN THE END, they stayed at her apartment and ordered pizza, eating at the little table that he dragged over to the window. Arlo had some champagne delivered too and during dinner they raised a glass to Arjun and Mason.

Cosima put down her glass. 'I need a soak in the tub, I feel gross. Wanna join me?'

IN THE TUB, she lay back against his chest, her whole body relaxing. 'That was a bit of a day,' she said softly. Arlo was tracing soap bubble patterns on her belly.

'You could say that. Cos...I don't want to overstep the mark here, but I'm worried. About you being here alone, about your safety.'

Cosima had known this was coming and was ready. 'I knew you would be but Arlo, I don't want to feel caged.'

He was silent for a moment. 'Are you saying moving in with me would make you feel claustrophobic?'

She sat up and turned around, cupping his face in her palm. 'Absolutely not. But I want us to live together because we *want* to live together, not because circumstances force us to. I hate being regulated; I don't think you realize just how much my life is organized by other people.'

'Okay.'

She sighed. 'Speaking of which, I don't want to tell Jack about today. We don't know if it was something to do with my father's enemies or just a random mugger.'

'Random muggers don't attack in broad daylight in the middle of crowded markets.'

She shrugged. 'I don't know then. But, Arlo, if we tell Jack, he'll make me leave New Orleans. He'll make me leave you.'

Arlo shook his head. 'He can't do that. You're not a prisoner, for chrissakes.'

'But the FBI could revoke our protection, and I won't risk Harpa's safety for my own happiness. As much as I love you, Arlo, I wouldn't be able to live with myself.'

She felt tears threatening and Arlo, seeing this, kissed her tenderly. 'I know, I know. Okay, we won't tell the pretty boy.'

Cosima laughed. 'That's so mean. Why don't you like him?'

'I like him fine. It's his roving eye I'm not so keen on.' But he grinned at her, and she flicked him with water.

'I think you and Harpa are crazy. He's just a friendly guy.'

Arlo pulled her to him. 'To be fair to Jack, I can't say I blame him. Look at you,' he trailed his fingertips down her spine then moved around to cup her breasts. 'Your chest should be a national monument.'

Cosima giggled. 'You loon.' But soon they forgot about the horrors of the day and made love for the rest of the night.

. . .

HARPA PICKED up Jack's call as she was driven into the city. 'Hey, dude...just checking in on me?'

Jack laughed. 'Well now, I just called to tell you Mikah Ray has a clean bill of health security wise.'

Harpa chuckled. 'It's so weird, you're like my dad checking out my dates.'

'If only I could check for douchiness, I could have saved you from Deacon.'

'Deacon who?'

'That's my girl. Have a great time tonight.'

Harpa said goodbye and shoved her phone back in her bag. She had showered and changed into a lilac dress which she knew set off her dark skin and hazel eyes, and sweeping her hair over one shoulder, fastened a simple gold chain which Cosima had given her before she left New Orleans, around her neck. Now, her palms felt sweaty, and she surreptitiously wiped them on the seat of the car. Sean was driving today with Tony in the jump seat.

'Tony...um...what happens if I want to....um...'

Tony grinned around at her. 'Relax. We'll be a discreet distance, but you'll have your privacy.'

'Okay, cool.' She was blushing furiously. Steve grinned at her in the rearview mirror.

'We will mock you mercilessly, however.'

Harpa scowled at him. 'I'm sure that's not in your job description.' But she giggled, her nerves easing somewhat. When they pulled up to the bar, she got out, sticking her head back in. 'Enjoy your Peeping Tom assignment.'

'Ha ha. Go have a good date, princess.'

SHE SAW him as soon as she walked into the bar, his tall frame leaning against the bar talking to the bartenders. He stood, smiling, as he caught sight of her and kissed her cheek. God, just the feel of his lips made her cheeks flame and her senses reel.

'Hi,' she said, breathlessly.

'Hello...thanks for coming out tonight. What are you drinking?'

After they had their drinks, they found a table and sat down. Mikah studied her, his eyes taking in her every feature. Harpa felt tongue-tied, desperate to say something, but kept getting lost in his dark eyes. Mikah leaned over and touched her face.

'So, pretty girl, tell me about yourself? All I know so far is your name and that you're an incredible cook. I take it that's your passion?'

She nodded, grateful to him for breaking the ice. 'It is – and thank you. I was so nervous about putting up that dish, especially as it's so different from the usual menu, but Stan's been an incredible mentor.'

Mikah smiled. 'He's a good guy. How long have you been working there?'

'Just over a month.'

That made Mikah's eyebrows shoot up. 'A month? And he's letting you take a lead? Wow.' He looked impressed, and Harpa relaxed a little.

'It was a one-off but yes, so generous, but that's Stan. Have you been going to his restaurant long?'

Mikah smiled. 'Years. Stan and I grew up together in Tacoma, we're practically family. I actually own half the restaurant.'

'So you're my boss too?'

He laughed. 'Technically yes, but not really. I stay out of the running of the place.'

'And you're an art dealer?'

He nodded. 'That's always been my passion. I got started young, I was lucky enough to be mentored by Randall Mallory so I understand what you're going through now. All work, all the time.'

Harpa grinned. 'You got that right – I'm at catering college too, so sixteen-hour days is the norm.'

'Only sixteen? Lightweight,' he teased, and she giggled. God, his voice, so low and mellifluous, was sending her heart fluttering, his smile, so wide and warm was intoxicating.

'You're really beautiful,' she blurted out and then stopped in horror as Mikah smiled. 'Oh god, I'm sorry, that just came out.'

'Why are you apologizing? Thank you...' He leaned forward and took her hand, 'Look, you're nervous; believe or not so am I, so let's stop playing games and say what we mean. I've wanted you since the minute I saw you. I want you in my bed, Harpa.'

Oh, dear lord, her vagina was already contracting with the thought of his cock plunging into it... 'In that case,' she said slowly and looked up at him from under her lashes, 'I say...why are we wasting time in this bar?'

Mikah grinned widely and stood, holding out his hand to her. 'My place is only a few blocks away.'

In the end, she would never remember how they got back to Mikah's huge apartment because as soon as they walked in, they fell on each other greedily, pulling their clothes off and kissing.

Mikah, towering above her, swept her into his bed and proceeded to kiss every part of her body until she was shivering with desire. When his mouth found her clit, Harpa moaned at the sweet sensations his tongue sent slamming through her body, and by the time he tugged her legs around his hips and launched his rock-hard, thick, long cock deep into her, she knew she was lost.

They fucked hard and long, never taking their eyes from the other's face, Harpa feeling every muscle in her body working as he plowed into her with rhythmic, powerful thrusts. His hands on either side of her head; her own were roaming over the hard muscles of his broad chest, his firm stomach. Harpa could feel her control slipping as he drove her onwards to a shattering climax that made her scream his name deliriously.

Mikah came hard, his cock jerking and pulsing as he shot his semen deep into her belly. He gathered her to him and kissed her deeply, murmuring her name over and over. They had no need for discussion afterward; indeed, Harpa did not want to talk, she just wanted this man to take over her body in whatever way he wanted to. He excused himself to use the bathroom and Harpa, feeling the cool air on her body, and her orgasm faded, slid her fingers into her sex and started to rub her clit, keeping it hard and sensitive. Mikah returned from the bathroom and nodded approvingly as he saw her fingering herself. She spread her legs wider so he could watch her and was delighted when he started to fist his cock at the sight of it, the long, thick member already at half-mast and growing. They watched each other masturbate until Harpa came; moaning and Mikah gave a long groan as he came, ejaculating onto her skin, then covering her body and thrusting his still rigid cock deep inside her.

They made love, again and again, Harpa losing any inhibitions as they screwed in every position, explored each other's bodies curiously, and taking their time.

Dawn was breaking over the city before they finally feel asleep, sated and exhausted and with a connection formed that neither of them wanted to break.

SABINE SMIRKED to herself as she watched the video footage her guy had sent her. His henchman rushing at Cosima Bedi with a knife, attacking her before her goons dragged him off, blood dripping from Cosima's arm. She had told him to wound, not kill, and he had done a fantastic job. She sighed happily; that should unsettle the princess enough so that when Sabine put the next phase of her plan into action, she would start to crumble.

Trouble was...Sabine had no idea what to do next. *Damn it.* She sat in her hotel bedroom, twirling a pen around a piece of paper. She wouldn't be able to afford to stay in New Orleans much longer, she knew so whatever she did, she had to do it quickly.

There was a quiet knock at her door, and she frowned. Who knew she was here? She moved cautiously to the door and then gasped as she opened it. *Naveen.* He smiled at her in that cool way of his.

'Sabine, you're looking lovely. May I come in?'

COSIMA THANKED THE CONTRACTORS, beaming at them. 'I can't believe how quickly and how well you've completed it,' she raved, 'I'm utterly amazed. Thank you. You'll definitely be my go-to guys from now on.'

The foreman, Mack, chuckled. 'Well, that's good to hear. We've actually really enjoyed this project; you may be the best project manager we've ever had.'

Cosima flushed with pleasure. 'Just make sure you tell my boss that; I think this was my big tryout.'

'Well, you all nailed it,' Arlo said as he came through the door, looking up at the resplendent new reception with its high ceilings, restored features and new furnishings. The focal piece was the stunning metal work staircase, a behemoth of a structure which Cosima had lovingly restored by a specialist. Arlo put his arm around her shoulders and grinned at them all. 'I just wanted to say to all of you; thank you from the bottom of my heart, you have made mine and Cos's vision come to life. There'll be a bonus for all of you in your paycheck, and I'd like to invite you all back for a champagne reception to celebrate the opening in a month's time.'

There was a round of applause and then the gathering broke up. Cosima kissed Arlo. 'I have a surprise for you,' she said, grinning. 'Let's go up to the penthouse.'

Arlo smiled. 'You mean, our place?'

'I do.' She deliberately gave him a hot look. 'Let's take the fast elevator.'

He laughed. There was no fast elevator. 'Let's go, kiddo.'

As the elevator reached their floor, Cosima told him to close his eyes and she led him into the living room. 'Okay.'

He opened his eyes and smiled. Cosima, who he'd given carte blanche to decorate, had painted the living room in neutral colors; navy, stone, and duck-egg blue, but had complemented the muted scheme with pops of color. Stuffed bookshelves, colorful prints and over the large fireplace, against the navy, she had placed three square prints of bright sari material in orange, turquoise and pink. Comfy couches for them to veg out on, a huge flat screen ('Boys must have their toys'); the penthouse was open-plan, so, at one end of it, the spacious kitchen stood with its polished counters. Wall-to-ceiling windows gave a view of New Orleans that was unequaled.

Cosima watched Arlo take it all in. 'You like?'

He grinned. 'I love. When did you do all this?'

'Well, the gang were working so well without me, I actually had plenty of time to do this, plus I had help of course. The rest of it is done too, want to look?'

She moved to show him, but he stopped her. 'You mean...it's ready to move into?'

She smiled. 'I guess it is. I thought you would want to move in when it opened, is that right?'

Arlo pulled her into his arms. 'If it's ready now, I want to be in here with you, in our home. Right now.'

She kissed him and grinned. 'There'll still be work noise...just to warn you.'

'I don't care, I want us to be living together, why the hell wait? Is that what you want?'

She laughed, throwing her head back. 'Of course! Hell yes!' She shrieked with laughter as Arlo picked her up and twirled her around. She wobbled dizzily when she was finally put down, and Arlo steadied her, grinning. He pressed his lips against hers. 'Welcome home, baby.'

She smiled. 'Welcome home.'

He ran his hands down her body, and she wriggled with pleasure but stepped away. 'Not yet. If we're really doing this today, then I have plans for you.'

Arlo grinned. 'In that case...what do you need to bring from your apartment?'

WITH STEVE and Roger's help, it took only the four of them to move her meager belongings. Cosima didn't want strangers picking over her stuff, so when Arlo offered to arrange movers, she shook her head. 'No, I want to do it – it's closure.' Cosima took one last look around the place, her expression sad. 'This was a nice place to live,' she said, 'Probably the last place I will have shared with Harpa. Damn, talking of which, I need to call Jack, tell him where I am.'

Arlo put his arms around her. 'Not tonight. Tonight just let him think you're staying with me – which you are. At my hotel – which you are – just not the one he thinks.'

She smiled but looked undecided. 'Really?'

'I promise it'll be okay.'

BACK AT THEIR NEW HOME, it was already evening, and the workmen had cleared out. They had food delivered and sat on their new couch eating it, relaxing. Arlo opened a bottle of red wine, and they toasted their new home. Cosima sighed happily. So good to be alone. 'I can't believe this is my life now,' she said, smiling at Arlo, her eyes soft. 'I'm so happy, Arlo, you can't even imagine.'

He smiled and kissed her. 'I can, beautiful, believe me. I love you so much, Cos.'

'As I love you,' she grinned as he pushed her back on the cushions, taking the carton of Chinese food from her hand and putting it on the table. He pushed his hands under her t-shirt and pulled it over her head, admiring the way her long, long dark hair tumbled over her shoulders.

'I do believe,' he said, his hands at the fastening of jeans, 'that's it's your birthday next week, Miss Bedi, and I'm trying to think of some way to surprise you.'

She chuckled as he yanked her jeans down. 'And telling me that doesn't hurt your cause?'

He shrugged, his fingers caressing her belly. 'Probably.'

'Twenty-nine,' she grimaced, 'Not sure I want to celebrate that.'

He groaned, laughing. 'You're making me feel old.'

'Never,' she sat up and moved so she was straddling him. She opened his shirt and kissed his chest, teasing his nipples with her tongue, 'I'll make you feel young again. Come to our bedroom and I'll show you your present...'

She led him to the king-size bed, swathed in white linen. 'Undress and lay on your stomach,' she ordered, and he grinned.

'Whatever you say, ma'am...' He did as she asked and lay down on the bed, propping his head hand to watch her. 'And what might that be?'

Cosima had taken a small closed basket from the closet and set it down on the nightstand. She grinned at him. 'This, my darling lover, is a box of treats for us to play with. I do hope you haven't got an early meeting in the morning because I have a feeling you're going to be...*up*...all night.'

He laughed at her wicked grin, and as she slipped out of her underwear, watched as she took a small bottle of monoi oil from the basket. 'We'll start with this.' She tipped a little of the oil onto her chest then followed it down her body with her fingers until she slicked it into her sex, never breaking eye contact with Arlo. He blew out his cheeks, his arousal clear.

'*Damn*, woman.'

She grinned and ordered him to lie flat, climbing on top of him. 'Sensual massage, sir?'

He grinned. 'Yes, please, ma'am.'

She poured some oil onto his back then smoothed her hands over his skin, up and down his back, her fingers working the knots in his muscles. Arlo groaned. 'That feels so good, Cos...'

'Hush now.'

She felt his laugh rumbling through his back as she worked on him. Her little hands roamed over his broad back, and she leaned down to kiss his ear, whispering 'I'm getting so wet for you, Arlo, can you feel how hot I am?'

She pressed her sex against his thigh, and he moaned. Cosima smiled, pressed her breasts against his back while her hand slipped between his buttocks and her fingers massaged his balls. 'I'm going to ride you hard all night, big boy....you can turn over now.'

Arlo flipped over, grinning up at her, his cock huge and rigid against his belly. Cosima took it in her hands, stroking and caressing, drawing the tip up and down her sodden pussy. Arlo gripped her hips hard as she guided him inside her, sighing as he filled her completely.

'*Christ*, Cos...you are so fucking beautiful...*god*...' He moaned as she thrust hard, taking him in deep, her hand behind her, still massaging his balls, urging him on, loving to see him so blissed out. She loved the feeling of him inside her, filling her; it was when she felt most alive, most beautiful. She wasn't a vain woman, but she loved that Arlo thought she was beautiful.

His hands were on her breasts, his thumbs sweeping over her nipples, back and forth, back and forth until the nubs were almost painfully sensitized. Cosima moaned softly as his fingers swept down her belly, circling her navel then slipped between her legs to caress her clit.

Their love-making grew so intense that the rest of the world seemed to slip away. When Arlo came, they bucked and moved together as he pumped streams of hot semen into her, and Cosima threw her head back and let out such a lovely moan, that his cock, still inside her, grew hard again. He cradled her as he flipped her onto her back and drove himself into her. She cupped his face in her hands.

'I love you so much,' she whispered, and he pressed his lips to hers.

'You are the love of my life,' he said simply, and they continued on until dawn spread its fingers across the sky.

***

'Good morning.'

Harpa opened her eyes and smiled at the gorgeous man who stood by the bed, a white towel around his hips. Mikah grinned down at her. 'You should always be naked, you know that?'

Harpa laughed and rolled over onto her back, stretching luxuri-ously. 'I think it might raise a few eyebrows at work, not to mention Health and Human Services.'

Mikah sat down next to her, running a hand down her side. 'Are you kidding me? Your bookings would quadruple.'

She laughed then smiled shyly. 'I had a great time last night.'

'Me too, beautiful.' He bent down to kiss her. 'What are you doing today?'

'I have to work this evening but for the rest of the day – '

'Spend it with me. I'd like to take you to lunch then maybe we get to know each other better. Have you had a chance to really see the city since you got here?'

She pulled herself up into a sitting position. 'Not really. I haven't even been to the Space Needle.'

'No way...' Mikah pulled a face. 'Dude, we need to go there first and then maybe a cruise around the bay, maybe see some orcas.' He stroked her face. 'Harpa Bedi...where did you come from?'

She felt a pang; affection mixed with sadness. Soon she would have to tell him about her past, her constant protection, and the restrictions that she'd gotten used to. She wanted to be just a girl who met a boy for a little while longer.

'You okay?' Mikah shifted so he could pull her closer. She rested her head on his broad shoulder.

'Absolutely, although I kind of feel I'm dreaming.'

She felt his laugh rumbling through his chest. God, he smelled of soap and fresh air. 'Believe me,' he said, 'This is real.'

LATER, as they left his flat, Harpa glanced quickly at the black sedan parked across the street and sighed inwardly. There was no getting away from who she was, the threat to her, but *God,* sometimes it made her feel caged and irritable. As Mikah opened his car door for her, she smiled up at him. It was strange, she felt so comfortable with him, her nerves of the previous evening gone. She thought back to what Cosima had told her about her decision to just go with it in the Maldives when she met Arlo...Harpa grinned to herself. At least she and Mikah had known each other's real names.

'Something funny?' Mikah, easing the car into traffic, grinned at her.

'I was just thinking about my sister. She met a guy this year when she was on vacation, had a fling, then when she came home, he came looking for her. She told me the best decision she ever made was to just go for it.'

'And so we did,' Mikah nodded thoughtfully. 'I'm looking forward to getting to know you better, Harpa Bedi.'

Harpa glanced in her side mirror; saw the black sedan behind them. 'Be careful what you wish for,' she half-smiled, 'there's more to me than meets the eye.'

'WHAT'S THIS?'

Naveen pointed at the file on her laptop. Too late, Sabine realized she'd left the folder containing the video of Cosima's attack open. She hesitated and Naveen smiled. 'Secrets?'

She shrugged, and with a sinking heart, she watched him click on it. He watched the brief clip.

'How did you get this?'

Sabine frowned – she had been expecting questions like 'Who's being attacked?' or 'Why the hell have you got something like this on your laptop?'.

'A friend sent it to me.'

'The girl being attacked?'

'No.'

Naveen studied her. 'Are you going to send it to the police?'

Sabine sighed. 'No.'

'Why?'

'Because the man who attacked her is the one who sent me the video.'

Naveen sat back in his chair. They were in her suite; the suite she'd downgraded to reluctantly. It was still luxurious, but somehow, Naveen's presence shone a spotlight on its inadequacies. Everything about the man radiated wealth: his exquisitely tailored suits, his discreet but expensive watch, manicured nails, his dark skin soft and clear. He was looking at her now, a slight smile on his face.

'You know who the woman in that clip was?'

She nodded. 'She's my ex-boyfriend's new whore.'

Naveen smirked. 'Her name is Cosima Malhotra, but I think you already knew that.'

Sabine was stunned. 'You know her?'

'Oh yes. And I'd appreciate it if you didn't send any more amateurs after her.'

Sabine straightened up. 'What I do is none of your business.'

Naveen chuckled softly. 'When it comes to Cosima Malhotra, it is very much my business.'

'Why?'

His smile both scared and thrilled her. 'Because I'm the man who's going to kill her.'

Cosima sat down at her desk, feeling weird about being back in the architect's office after all these months at the site. It was the last day of remodeling at the hotel, and Cosima felt a little sad at saying goodbye to the workers. Jennifer, another architect, greeted her with a smile.

'Hey you, long time no see. I swung past the hotel this morning. It looks amazing. Almost made me wistful for the old days before I got stuck making factories.'

Cosima grinned. 'Don't give me that, you love it.'

'I do,' Jennifer admitted, flopping down in the chair opposite Cosima. 'So, how's the divine Mr. Forrester?'

Cosima suddenly got very interested on her computer screen. 'Um...'

'Cos...we all know, it's okay,' Jennifer was grinning at her, and Cosima couldn't detect any malice in the older woman's expression.

'I just don't want to be seen as unprofessional,' she said in a low voice. 'Arlo and I met before this job, and he...came to find me. The hotel is separate from that...kind of.'

'Cos, really, it's romantic. And it's given our whole office some-thing to gossip about,' she laughed as Cosima looked appalled. 'Relax, chick, I'm kidding. But good for you, he's gorgeous. And rich. And sweet – god, I think I hate you.'

Cosima laughed, grateful for the other woman's humor. 'Thank you, he is very special to me.' She pondered telling Jennifer that she was now living with him but decided against it – at least until she'd told Harpa and Jake. Jake! God, she'd forgotten about him, *shoot.*

After a while, Jennifer left her alone, and Cosima took out her phone to call Jack. She got his voicemail and left a message, then went back to work.

A half hour later, Tal called her into his office, his face creased with concern. 'Cosima... did something happen to you recently?'

She suddenly felt cold. 'What do you mean?'

He nodded at her still-bandaged arm. 'You told me you hurt your arm in a fall.'

'So?'

He motioned for her to sit down then turned his laptop around. Cosima watched in horror as a video of the attack played out on the screen. Her hand at her mouth, she watched as her attacker slashed at her, then her own reaction, bent double clutching her arm as Steve and Roger took the man down. The video wasn't a fuzzy, handheld camera – it was shot in such a way that the camera person obviously knew the attack was about to happen. Underneath the clip, the title read: 'Attack on Cosima Malhotra, New Orleans' and the date of the attack.

Oh, damn it, damn it. 'Yes...that happened but we were trying to keep it quiet because...*god,* how long has it been on the internet?'

Tal, his old eyes filled with worry, checked the timestamp. 'About twelve hours. Look, Cosima, with your situation, maybe you should call your FBI guy.'

Her eyes filled with tears. 'He'll make me leave, Tal. He'll make me leave all of you, Arlo, the hotel, New Orleans.'

'It's your life at risk, Cosima. Obviously this,' he nodded at the laptop, 'means they're still after you.'

She shook her head. 'That's the thing, Tal; it was a weird attack like he only wanted to wound me, not kill. It was a warning – '

'*Exactly.* Look, no one wants you to leave, least of all me. But I'd rather you be alive and well.'

Cosima nodded, wiped a tear away. 'I know. Look, I'm going to call Arlo.'

'Do that, and then call your guy. Take the rest of the day, Cos, this is more important than work.'

Cosima thanked him then went to call Arlo. He picked up on the first ring.

'Hey beautiful, you okay?'

Cosima could have cried at the love in his voice. 'Not really, baby.' And she told him everything.The tone of his voice changed immediately.

'Stay there, I'm coming to get you.'

Cosima put her phone in her bag and went to the restroom. *Jeez, could this really be happening?* As much as she took the threat to her life seriously, she was far more terrified of having to leave Arlo and her friends here in New Orleans. For crying out loud, she'd just moved in with her gorgeous lover, why now?

She sighed and bent to splash water on her face. In her haste, she cranked the faucet too hard, and the water splashed all over her. She cursed and reached for the hand towels...only to encounter an arm. Water streaming in her eyes, she jerked away and gasped. Someone grabbed her from behind and a cloth soaked in chemicals was pressed to her nose and mouth, and as she sank into unconsciousness, she only had one thought...

I'll never see Arlo again...

END OF PART TWO

3

TORN AND TORMENTED

A Billionaire, Bad Boy, Romance

Harpa Bedi stood on the viewing deck of Seattle's Space Needle and gazed out over the city. God, how had she not done this her first day? Seattle stretched out below her, the sun glittered off Elliott Bay; in the distance the Olympic Mountains and Mt. Rainier stood out against the skyline. Harpa squinted and pointed to the right of the big mountain at the faintest outline of another mountain on the horizon. 'Is that...?'

'Mount St. Helens,' Mikah Ray said, sliding his arms around her waist and hugging her to him. 'Beautiful, isn't it?'

'The mountains look painted on the sky,' she said in wonder and Mikah chuckled.

'I guess they do. Living in Washington all my life, I kinda got used to them but yeah, it's an amazing sight.'

She turned in his arms and gazed up at him. '*You're* an amazing sight,' she said, her voice thick. 'Thank you for bringing me up here.'

He smiled down at her. 'Well, you're very welcome.' He pressed his lips to hers. 'Wanna go grab some lunch?'

It had been only a few weeks since they had met but already Harpa was smitten. *Big time.* Mikah was erudite and funny, laid back and just so... 'Cool,' she thought,' he's just so *cool.*' She felt relaxed in his presence.

After that first night, they had spent every free moment together. They had talked a long time about their lives; at least, Harpa had given him a carefully edited version of hers. She didn't want to burden him with all the crap going on in her life. She told him about Cosima, about Arlo, about moving away from her sister for the first time. Mikah, in turn, told her how he'd started out in the business, his first tentative steps into the art world. His tutelage under one of the world's foremost art experts, Randall Mallory, had quickly turned into a lucrative career, and now Mikah found himself head of a business which made millions, if not billions, a year.

'I would worry that Randall would think I'm stealing his business, but he's moved more into philanthropic foundations for the arts now; a couple of his daughters-in-law are artists. I'm not that selfless yet, I'd like to make sure my future – and those of my staff – are secure first. Even with the recession, we've managed to still make a profit, so we're very lucky.'

'Rich people still need their toys,' Harpa quipped, and he grinned.

'Exactly.'

They'd never gotten around to doing all the tourist things Mikah had promised on that second day, too busy exploring the other's body, fucking, loving, laughing.

Now, finally making it out of Mikah's bedroom, they sat in one of the seafood restaurants on the waterfront and Harpa told him about the hotel Cosima was remodeling for Arlo. 'You should see it,' she raved, 'God, I wish I had Cos's eye for that kind of thing.'

'You have other talents,' Mikah grinned, and as she flushed, he relented, 'I mean, your food is incredible.'

Still scarlet, she waved away his compliment. 'You've only had one dish.'

'I can tell.'

'Psychic?'

'Absolutely,' and they laughed. Mikah took Harpa's hand, linking his fingers with hers. 'Look, Harpa, it's been a while since I connected with someone like I have with you. I'd like to see you exclusively; is that something you would consider?'

She was charmed by his old-fashioned manner. 'I would, very much.'

'Good.'

HE DROVE her back to her apartment and then whistled when he saw the building. 'Oh, *that* Arlo Forrester. Should have made the connection.'

'Do you know him?'

'I've met him a couple of times, just to say hi. He seems like a good guy.'

'He is, he's the best. He's crazy about Cos too, it's really sweet.'

'If she's anything like you, I'm not surprised. Can I see you later?'

Harpa looked doubtful. 'I'll be at work until about one a.m.'

Mikah smiled and leaned over to kiss her softly. 'I'll pick you up,' he murmured against her lips and Harpa felt her stomach dissolve with desire.

'Okay,' she whispered, closing her eyes and relaxing into the embrace. God, he was intoxicating.

When she finally made it back to her apartment, her whole body felt different, her mind a delirious, delicious fog of lust and happiness. She showered and changed, then grabbed her cell to call Cosima. The phone rang and rang until it clicked onto voicemail.

'Hey, sis...it's me. Have I got some news for you...'

· · ·

JENNIFER LYONS SAT her desk in the office, sending an email and looking up periodically. Cosima had gone to the bathroom at least ten minutes ago and hadn't come back yet. Jennifer, very fond of the young architect, hoped she wasn't unwell; Cosima had come out from Tal's office looking very green. Jennifer wasn't worried that she'd had words with Tal – no one ever had a bad word from Tal – and Cosima was such a rising star and a hard worker there was no way Tal was unhappy so...

Pregnant? Maybe, thought Jennifer with a smile. Cosima and Arlo Forrester were clearly crazy about each other, but it was too soon in their relationship to have that decision to make. *Ah, screw it,* she thought and got up to seek Cosima out. She pushed open the door of the bathroom and stopped. Cosima's purse lay on the floor, the contents scattered across the linoleum. Jennifer frowned. 'Cos? You okay?'

She checked the stalls, but the bathroom was empty. Her heart began to beat a little faster and when she turned she saw it. The blood on one of the basins. Not a lot, but a smear of it. *Oh no...* She ran out into the hallway and looked around. The fire escape was open, just a little, she ran to it. It opened out into a wide parking lot, and Jennifer ran out, scanning around, her breath coming in panicked gasps. One of Cosima's shoes lay abandoned on the asphalt.

Jennifer ran back in, tears starting to fall down her cheeks, straight to Tal's office, not bothering to knock. 'Tal...' She couldn't get the words out, and the elderly man shot up from his desk and came around to comfort her.

'What? What is it, dear?'

Jennifer could not contain her sobs. 'It's Cosima...Tal...I think she's been taken.'

ARLO REMEMBERED every moment from the day his brother Mason had been murdered. The sympathetic policeman who had come to his office. *I'm sorry to inform you...*

Even now, all these years later, he still felt that nausea, that clenching of his chest, the shattering grief.

And now it was happening again. He sat in the back of the police cruiser as they drove him to the station, numb, his mind blank with terror.

Cosima was gone.Abducted.Taken from her place of work in broad daylight. *Oh God. Oh God. Oh God.*

Every scenario ran through his head, all images of Cosima being murdered, horribly, brutally. He didn't know how to stop them.

'We've called her liaison, Jack Hampton, he's on his way. He was flying in to see her today; did you know that?'

Arlo shook his head. 'No, I didn't. Good, though, he'll know what to do.' His voice sounded weird, disconnected like it didn't belong to him. He wanted to shake himself, yell at himself to wake up, think, and make a plan. The shock was paralyzing.

At the station, he was given hot coffee and lead to an interview room where a young, good-looking detective sat down with him. Det. David Hanks, dark-haired and blue-eyed, studied him.

'Mr. Forrester...can you tell me about the last twenty-four hours with Cosima, please? Obviously, I don't mean to pry but anything you could tell us that's relevant. And I'd like to know about this.'

He handed an iPad to Arlo and Arlo watched the video of the market attack on Cosima. *Oh god*...he was so stupid – her enemies had found her and so terrified he had been of her having to leave New Orleans, he'd gone along with her plan of not telling Jack. *Damn it...*

'Yeah, I'd quite like to know about that, myself.'

The two men turned to see a very grim-faced Jack Hampton staring at Arlo. 'What the *fuck,* Arlo? Why the hell wasn't I informed about this?'

For a moment, Arlo struggled to find the words then... 'Cos didn't want to tell you; she thought you might insist on her leaving.' He winced; he didn't want to blame Cosima for that decision, but it was the truth. 'We both agreed.'

Jack threw a file down on the table. 'Well, fucking congratulations, Arlo, that decision has probably gotten her killed.'

Arlo jerked back in pain. 'Stop. Please, help me find her.'

Jack stared at him coldly. David Hanks nodded at the file. 'What's that?'

Jack's eyes were icy. 'It's a collection of the multiple death threats we've accumulated for Cosima over the years. The threats have ramped up this year. In that file, Arlo, is the way her enemies intend to kill her, every last detail. I want you to read that file and realize what a dumb fucking mistake you've made, what they'll do or are doing to her right now. Sick fucking stuff. And all because you couldn't give up screwing her long enough to consider her safety.'

'That's *enough*,' David Hanks stood, his voice hard. 'I don't know how things are done in the FBI, Agent, but here we take care of the next of kin.'

'Oh God,' Arlo said suddenly, 'Harpa...what the hell am I going to tell Harpa?'

'Nothing,' Jack said. 'Nothing yet. We check out every place we think she might have been taken.' He looked at David. 'You realize, Miss Malhotra's abduction and probable murder will be an international incident, yes? The U.S. Government had always supported the family of Arjun Malhotra against terrorism and if we're found to have dropped the ball, the ramifications of that...'

'Let's just all cool our boots, okay? One thing at a time. The only thing I care about at this moment is finding Cosima alive and well.' David Hanks' manner was calm, and Arlo found himself liking the detective.

Arlo sighed and closed his eyes. 'I'll tell you everything leading up to today,' he said, then remembered. 'Jack, there's something else you should know. Cosima and I are now living together at the hotel. She moved in with me a couple of weeks ago.'

Jack's jaw was clenching, the muscles tensed. 'We need to have a serious talk about what you two think my job is and what I should know.'

He slammed out of the room and Arlo sighed. 'Look, detective, I have a whole fleet of security detail that can help you find Cosima.'

'I believe she had two men on her watch, outside the office?'

Arlo nodded. 'I know, it seems ineffectual, but she didn't want to be 'watched' all of the time and have them intimidating everyone in the office. The office was deemed safe.'

'But it wasn't.'

'No. It was shoddy planning on my part, and I can't forgive myself. We have to walk a fine line between safety and intrusion...'

'Mr. Forrester – Arlo – don't beat yourself up. The hard truth is, no matter how many bodyguards a person has, if someone's determined to get to them, they will. The abductors took a huge risk taking her in broad daylight at her place of work – at the same time, it was a genius move. No one would have expected that. It's like when we send our kids to school – we think they're protected and safe then some gun nut walks in.'

Arlo half-smiled. 'You're not reassuring me.'

David sat back down opposite him. 'I won't treat you like Agent Hampton but neither will I sugar-coat things. It's bad.'

Arlo nodded, his entire frame slumped. 'I know.'

'I'll leave you along for a moment.' He patted Arlo's shoulder then reached for the file Jack had left.

'No, leave it. I want to see it.'

David looked doubtful. 'I think...'

'Please. I need to read it.'

David nodded. 'Okay. I'll give you some space.'

'Thanks.'

When the door closed, Arlo reached for the file and then hesitated. What horrors lay within those pages? Would he be able to function if he knew what was probably happening to Cosima right now? *God...*

He closed his eyes, pinched the bridge of his nose. 'Cos, I'm so sorry...I love you...please, please be alive, *please*...'

And he opened the file and began to read.

.   .   .

COSIMA DRIFTED SLOWLY BACK into consciousness. She felt the need to throw up but drew in some air to stop herself because she could feel her mouth was taped. Her eyes were also blindfolded, her hands tied behind her, her ankles bound. She was lying on what she assumed was a bed – it was soft under her body.

Why aren't I dead? That had been her first thought, and she wondered again now. She always assumed that if her father's enemies took her, they'd put a bullet in her head or cut her throat and dump her body somewhere. But this...

When she had been attacked in the restroom, as the darkness had come, she'd struggled wildly, twisting out of her attacker's grip only to smash her head on one of the porcelain sinks. Instant blackness. Her head screeched with pain – concussion no doubt. She lay still, realizing she could not hear anything either; her ears felt plugged. The only sense she had fully functioning was her sense of smell, and she breathed in a lungful of air. There was an undercurrent of something; fetid, swampy. She must be near the bayou. So that was their game plan – her body thrown to the alligators like so many other murder victims and Arlo and Harpa would never know what happened to her.

Suddenly she froze. There was a change in the room, she could sense something – someone. When cold fingers touched her face, she whimpered. Her ears were unplugged.

'Ssh,' a whispered male voice, gravelly, muffled, disguised. 'Don't struggle or I'll put a bullet in you. Nod your head if you understand.'

She nodded.

'Good.' Her abductor stripped the tape away from her mouth, and she gasped. A drinking straw was placed between her teeth. 'Sip.'

She did, the swirl of fresh cold water was blissful in her mouth.

'Good girl.'

He hauled her into a sitting position and took her blindfold off. He was dressed in head to toe black, a balaclava covering his head and a mask, a dumb goat's head mask. She blinked a couple of times, realized her left eye was sticky with blood. Her abductor – Goaty - brought a bowl of warm water and washcloth and gently washed her face. She saw the water turn red and felt a wave of dizziness.

'It's a pretty nasty cut, pretty girl. You shouldn't have fought me so hard.'

Her mouth was dry again. 'Who are you?'

Goaty said nothing, just continued to clean her wound. Now her eyes were used to the light, she saw she was in a bedroom – and a pretty plush room at that. She was confused – she had expected a broken down shack or somewhere – not this. The ceiling was high, at least double what she was used to in modern homes, the windows large – and barred. The bed she was sitting on was huge, king size, swathed in mosquito netting, the sheets pearly white and new, the pillows plump and comfortable. There was a vanity unit, and now she saw a small room leading off – a bathroom. Against the far wall, were boxes and boxes of food and toiletries, bottles of water stacked up as if someone was stockpiling for the end of the world. The room itself was huge, beautifully decorated. Goaty finished his cleaning and followed her gaze.

'You like?'

She didn't answer, just stared back at him for a long moment then looked away. On the nightstand, a gun with a silencer screwed onto the muzzle. She felt sick.

'This room is your new home, princess,' he said, and she cringed at the sing-song, creepy way he spoke, neither male nor female, barely human. 'At least until I decided it's time to kill you.' He picked up the gun and pressed it to her belly. 'Bang, bang, bang,' he said and chuckled, putting the gun back down. He nodded to the door. 'The door is reinforced steel, the windows are barred and alarmed, and you are being watched all the time.'

He tipped her chin up with his finger, and she saw in the far corner of the ceiling, the telltale red blink of a camera. 'There is no possible means for you to escape, my lovely Cosima. You *will* die here. But in the meantime, you must enjoy the time you have left. There's plenty of food – I'm afraid it's all cold, can't risk you burning down the place or trying anything stupid, but there is a small refrigerator in the bathroom there. I'll bring you fresh fruit and produce if you behave, otherwise you'll be living on crackers and cold soup.'

He cupped her chin with his hand, making her look at him. 'There are some clean clothes for you and you can wash things in the sink. I will come to visit you, and you will be gracious and thankful for every day I choose to keep you alive. You will give me whatever I want, princess, do you understand?'

She stared at him, the dizziness in her head not enough for her to misunderstand his meaning. So she was here as his sex toy for as long as he kept her alive. *Oh god...*

'Kill me now,' she whispered. 'Kill me because I'm never going to give you what you want.'

He chuckled. 'Yes, you will, my beautiful Cosima. You will give me everything.'

Hot tears of anger spilled down her cheeks. 'Why? Why are you doing this?'

His hand went to the nape of her neck and fisted the hair back there, holding her head rigid. She winced at the sharp pain of her hair being pulled, but Goaty leaned in, nuzzling her neck.

'Because I can,' he whispered, and he pushed the mask upwards so he could grind his lips onto hers, rough, violent. Cosima tasted blood.

He released her, laughing, pulling the mask down before she could get a glimpse of his face. 'I'm going to go. Turn over, lay on your belly, and I'll release your hands and feet. Try anything and I'll empty this gun into you.'

She complied, giving an involuntary sigh of relief when her hands and feet were freed. Goaty rolled her back onto her back, and stood over, pointing the gun at her belly. 'There will be no point screaming. There's no one around to hear you, Cosima. There will be no one to hear you beg for your life the day I come to kill you – although I might just record your murder and send it to your bastard lover. Won't that be a treat for him?'

'You are a sick fuck,' she said, finally, her voice scratchy, her throat dry. Her abductor bowed mockingly.

'Next time I visit, Cosima...we'll have a little fun.'

He went to the door and opened it, and she saw it was indeed thick steel. Her heart thudded as it slammed shut, and she heard the deadbolts lock. As soon as she heard his car start outside the window, she was up, off the bed and running to the little bathroom where she did what she had wanted to do as soon as she awoke to this nightmare.

She threw up.

HARPA TRIED CALLING her sister again when she went on her break that night. She told herself it was okay, that Cosima was probably busy with organizing the opening of the hotel. Harpa wanted to know what day Cosima wanted her to fly back to New Orleans to attend – she'd already cleared it with Stan, and now, she was wondering, could she bring Mikah? She hadn't asked him yet, but more and more, she wanted to be there with him, for him to meet her beloved sister, to say hello again to Arlo – *my family.* Her heart warmed at the thought; her sister and her *almost* brother.

Her mind briefly drifted to her mother in London. It had been years since Monica Lascelles had bothered to call or write her daughters. Harpa knew Monica didn't even know they'd left New York and she didn't care; her mother had been nothing but a burden to them. Cosima had been Harpa's mother for most of her formative years, despite there only being two years between them.Monica didn't even care that there had been a bounty on her daughters' heads since Arjun's murder.She was devoid of any mothering instinct, and Harpa wondered again how they could have been born of her. *Especially Cos,* she thought now, *she has such a big heart whereas I can be a little ruthless if I want. Yeah, yeah, kid yourself,* she smirked.

She went back to her station in the kitchen and busied herself with prep and didn't see Sean and Tony enter and chat quietly with Stan until she was making the spice paste for her dish. She smiled at them.

'Hey you two, got too hungry?'

Tony looked uncomfortable, but Sean grinned. 'You know it. Listen, can we have a quick word?'

She beckoned them over to a quiet corner. 'What is it?'

'You may see an increased security presence over the next couple of days. Nothing to worry about, just a precaution.' Tony's voice was low, and Harpa's heart began to thud.

'Is this why Cosima's gone radio silent? What's going on?'

Sean and Tony looked at her. 'Something like that. Just some undesirables flew into the country so we're keeping an eye out that's all. I'm sure Cosima will call you when she can.'

Harpa felt a little sick but nodded. 'Okay, I get it. Can I still hang out with Mikah?'

'Of course,' Sean said, patting her arm, 'There just might be extra security around his building. Does he know about your situation?'

She shook her head. 'I know I should tell him but I don't want to freak him out yet.'

Sean and Tony exchanged glances. 'Maybe you *should* tell him,' Tony said softly. 'If we need to extract you fast then it could get difficult.'

She blew out her cheeks. 'Okay. I'll think about it.'

But later, when Mikah came to collect her and drive her back to his place, she couldn't do it, couldn't sully his good mood, his romantic plans for them. Instead, they ate the leftovers she brought home straight from the foil dish, sitting at his breakfast bar, then showered together.

Mikah ran his fingers through her wet hair. 'Have I told you how beautiful you are today?'

She grinned, tipping her face up for a kiss then spluttering at the water hit her full force in the face. 'Didn't think that through, did I?' She laughed, and he cranked the water off.

'Let's get dirty again,' he said in a low growl, and her whole body responded.

'Let's...'

He lifted one of her legs up high and pressed her against the cool tile of the shower. He dropped to his knees, hooking her leg over his shoulder. His fingers found her sex and he gently spread the folds of her labia, his tongue sweeping up her cleft to her clit. Harpa shuddered as he made contact, sucking and nibbling at the small nub until it grew hard and red, her cunt swelling and pulsing as he attended to her.

Harpa moaned, and she felt his mouth curve up in a smile. 'You like that, pretty girl?'

She nodded, breathless and he gave a low chuckle. He scooped her into his arm and carried her to his bed. 'Then we'll just have to keep doing it...'

He went down on her again, and as he worked her clit, his long, thick fingers slid inside her, rubbing, massaging, finding that tender spot inside her, her sex growing moist as he worked. Harpa felt a frenzy of ecstasy screaming through every cell in her body as she shivered through an orgasm and then his mouth was on hers, and his titanium-hard cock was plunged deep into her swollen cunt, hard. He pushed her knees to her chest, sinking balls-deep into her and she smiled up at him as he drove himself into her, almost violently, the need and desire on his face as thrilling as the feel of his cock nailing her to the bed.

Her fingernails dug into his buttocks willing him deeper, deeper with every stroke; his cock seemed to get bigger, thicker, her vagina stretching to accommodate his size.

Mikah kissed her thoroughly as they fucked, and she loved how he could be so rough, so masculine while being so tender. She'd never experienced that in a lover before, and the way her body reacted to him was a revelation to her. At the slightest touch, her skin would flame, her sex would pulse and swell, her heart would clatter loud enough so she thought he might hear it.

Now, he groaned as he came, his thick cock jerking, spilling his seed into her belly. Harpa arched her back, feeling her belly against his as she reached her own climax then fell exhausted to the bed. They both were breathless but Harpa, grinning, climbed down his body.

'Your turn, big guy,' and she took his still hard cock into her warm, ready mouth, suckling at the salty remnants of his cum, teasing the tip, fisting the root with her hands until he was shuddering and groaning under touch, coming again quickly, shooting onto her waiting tongue.

Afterward, they lay, sleep coming over them, murmuring to each other. Harpa had just fallen asleep when she heard her cell phone buzz. She ignored it at first, letting the call go to voicemail but when it rang again, she rolled out of bed, groaning and went to find her purse.

Mikah, awoken, followed her and she smiled at him apologetically as she grabbed her phone. 'Sorry baby. Hello?' She recoiled in shock. 'Mom? Is that you?'

Her mother was crying hysterically, and Harpa could only make out the words Cosima...and knife. *Oh god, oh please, no...*

'Mom! Calm down! Has something happened to Cos?' She listened as her mother tried to explain. 'What video?'

MIKAH WATCHED his lover as she spoke to her mother, a myriad of emotions on her face. Fear. Sadness. Irritation. Then a blankness.

'I see,' Harpa said. 'Yes. I'll call him. Yes, I'll call you back, Mom, what's your number there? Oh, of course, yes. Give me a half hour.'

She ended the call and just sat there for a second, staring at the floor. When she looked up, her face was set, angry. 'I have to go home.'

Mikah frowned. 'What's going on, Harp? Is everything okay? Is your sister...'

'I have to go home.' She scrambled to her feet and skittered into the bedroom, pulling on her clothes. Mikah pulled his jeans on.

'Of course, I'll take you but – '

'It's okay, I have a ride.'

'What...wait? Harpa, what the hell's going on?'

She was at the apartment door now, and she turned and looked at him. 'I'm sorry, Mikah, you don't want any part of this...I'm sorry.'

Mikah stepped towards her. 'Talk to me,' he said fervently, his hand reached out towards her. Her eyes filled with tears.

'I can't,' she whispered and then she was gone. Mikah stood in the middle of his apartment, not believing what had just happened. *What the actual fuck?* He thought about following her, but she clearly wanted to be alone...instead, he went to the window in time to see her crossing the street and getting into a black sedan. It pulled away from the curb followed a second later by a second car.

Mikah shook his head. *I do not understand what just happened here.* He glanced at the clock. Ten after three. Exhaustion was setting in, he could feel his body drooping, but his mind was in overdrive. He rubbed his face then went to grab a bottle of water from the cooler. He had to be up in three hours for a meeting, and he hadn't minded about the lateness of the hour when Harpa was here and he was buried deep inside her velvety, soft body.

What the hell? He asked himself for the hundredth time. *Think. Think.* He grabbed his laptop and fired it up, glanced at his calendar for the day. Underneath the morning meeting, he blanked out the rest of the day and wrote eight words in capital letters.

FIND OUT WHO THE HELL HARPA BEDI IS.

Someone was banging on the penthouse's door. Arlo, who hadn't slept, opened it to see Jake, grim-faced. 'Harpa called me, hysterical. Her mother – her *mother,* of all people – rang her to tell her about the video. She wanted to know why the hell you or I or Cosima hadn't told her about the attack. Has she tried to call here?'

Arlo nodded. 'I didn't pick up,' he sighed and stepped aside to let Jack in. 'I didn't know what to say to her, and I knew she'd ask where Cos was...so I funked it.'

Jack studied him. 'You look like shit.'

'Tell me about it? Any news, anything?'

Jack shook his head, and Arlo groaned. 'I cannot just sit here and do nothing, Jack, I'm going crazy.'

'You're not going to do nothing. You're coming with me to Seattle. We need to tell Harpa before the press gets hold of it. Get in the shower, Forrester, we leave in an hour.'

COSIMA SAT UP IN BED, a panic attack beginning to build inside her. It wasn't a new occurrence; she'd been woken by them ever since the Goat had last been there. From her reckoning it had been seven days since he brought her here, and in that time he had visited twice, each time threatening her, telling her what he wanted to do to her. Still concussed, she had pretended to be asleep on one occasion until he'd laid on top of her then she'd panicked and bucked to get him off only to be met with mocking laughter. She'd gone through the entire place looking for a way out or something she could use as a weapon. But he'd been thorough. The camera blinked, constantly reminding her she was being watched all the time; she wondered if he had accomplices. *Probably,* she decided and made herself feel better by periodically making obscene gestures to the camera. Well, he did say she was going to die here, so what difference did it make? The only good thing when he visited was that he brought hot food for her, and had so far not forced himself on her. She knew it was only a matter of time.

There was a camera in the bathroom too, but she found if she ran a bath instead of showering, she could turn her back on him – plus a soak gave her something to do except stare out of the window. She was indeed in the bayou, she looked out onto trees heavy with Spanish moss and in the distance she could see the swamp, fizzing with mosquitoes and bugs. In the evening, she would sit on the window seat and watch the fireflies. It was better than trying to escape, getting nowhere and screaming – although she still did that too.

Tonight, her throat felt scratchy and raw from screaming. She ate a few Saltines and some fruit from a plastic cup and dug around in the small pile of paperback books he'd left. No, *Harry Potter*, she thought with a pang, then remembered she'd been reading *'Prisoner of Azkaban'* the night she'd meet Arlo in the Maldives.

*God, that night…*they'd walked back to her little villa which stood out in the ocean and made love all night. It had been a revelation to her, for once losing all her inhibitions, enjoying her own body as much as his, completely giving herself over to the sensual pleasure. She had never experienced anything so animal and yet so tender, so masterful and yet there was a vulnerability there too, from both of them. A true connection, a trust was built on that first night that had been built on in the months they had been together. She closed her eyes now and thought about Arlo, naked, all viral male, his broad shoulders, that hard, hard chest, the defined abs, the slim hips, and his long, thick cock. Cosima moaned and rolled over onto her stomach, curling herself up into a ball. That last night with him, one of their last nights as sole occupants of the hotel, had been the most exciting, the most adventurous yet.

She had promised him they would play with her box of treats, and they did; silken rope to bind each other, dildos, vibrators, paddles. They experimented freely with them, always taking care that the other was open to the kind of thing they were trying. Cosima found she loved to be bound while he fucked her; Arlo loved it when she used a vibrator on his ass while she sucked him. Not everything worked, of course, and they had many times when they would fall about laughing. Such perfect trust, perfect love. Joy. She remembered what Harpa had said to her those months ago; that now her life had joy…maybe this was the price she was paying for that happiness.

She stuck her fists into her eyes, trying to stop the tears. She didn't want that motherfucker seeing her cry. She rolled off the bed and walked to the camera. 'Fuck you!' She screamed it at the camera. 'Fuck you, you cocksucker! Come get me, asshole, come kill me because you will never have me…*ever*.'

She hoped he could lip-read. 'Asshole.' She turned away from the camera, anger, rage flooding through her, she cast around for anything – anything – she could throw at a window, break it, and scream her lungs out. But there was nothing. In the end, she went and sat in the bathtub and cried.

HARPA STARED at the two men for the briefest moment before her legs went to jelly, and she crumpled to the ground, hyperventilating. Arlo darted forward and cradled her in his arms.

'No, no, no, no....' Harpa was struggling to breathe, her hands clawing at Arlo's back.

'Sweetheart, sweetheart, breathe...' Arlo rocked her gently, but Harpa would not be calmed. Cosima was gone....probably dead....*no, no, not my sister, please...*

She heard Arlo talk to Jack.'Get a doctor, she needs a doctor...'

Why the *fuck* were they worrying about *her*? 'No...' she gasped, 'No, no doctors. I don't understand, how did this happen? When did this happen?'

They told, and she lost it again. '*Seven fucking days?!* My sister has been missing for seven fucking days, and you didn't tell me?' She was screeching now, but she didn't care.

They were in her apartment and it was mid-morning. She had been trying to call Cosima all morning, had watched that terrible video of her sister being attacked with a knife over and over until she was half-crazed. When she saw Arlo and Jack together at the door – and no Cosima – she'd known, but it wasn't until they said the words that she'd believed it.

Cosima was gone.

She turned back to the men, studied them. Jack's face was pale, drawn, but it was nothing to the sheer hell on Arlo's face – his eyes... she found it hard to look at the pain deep within them.

'So what now?'

Jack cleared his throat. 'I'd like to take you back to New Orleans – we think the abductor has her somewhere in state – '

'Based on what?'

'The alarm was raised soon after Cosima was taken and we locked down the airports, the ports, the rail stations, bus stations.'

'He probably took her in a car – they could be anywhere.'

Jack inclined his head. 'Yes. But we want you back in New Orleans, with Arlo, so we can keep you all together, it's safer that way.'

Harpa closed her eyes. She tried to force her mind to get past the overwhelming terror that was flooding through her. *Cosima...*

'I have a life here. I would have to talk to Stan...'

'Already talked to him, it's cleared. Anyone else?'

She didn't answer him. She'd known Mikah a month – did he really need to be dragged into this crap? She liked him – a lot – there was no doubt, and the connection they had was thrilling but, Jesus, involve him, and he might end up dead or with the same look in his eyes that Arlo had now.

'Harpa,' Arlo spoke now, his voice gravelly with exhaustion and pain, 'I couldn't bear it if something happened to you too. I won't permit it.'

Her eyes opened, and before she could stop herself, she snapped at him. 'Like you did such a bang up job of protecting my sister?'

She could have bitten her tongue off, but he nodded. 'I know. I will never forgive myself.'

Harpa sighed. 'I'm sorry, I didn't mean that.'

'Doesn't make it any less true.'

There was a knock at the door. Jack looked irritated. 'I told them to stay downstairs.' He went to the answer the door. It was Sean.

'Sorry, but there's a guy downstairs insisting on seeing Harpa. Name's Mikah Ray.'

Arlo looked up. 'Mikah Ray?'

Harpa colored. 'He's my friend.' She looked at Jack. 'I need to talk to him if I'm going back to New Orleans with you.'

Jack didn't look happy but nodded. 'We'll give you some privacy.'

'Thank you.'

Mikah was at the door before the two men left and he shook hands with them both, smiling at Arlo. 'Good to see you, man.'

Arlo nodded. 'You too, buddy.'

When Harpa and Mikah were alone, he took her in his arms. 'What's going on, Harp?'

The way he used Cos's nickname for her was the thing that finally made her break, and she burst into tears. He cradled her in his arms, trying to soothe her.

'My sister's been abducted...and she's probably dead by now,' she said between sobs. 'I can't bear it, Mikah, I can't.'

'Oh, sweetheart...'

Eventually, her sobs subsided and she stepped away from his embrace, smiled at him. 'I have to go back to New Orleans while they look for her.'

Mikah nodded. 'Of course. I'll come, I can move some things around and – '

'No.'

He rocked back. 'No?'

Harpa touched his face. 'I adore you, Mikah, which is why I don't want you to come. I don't want you to be messed up in my family's crap.'

Mikah shook his head. 'I don't understand.'

'I know you don't. Just trust me enough to know that this is for the best.'

Realization dawned. 'You're breaking up with me.'

She nodded, her eyes filling with tears. 'It's for the best. Mikah, this last month with you has been the best of my life, but we have to end it. I cannot risk your life.'

'No, wait...my life? What the hell is going on?'

Harpa wiped away her tears. 'It'll be in the press soon, and then you'll understand.' She stepped closer to him, stood on her tiptoes to kiss him. 'I'll never forget you, Mikah.'

Mikah took her shoulders and pushed her away. 'No, this is insane. I want to be there for you...'

'No.'

'Why?'

'I don't want this.' *God*...she remembered Deacon saying those very words to her and now she was wretched, saying them to this glorious man.

Mikah stared at her in disbelief. 'Don't push me away. Please, Harpa, I care too much for you to do that.'

'I'm sorry.'

He stared at her for another long moment then turned and left, slamming the door behind him. Harpa crumbled as soon as the door closed, sobbing silently into her hands. She heard Arlo and Jack return, felt Arlo put his arms around her. For a long time no one said anything, then Jack cleared his throat.

'Come on, guys,' he said softly. 'Let's go home.'

Nine days gone...

SOMETHING WAS WRONG. Very wrong. Cosima hunched over the toilet and threw up until there was nothing left to bring up. Her stomach cramped and clenched, and she retched again, slumping breathless to the floor. The pain in her stomach was excruciating. She crawled back to bed, drenched in sweat, her hair sticking her face, both freezing cold and boiling hot.

How she got sick, she didn't know, unless it was food poisoning from something he'd brought her. He'd visited last night, bringing her a tray of hot food – well, lukewarm by the time he'd gotten here – but it had given her hope that civilization wasn't too far away and if she could just find a way out...

But now, running was the last thing on her mind. She curled up on the bed, in full view of the camera, hoping he would see, that he would take pity...what was she thinking? He was an animal, he didn't care...again she wondered why the hell he didn't just kill her and have it over with. *Because he is a psycho, you dumb woman,* she thought to herself. She closed her eyes and prayed for sleep, oblivion, anything. With her physical and mental defenses down, she was laid wide open for anything he wanted to do to her...and at this particular moment, she didn't care.

She didn't know how long she had slept for, but it wasn't until she felt him touching her that she opened her eyes.

'Jesus, you're burning up...'

Hovering between awake and unconsciousness, she heard him go into the bathroom and run a bath. When she felt him start to undress her, she moaned in protest.

'I gotta get your temperature down, stop fighting me.'

She did, having no energy. Goaty undressed her then carried her into the bathroom, lowering her into a very cool bath. She cried out in protest and shivered violently, but he washed her, soaking a cloth in the water and putting it against her burning forehead to quiet her down. Soon, she was sinking into unconsciousness again and didn't feel him lift her out of the tub.

When she awoke he was gone, but on the nightstand were two aspirin and some vitamin tablets. She took the aspirin and one of the vitamins, seeing a basket of fresh fruit on the chair next to the bed. She swallowed some water carefully, found her stomach could take it, but decided not to try to eat anything yet. She had no idea of how much time had passed, but a couple of hours later, she heard his car.

He came in, saw her sitting up, reading, and nodded. 'Feeling better? Good.'

He put two more aspirin on the nightstand. 'Why don't you just leave the box,' she said, 'save you from having to keep coming out here?'

He chuckled. 'And have you take a bunch of them and deny me the pleasure of killing you? I don't think so, beautiful.'

She studied him. The balaclava, the mask, she really couldn't see anything of him. 'Why haven't you killed me yet?'

He didn't answer.

'Seriously, why all of this?'

Another silence then. 'Because I want to savor the moment.'

His answer made her feel like throwing up. *Sadist fucker.* 'How are you going to do it?'

'I'll put a bullet in your belly and watch you bleed slowly to death. Is that enough detail for you?'

She wanted to scream. 'Then do it.'

He laughed. 'Not yet.' He bent down and splayed his hand across her stomach. 'Haven't you heard of anticipation, Cosima?' He pushed his forefinger into her navel, hard. 'Next time it won't be my finger but the muzzle of my gun and then...*bang.* I imagine the pain will be...unimaginable.'

She stared up at the eyes of the mask, trying to see anything human in him. 'You're a sick *fuck*.'

He laughed. 'Yes. Now, I'm going to go, is there anything else you need?'

'Yes.'

'And what's that?'

'I need you to go fuck yourself.'

He laughed again. 'See? This is why you're still alive, you make me laugh, Cosima. And next time I see you, you'll give me something else too.'

He leaned in and nuzzled her neck; Cosima shrunk away from him. 'I can't wait to taste your sweet little cunt, Cosima. I'm already hard for you, can you tell?'

He grabbed her hand and pressed it against his erection briefly then laughed and left the room, the door clicking shut behind him.

Cosima was trembling violently, but she sucked in a few deep breaths calming herself. So now she knew his plan, knew he planned to rape and murder her, and so Cosima, for the first time, had an advantage. Because she wasn't going to go along with his plan.

She was getting out of here even if it killed her to try.

THE NEWS of Cosima's abduction broke nationally then internationally ten days after Cosima had gone missing. The Malhotra family history was dredged up and analyzed over and over; several groups known to be enemies of Cosima's father and grandfather were quick to disassociate themselves from the kidnapping. '*Although we have historical ties to the family, and in the past have actively sought the deaths of anyone related to the traitorous Malhotra family, in these more enlightened time, we do not seek retribution from innocent children. We wish and hope that Ms. Malhotra is found alive and well.'*

'Bullshit,' said Harpa, fiercely. 'They're probably having street parties. Wait until they find Cos's body, they'll have posters made.'

'She is *not* dead,' Arlo growled, getting up from the couch.

Harpa felt bad. 'I'm sorry, Arlo, I didn't mean to say she's dead. There is hope.'

She had been staying at the penthouse of the hotel, sleeping in the guest room, which had been a blessing and a curse. She felt close to Cosima here, seeing her sister's things, her books, her jewelry. Arlo had come home one day to find Harpa in her sister's closet, holding onto the sari she had been saving for a special occasion, sobbing. He had gently lifted her up and sat her on the couch, listening as she rambled on about Cosima, random memories. It had brought her closer to Arlo. She had apologized for blaming him; she knew it was killing Arlo that he hadn't protected Cosima enough.

'No one could have seen this coming,' she told him over and over but to no avail. Jack had been updating them daily on progress, but she knew Arlo was frustrated. He was using every means open to him as a civilian to try and find her; hundreds of detectives countrywide were searching every 'Outhouse, doghouse, farmhouse...' He had intoned and half-smiled.

They spent all day trying to figure out what to do next. Worst of all, when the news broke, Monica Lascelles had gone public too, playing the brokenhearted mother of the victim to a tee.

Harpa and Arlo watched her press conference on the t.v. and, afterward, Harpa turned to Arlo, a strange smile on her face. 'Arlo, you've just seen our birth mother at her finest. Did you notice she didn't say Cosima's name once? It was all '*my* daughter', '*my* loved one.' She made Cosima's abduction all about *her*.'

Arlo was grim-faced. 'Harpa, I can see exactly why you and Cos don't have anything to do with her. What a piece of work.'

'Yep.'

But then Monica had decided she was coming to New Orleans and bringing her whole entourage. 'It's going to be a circus.' Harpa groaned, then grabbed Arlo's hand. 'Whatever you do, don't offer her anything – no hotel rooms, no special favors. She will leech onto you and never let go.'

'How on earth do you and Cos share DNA with her?'

'Lord knows. I have a fantasy that one day we'll find out she used a surrogate.' Harpa clasped her hands together. 'I send up a prayer about that nightly.'

She smiled, and Arlo was glad she still retained some of her sense of humor; it reminded him so much of Cosima.

God, he missed her so much, it was like his heart was being torn to pieces thinking she might be dead. Every day he would sit, his eyes closed, trying to remember the soft velvety feel of her skin, the flush of her skin when she came, her kiss, so sweet and tender. Her smiling eyes haunted him.

He felt so helpless; Jack had warned him not to get in the way of the official investigation, and so he was tied on how much he *could* do. He had his contacts come up with lists of abandoned buildings in the New Orleans area and wider Louisiana, but she could be anywhere. *Anywhere. Just be alive, please,* he prayed constantly. If she was still alive, then there was hope, and he desperately needed to cling to that.

The hotel's grand opening had been postponed, and now it echoed with silence, the workman having cleared out four days previously, and Arlo and Harpa had been left alone. They'd talked, of course, endlessly about what to do, what they could do to find Cos, but also about plans for the future as if saying the words would strengthen the possibility of Cos's safe return.

Their little self-contained unit was broken when Monica Lascelles arrived. She summoned them to her hotel room and subjected them to hours of self-pitying grief before finally asking Harpa about her own life. Harpa gave her the bare bones of her life in Seattle.

They were sitting at dinner in one of Seattle's finest restaurant – a private table, Monica had announced loudly, making sure everyone in the room heard. Arlo couldn't believe this brash, vain woman was Cosima's mother.

Monica kept dabbing at her eyes as she talked about her loss. '*Cos isn't dead*,' Harpa said between gritted teeth, but Monica wasn't listening.

'It's different for a mother,' she said, 'it's a physical pain to know your child might be in danger. It's that blood link.'

'Cos and I share the same DNA,' Harpa said archly, 'We share a deeper bond than you have ever had.'

Monica rolled her eyes and turned to Arlo. 'She always gets like this, forgive her, so competitive.'

'I've never found her to be so,' Arlo said calmly, and Harpa flashed him a grateful smile. Monica ignored his words.

'When I saw that video...my god, my baby, attacked with a knife, I felt a...chasm open up inside me. Raw, raw pain, agony, really.'

'Mom.' Harpa toyed with her cutlery, 'Do you realize that since you came to New Orleans, you haven't said Cosima's name once?'

Monica rocked back. 'Don't be silly, of course I have. This is what I mean,' she said to Arlo, who gazed back at her coolly. Harpa could barely control her temper.

'No, you haven't. Not once. You don't know the Cosima we do: funny, brilliant, artistic, warm, kind, erudite. You don't know that she loves, *loves*, Harry Potter; the books *and* the movies. You don't know that her favorite musicians are Billie Holiday and Johnny Cash, or that she hates wearing nail polish on her fingers but always wears it on her toes.'

'That she sings when she's cooking' Arlo joined in, 'Or that she winds her hair around her finger when she's concentrating on something. That she loves with her whole heart.'

'That she's the best person I've ever known,' Harpa's voice was shaking now, 'that she is my sister, my mother, my father, my best friend. That when she met Arlo, she found her soulmate. You don't know any of this.'

Monica was stunned into silence, looking away from her daughter. The waiter came with the wine then, and she made a great show of flirting with him and discussing the different vintages with him. Harpa looked at Arlo who winked at her and mouthed '*Way to go.*'

AFTER DINNER – which, of course, Arlo paid for - Monica wanted them to go back to her hotel for drinks but seeing Harpa's stricken face, Arlo made their excuses and they left, both sighing with relief.

'She's a goddamned parasite,' Harpa raged in the cab back to the LaBelle. 'Did you notice her flirting with you? Gross.'

Arlo laughed. 'Thanks.'

Harpa chuckled. 'You know what I mean. God, you know what, I feel like doing a DNA test to try and prove she's not our mother.'

He looked over at her. 'You think that would tell you anything new?'

Her shoulders slumped. 'No.' She sighed. 'We look too much like her for it to be in doubt. Well, I do. Cos has always taken after Dad; her features are softer than mine.'

'You're both beautiful, and on the inside too, which is what matters.'

Harpa grinned. 'You been reading *Cosmo*? Are you seriously telling me you would have noticed Cos if she didn't look like she does?'

Arlo nodded. 'I am saying that – maybe it would have taken me longer than a millisecond – but there's something that shines out from your sister and it's not about physical beauty.'

Harpa's eyes filled with tears. 'You're right.'

Arlo squeezed her hand. 'We're going to get her back, Harpa, I know it in my bones.'

IT WAS ANOTHER BAD DAY. The sickness she thought had left her was hanging on, and she felt wiped out. She had read all of the books Goaty had left for her, and now she was curled up on the bed, staring at the tiny red light blinking on the camera. She'd been doing that for hours, but she didn't know why. Eventually, she grabbed a bottle of water and some saltines then went to bed.

Waking in the middle of the night, she stumbled to the bathroom to pee, then climbed back into bed. *Maybe I'll die of this virus,* she thought and remembered his words about killing herself and robbing him of the pleasure. She lay back down and turned on her side – and stopped. The red light wasn't blinking. There was no red light at all. She sat up and stared at the darkened corner of the room. Did that mean he wasn't watching? The moon was full outside, and its light streamed in on the huge windows.

Suddenly Cosima felt the adrenaline coursing through her. Maybe he was asleep; maybe he watched until she fell asleep, then turned in himself – after all, he was human, wasn't he?

What can I do? What can I do? She looked around wildly, desperate not to waste this opportunity then realized she was hyperventilating. *Calm, calm.* She sat back on the bed and breathed deeply. *Calm. Think. Think.* She got up and moved around the room, running her fingers over everything in the room. The bed was iron, welded, no loose parts. In the bathroom, she felt each tile, but they were cemented in place. The faucets too were old; time had encased them in their fittings. The shower head was fixed.

Damn it, damn it. She walked to the bathroom door and gazed out over the bedroom again. Her eyes settled back on the bed...then she dropped to the floor and crawled across it. Gingerly, she felt under the bed, wary of spiders and bugs and felt around. The floorboards were wooden in this room, and as she moved her hand around, she felt how rough they were. Maybe she could break off a splinter, use it as a weapon? Maybe. She wriggled under the bed, and when she was halfway across, she heard it. The squeak of the floorboard under her. She moved again, and it squeaked. Her throat felt full of nerves and anticipation. Squeezing her body around so she lay flat on her stomach, she found the squeaking floorboard and traced along it until she reached the screws that held it in place. A screw was standing a little proud of its fixing, and she eagerly attacked it, twisting the metal with her fingers. When she felt it give, she whooped and unscrewed the whole thing. She clenched the long screw in her fist. *A weapon.* Shove this in his eye, or his throat, or his scrotum, which might give her time to get away. It was a small hope, but it was still *hope*. She felt along the board to try and unscrew the second fixing. This one was deeply buried in the wood. *Shoot.* Well, maybe this was a start. She wriggled out into the moonlight. Still no red light. It must have been an hour at least. She hid the long nail under the mattress, at the far corner of the bed. Maybe she could use it to pry a tile free or something.

Cosima felt something she'd hardly dared to hope; that she might be able to fight back. That small piece of metal might be the thing that saved her from the monster that held her here, who planned to rape and murder her. At least, she had to try.

She watched and counted the minutes until the red light of the camera flickered back on just before dawn then she closed her eyes and sleep more soundly than she had for days.

MIKAH RAY SAT in the auction house, staring unseeingly at the pieces up for sale. Usually this was his happy place, his hunting ground, but since Harpa had left Seattle and the news of her sister's abduction had broken, he couldn't think of anything else. After the bidding was over he filed out with everyone else then felt someone drop into step beside him.

'Dude, what's with you? I was expecting a fight on that Hockney miniature.'

Grady Mallory grinned at his friend and Mikah shrugged. 'Just wasn't feeling it today.'

Grady studied him. 'What's up, bro?'

Mikah stopped, hissed out a sigh. 'You got time for a drink, Grady? I need to talk to someone about...something.'

'Sure thing,' Grady looked at his watch. 'I'm picking Flori up at four but until then, I'm all yours. O'Shea's?'

At the bar they ordered a beer and some chips and salsa and sat down. Grady twisted the cap of his beer. 'So, what gives?'

'I was seeing someone, briefly. Was crazy about her too, then...did you see the stuff in the news about the girl who got kidnapped in New Orleans?'

'Wasn't she Indian royalty or something?'

'Yeah...well, it was her sister. Harpa. They lived under assumed names, Harpa just came to Seattle to train as a chef, which is where I met her. Then all this happened and she just...left. Checked out. Didn't want me to be involved with, as she put it, 'all this crap'.'

'Sounds fair enough but I guess you think otherwise?'

'I can't stop thinking about her, man. I think we could have built something really special, you know?'

Grady nodded and was silent for a moment, considering. Mikah watched his friend's expression. 'I thought I'd asked you since you've had some experience with this kind of thing.'

Grady nodded. It had been a couple of years since his girlfriend Flori had been attacked and stabbed by a psychopath named Gregor Fisk, who had gone on to kidnap Grady's sister-in-law, Quilla. Quilla had escaped Gregor's hands but nearly died in the process. The whole sordid saga had been gone over and over in the press so many times, Mikah knew the entire story.

'What would you do?' he asked Grady now, his need for some kind of approval growing. 'Should I respect her wishes and stay away, or go find her and tell her that her problems are my problems and that I'm not going anywhere?'

Grady smiled sadly. 'I know what I did; I stuck around...but then it was *my* family Fisk was targeting – and although I didn't know it, I was already in love with Flori. I don't know how to advise you. If you're serious about her, I say go for it but don't crowd her. Just say 'I'm here, I'm not going anywhere, whatever you need, whatever you want."

Mikah nodded. 'That's good advice, man.'

'But?'

Mikah smiled. 'How'd you know if you're serious about someone?'

Grady grinned. 'Is she the first person you think of when you wake and when you see something funny? Can you get the feeling of her skin out of your head?'

Mikah nodded. 'All of those things and more...I just hope I can convince Harpa.'

HE PULLED up to the house around noon. He'd been watching the feed all morning, seeing her sleeping soundly. She still looked sick, but at least someone of her character was coming back. He laughed every time she passed the camera and stuck her middle fingers up at it, or mouthed *'Fuck you'* at it. He loved her spunkiness as much as the feel of her soft skin. God, he'd miss her when she was dead, but still, knowing he would be the last person she would ever see made up for that. He would cradle her in his arms after he shot her, watching her bleed out, hearing her last desperate gasps for air, for life, and he would kiss her as the light went from her lovely eyes.

He got hard just thinking about it.

He looked up at the window as he got out of the car. He always expected – hoped – she would look out at him and smile, wave in greeting. *Fat chance, pal.* Cosima hated him with the fury of a thousand suns.

But today, he grinned as he climbed the stairs to her room, today would be different, today would be tender, and loving...today would be the day she gave him everything...

COSIMA DIDN'T LOOK up when he entered the room, just stuck her middle finger up. Goaty chuckled. 'And good morning to you, beautiful. I have a treat for you today.'

'Shove your 'treat' up your ass.'

He laughed again, and she slammed the book she was pretending to read down on the bed. 'Look, asshole, just fucking shoot me. Or let me go. I'm never going to give you what you want.'

He pulled up a chair and reached into his backpack. For a second, her heart stopped, thinking he was reaching for his gun, but then he pulled out a paper cup and a bottle of bourbon. He poured some into the cup and handed it to her. 'We're just going to talk. Drink.'

She threw it at him, and he laughed. 'Should have seen that one coming but God, Cosima, what a waste of the good stuff.'

He pulled out the bottle and another cup, poured them both drinks. He pulled up his mask to drink and Cosima stared at his mouth, trying to memorize it on the small chance she got out of here. Almost absentmindedly she sipped the bourbon. It warmed her blood.

'What do you mean, talk?'

He reached for the bottle again, and she wondered why he kept putting it back in his bag. Maybe he was scared she'd make a grab for it, smash over his head. *Well,* she thought, *that's exactly what I would do.* He refilled her cup.

'That. Talk.'

She took a huge gulp of the liquor. 'Let me go.' *Well, what else am I going to say?*

He shook his head. 'No. These four walls are your prison, Cosima. They'll be your coffin too.'

'Why? Why are you doing this? Is this about my father? You're not Indian, your hands are white....have they hired you to do this to me?'

He didn't answer, just kept staring at her through the grotesque goat mask. He poured another drink, and she threw it back, now wanting the oblivion. *Stop,* her subconscious told her, *stop now. Losing control will not help you.*

But she didn't listen. A quarter hour later, the room wheeled and swayed, and her vision became hazy. But...she didn't feel drunk, she just felt disconnected, absent. Her body felt alien to her. She squinted at Goaty. 'What's stopping me from getting up and walking out of here, right now?'

'Apart from my gun? Nothing. Go ahead. Try.'

She shook her head. 'You'll shoot me.'

He laughed. 'Well, okay then, say I'm in a good mood, and say I give you a shot - so to speak – at escaping. Go ahead. I promise I won't shoot you.'

He was mocking her, but she couldn't waste the chance. She got unsteadily to her feet and walked to the door, stopping to look back at him. He hadn't moved. Shakily she put her hand on the door handle and turned it, pulling the door open. The rush of fresh air assaulted her senses, made her head whirl and her stomach roil. She sucked in lungfuls of it and tried to walk out into the house. It was huge, a mansion, maybe a plantation house, grandly decorated, the wide upstairs hallway led to a grand staircase. Cosima tried to walk toward it, but every step was like walking in treacle. What the hell was wrong with her? She pulled herself along to the staircase then slumped to the ground. Jesus...she couldn't breathe....couldn't think...*Arlo...Arlo, please...help me...*

Too late, she realized she had been drugged, and as Goaty, mocking her, laughing at her attempt to escape, yanked her into his arms, she managed to gasp out the words. 'What did you give me?'

He chuckled nastily. 'Just a little something to make you more...friendly...'

Oh god...no...not that, please...Arlo...Arlo...

Mikah checked into the hotel in the French Quarter, dumped his bags then went straight out into the crowded streets. He wanted to scope out the place, see the hotel where Harpa was staying. Some helpful private dick of the Mallorys had helped him out, easily finding out the information that Arlo Forrester, once a resident of San Francisco – had now permanently relocated to the Big Easy. Mikah stared up at the refurbished hotel in admiration. *Cosima and Arlo Forrester have some major talent,* he thought. He didn't linger, couldn't risk Harpa seeing him and freaking out. He had a plan and that plan meant taking advantage of the few times he'd met Arlo. With the man grieving for his lost love, Mikah didn't want to take advantage, but he thought he might try, contact Arlo, see if he could help, maybe set up a meeting...

God, could that plan be any more passive-aggressive? Mikah shook his head and went to find a coffee house to settle in and plan what he was going to say.

. . .

COSIMA OPENED her eyes to see Arlo gazing down at her. 'Hey, beautiful...'

'Arlo...' she whispered and smiled. He smoothed her hair away from her face.

'I missed you so much, baby, so much....' He pressed his lips to hers, and she kissed him back, feeling the softness of his mouth on her own, and his tongue gently massaging hers. His hands were on her body, and she realized she was naked. She smiled and coiled a leg around his waist.

'I want to be inside you, my darling Cosima...' and with one thrust. He drove his cock deep into her velvety sex. She gasped at the quick pain and then moaned as he found his rhythm, urging him on... 'Arlo...'

His hips grew rougher, and the look in his eyes grew colder as he rammed his cock harder into her...she didn't understand the look in his eyes...and now he was scaring her...and now it wasn't Arlo but Jack thrusting into her....no, *wait*....now it was her childhood friend, the one who wanted to kill her..Naveen.....no...his face wasn't human...*it wasn't human...*

She bucked and screamed for him to stop but he cuffed her hard around the face and stunned her. She could not fight as he pinned her hands to the bed and grunting loudly, he came, and she felt the hot rush of his semen, his disgusting seed, deep in her belly, and she started to sob.

'Don't cry, Cosima, this was inevitable...ssh, don't cry, it won't be long now...soon you'll be dead, and this won't matter...'

She didn't stop crying for hours after he left, then, exhausted, fell into a nightmare-heavy sleep. When she woke, she wished she was dead. There was no spark of hope left in her as she sat in a freezing cold bath, leaning her head against the cold tile. She had no tears left now; her skin and eyes felt desiccated. She closed her eyes and took slow, deep breaths.

Never again. That monster would never touch her again. She would attack him, make him shoot her, or – if it was even possible – get the gun from him.

Yeah right. She sighed...and then it hit her. His gun. His gun with a silencer on it. If she was in the middle of nowhere, why would he need a silencer? She sat up. God, how had she missed that?

She could hardly wait until the middle of the night when the red light on the camera blinked off. As soon as it went out, she darted up, grabbing the small screw she had squirreled away and found a window that wasn't immediately noticeable from the middle of the room. He'd lied about her being alone in the area so maybe he'd lied about the windows being alarmed; using the sharp end of the screw, she scrapped away at the window's surround. The house, while magnificent, was old and the cement that held the window in place crumbled easily away. It still took her most of the night to do one side of it and by the time dawn was breaking, she was tired. She had checked the camera all night, every few minutes but it wasn't until she had brushed her teeth and washed her face that it blinked back on. She guessed the feed had been down about six or seven hours. Over the next few nights, she'd loosen the window pane and lift it out and spend the night screaming out of it in the hope that someone, somewhere would hear her.

Cosima's mind was buzzing now; she would try again to loosen the floorboards beneath her, see if she could drop through to the floor below. She didn't care how crazy the plan, she was determined she would try anything to survive. One thing was for sure; she'd never accept anything from him again.

'Five days,' she murmured to herself, 'five days and I will be out of here, or I'll take that sharp-edged screw and open my own wrists. You don't get to tell me what to do, motherfucker, you don't get to decide what happens to me and my body.'

She got into bed and slept soundly for the first time in days.

ARLO NODDED as the make-up artist took the shine off his forehead and Jack, his face rigid with disapproval, asked him again if the television interview was a good idea.

'I'm sick of doing nothing,' Arlo said firmly. 'The kidnapping is already headline news, and I want to get the message out that at the end of the day, regardless of her family, Cosima is an innocent victim, that whoever has taken her will be guilty of killing someone who only does well in this world. That whatever the crimes or perceived crimes of her father and grandfather, Cos is loved and cherished.'

He let out a long breath. 'God, Jack, I just want them to know what they'll be destroying for absolutely no reason.'

Jack sighed. 'Arlo...can't you think of any other way...?'

'Jack, you're the one who's put a block on my guys searching for Cos, on me going public with a reward for information.'

'To stop your guys prejudicing the FBI investigation, that's why I shut them down. And I did that *after* they'd searched your hit list of abandoned sites in the state. As for a reward – we'll get a million crazies and not one useful piece of information. Trust me, Arlo, I've done this before.'

'Not knowing is driving me crazy.'

Jack sighed. 'Arlo, have you considered this may not be the work of Arjun's enemies? That it might be a stalker? Or even...and I hate to say it...the work of your ex-girlfriend?'

Arlo gave him a chilly smile. 'I doubt Sabine would have a clue how to pull this kind of thing off, and she may be a world-class bitch, but she's not violent. And, yes, I have thought about it being a lone stalker...after all, the group in India wouldn't bother to kidnap her.'

'No, they would have slit her throat in her workplace restroom, quick and cold.'

'Jesus, Jack!' Arlo looked sick and angry. 'Do you not think before you speak? Do you know how many nights I've lain awake imagining every kind of horrific scenario?'

Jack looked shamed. 'Sorry. It just doesn't make sense to me, none of it. When I thought it was her family connections but....'

Arlo nodded. 'Yeah.'

The floor manager came to find Arlo. 'We're ready for you, Mr. Forrester.'

Arlo stood and pulled off the paper bib the make-up artist had given him. 'Okay.' He followed the floor manager out but stopped by the door and turned to look at Jack. 'Jack...I have to do something. I have all this money and influence, and I couldn't save the one thing I hold most precious in this world. Let me do this.'

Jack was quiet and then nodded stiffly. 'Okay. Okay, Arlo.'

COSIMA IS MY LOVE, my heart. Please, whoever you are, stop and look at the beautiful, brilliant woman in front of you, the woman you are keeping from her family. Imagine she is your daughter, your sister, or the love of your life and examine how you would feel in my position. If it's money you want, you can have it. If you're holding her because of her family's history...you are punishing Cosima for the sins of her fathers; she has nothing to do with those old arguments and differences. And if you are holding her because you think you feel something for her...I know how you feel. She is incredible. But love is not a negotiation, love is not control, love is not imprisoning or harming the one you love. Please...set Cosima free, let her come back to her family. Thank you.

SABINE CLICKED OFF THE TELEVISION, her mouth curling up in a sneer. *Revolting,* she thought to herself, ignoring the sharp pain in her chest. Arlo would never have spoken about her the way he spoke about the fucking princess. When she had heard Cosima had been abducted, she had felt a certain glee – she was convinced Naveen – her occasional lover - was behind the disappearance. She hadn't seen Naveen since the news broke that Cosima was missing, and she was feeling the absence – especially of his magnificent cock drilling her to the bed – but seeing as he was doing her dirty work for her, she'd let him off. Sabine had also sat through a desperate, pathetic, overwrought Monica talking to Diane Sawyer about her 'darling daughter' earlier that day which had put Sabine into an even better mood.

Now she reached for her cell phone. Really, the timing couldn't be better. She pressed the call button and waited. When he answered, she dropped her voice to a warm purr. 'Arlo, darling, I'm so sorry. What can I do to help?'

. . .

HE COULDN'T STOP THINKING about her, her skin, the brief moment when the drug in her bourbon had made her hallucinate, think he was Arlo. Her smile. God, it made him hard just thinking about it. The moment his cock had plunged into her, he had felt like a king. Triumphant. When she'd started to fight him, the power and control he had over her...

He was seriously rethinking killing her. What if, instead, he just kept her, wore her down, and made them into a family...could she be his? Forever?

She would have to be broken, he decided, so much that she would do anything to live, even submit wholly to him. Forget the past, forget Arlo Forrester, and even forget her sister. He would take her away, somewhere no one would even think to look for them. It wasn't as if he didn't have the means or the imagination to keep her away from the rest of the world for as long as he needed. The house on the bayou had been a good prison, but now he was getting edgy. It was too near New Orleans, too close to civilization. It only took one gator hunter out on the bayou to come across the house...

Yes. He would begin to plan the move, find a good base...put the plans into motion. In the meantime, he had one way of distracting the people looking for Cosima, and he smiled to himself. He was going to enjoy this.

JACK CALLED at the hotel just after seven a.m. and by the look on his face, it wasn't good news. Harpa huddled close to Arlo, and he put his arm around her, pressed his lips to her temple to comfort her. Jack sat opposite them.

'Guys,' he began slowly, 'I don't know....this is the hardest...'

'Oh no, no, no,' Harpa crumbled, and Arlo gave a low moan. Jack, his own face betraying his grief, held up his hands.

'We've found a body...now, look. It may not be Cos...I haven't personally seen the body yet. We got a call an hour ago, up near

Baton Rouge. A young woman of Asian heritage was found, bound and stabbed to death. She matches Cos's description but...I don't know, something about it seems hinky. I'm going up there now, and I'll call you, straight away.'

Harpa and Arlo looked at each other then turned back to Jack. 'No,' said Arlo, 'We're coming with you.'

Jack shook his head. 'No. I'm sorry but no...if it is Cos, I don't want you seeing her like that.'

'That's not your decision to make,' Arlo was angry now, 'you may have known her longer than I, but she is my love. I need to see her, Harpa needs to see her.'

'And if it is Cos, you will – *after* we've released her body, *after* we've prepared you and her. Harpa, does Cos have any tattoos, birth-marks, scars I should know about?'

Harpa shook her head. 'No...god, please, don't let it be her.'

Jack stood. 'Look, I'm sorry. I'm sorry for all of this. I'll call you when I know more.

And he was gone.

Arlo and Harpa hugged each other, the room suddenly cold despite the temperature of the day.

'Please tell me it's not her, Arlo, please,' Harpa's voice was barely audible. Please tell me I'll see my sister again.'

But he couldn't.

Cosima replaced the window pane back in its setting, her throat red raw from screaming for most of the night. Nothing. No one. The sky was lightening on the horizon, and she knew it wouldn't be long until the camera switched back on. She crawled under the bed and had another go at trying to loosen a floorboard. A half hour later, she screamed in frustration and gave up. The boards were just too firmly screwed down for her to make any difference. She lay on the floor for a few minutes, breathing hard.

Okay, okay, she thought. *Plan B...whatever that might be.* Two days of her deadline were up, but she refused to believe there wasn't something she could do so save herself. She went and took a quick, cold shower then sat down on the toilet to pee. As she stood and flushed, her elbow caught the heavy porcelain lid on the cistern and pain shot through her elbow. But she barely noticed. The lid had moved. It had shifted. She froze. At that moment, the bathroom camera blinked on.

Cosima didn't look behind her, didn't acknowledge the sharp pain in her elbow from whacking it on the hard porcelain. Instead, she moved like an automaton, washing her hands and brushing her teeth. She moved deliberately, casually, but inside her, the adrenaline was screeching through her system.

She got into bed and pulled the covers over her head, letting out a shaky breath. How had she missed it? She didn't know whether to laugh or cry and at that moment, she knew.

Today was the day she was going home.

JACK CALLED them from Baton Rouge. 'I'm about to go in. Are you sure there are no identification marks I could look for? Because...*god*...the girl has been dead a few days and in this heat...'

Harpa dashed to the bathroom to throw up. Arlo, feeling sick, gripped the phone tightly. 'No. We're sure. Please, Jack...'

'Stay strong, Arlo. I'll call back soon.'

Arlo put his phone down on the table and closed his eyes. There were so many emotions whirling around in him: fear, despair, grief. He sucked in a big breath and went to find Harpa. She was sitting on the side of the bath, the room stank of vomit. 'I'm sorry,' she said, tears rolling down her cheeks. Arlo shook his head.

'Don't be silly,' he opened a window then grabbed a face cloth, running under the cold water. He wiped her face gently, then sat down next to her, his arm around her shoulders. Harpa leaned into him.

'Arlo...if it is Cos...I want you to know that she was the happiest she had ever been when she met you. She loved you so much...'

Arlo's voice was gruff. 'I know. She was my world; no, screw it, she *is* my world. She's coming back to us, I know it.'

· · ·

COSIMA HEARD his car door slam, and she darted into action. The porcelain lid of the cistern was heavier than she'd reckoned but despite her screeching muscles, she got ready, her heart beating at a hundred miles an hour.

As he opened the door and stepped in, she brought it down on the back of his head with as much force as she could muster. He dropped immediately, and the aftermath was so silent, she stopped there blinking for a second. Had it really been this easy?

He didn't move, didn't groan. She dropped to her knees beside him and went through his pockets, found his keys. Without another thought, she ran, down the flight of stairs to the front door. *Locked.* Her hands trembling violently, she tried each of his keys. Finally, she yanked the door open and stepped out into bright sunlight. His car stood on the driveway and ignoring the gravel tearing into her bare feet, she ran to it. When it started the first time, she almost screamed with relief. Tugging the stick into reverse, she turned the car around...just as he appeared at the door. The goat's mask was even more terrifying; its calm visage in sharp contrast to his obvious rage. He raised his gun and fired. Cosima ducked and pressed her foot hard down on the gas, the rear window shattering behind her. She didn't care, with every second she was freer – a bullet zinged along the side of the car but then she was at the end of the drive and pulling onto what looked like a normal highway. She really had been *this* close to civilization this whole time. *Motherfucker.* Cursing loudly, she drove along the highway, speeding, not caring if she was stopped – she wanted to be pulled over by the cops. The cops were safe, they'd get her home. Finally, she saw the sign for New Orleans...six miles. Six miles? God...*I'm coming home, baby...*

I'm coming home...

ARLO AND HARPA stared at his phone as the screen flashed up with Jack's number. Harpa moaned softly, but Arlo took her hand in his.

'We have to know, Harpa.' He pressed the speaker phone button. 'Jack?'

'Hi.' He paused and Harpa started to cry. 'Guys, we couldn't make a positive identification. The body is too decomposed. If it is Cos, then she was killed almost as soon as she was taken.'

Arlo had trouble breathing. *No. No.* 'Then it can't be her. I'd know, I'd sense if she were dead.' He felt Harpa squeeze his hand.

'Jack...do you think it's her?'

Jack sighed, his own voice racked with pain and grief. 'I wish I could say positively one way or the other, Harp, I really do. I don't want to believe it's her but the height is right, the victim has long dark hair, dark skin that matches Cosima's own skin color. Until we have DNA proof...'

'Until we have DNA proof,' Harpa said, her voice suddenly strong, 'We are going to believe it's not her, okay? Okay, Jack? Okay, Arlo?'

Arlo nodded, but his eyes were hooded and dark. Jack sighed. 'It can't hurt to think like that. I certainly don't want to think it could be her...although it *is* someone.'

'Someone's daughter, sister, lover,' Arlo repeated in a monotone. 'There is no good news here for anyone.'

'Yeah.' Jack's voice was low, and Harpa unconsciously reached out her hand as if she could comfort him through the phone. She dropped her hand.

'Jack...I can't even imagine what it must have been like to see that.' She glanced at Arlo. 'We both know how much Cosima meant...*means*...to you.' Arlo nodded and cleared his throat.

'Yes, we do, and we want you to know, Jack, we're grateful for everything you've done for us, for Cos.'

'Thanks, man. Look, I'm going back to New York to see where we're at for a couple days then I'll be back. We won't stop looking for her, believe me.'

Arlo ended the call and hugged Harpa. 'There's still hope.'

She nodded. 'Look, I think I need a shower and some food. Then maybe I can think straight.'

He nodded and she padded into the room. Arlo stared after her, not really seeing anything. He rubbed his face with his fingers, trying anything to relieve this numbness he was feeling. He really believed what he had told Jack, that he would know if Cosima was dead. No, it wasn't possible. He closed his eyes and sighed. *Come home.*

Steve, one of Arlo's security team, knocked and came in.

'Sorry to disturb, boss, but there's someone here who wants a word.'

Arlo's eyebrows shot up. 'Not press.'

'No. It's Mikah Ray.'

Arlo half-smiled. 'Send him up.'

MIKAH RAY RODE THE ELEVATOR, feeling sick with nerves. Which was a new feeling for him – for the love of God, he was a successful businessman, someone with influence, connections, and yet he was *terrified*. Terrified that Arlo would turn him away and not listen to him, scared Harpa would lose it when she saw him. Mikah's hand hovered over the stop button. What was he doing bothering this family at this time? For what? His hard-on?

No. Because it wasn't just about sex…he wanted to be part of Harpa's life, to be there for her now, in this hell she must be living. He wanted to be the one she leaned on – and yeah, that was monumentally selfish, but he couldn't bear to know she was in so much pain, and he wasn't able to do anything. His hand dropped; *no*, he was going to do this, and if she rejected him now, then that was that. It was over.

He stepped out into the foyer and Arlo Forrester was there to meet him. Mikah felt a jolt of sympathy when he saw the pain in the other man's eyes.

'Man, I can't even imagine what this must be like for you. I'm here for you, for Harpa, for whatever you need.'

Arlo half-smiled as he shook Mikah's hand. 'Thanks, dude. Listen, I think you may be what Harpa needs right now, but it's up to her. I'm all for whatever it is you need from her but…'

'I know. Just five minutes is all I ask.'

Arlo nodded. 'Okay. Come on in, she's just in the shower.'

Mikah followed Arlo into the penthouse and whistled when he saw it. 'Dude, this place is magnificent.'

Arlo smiled sadly. 'All Cosima; she has a great eye.'

'You're telling me, *wow*.'

Arlo thanked him. 'Look, I'll just go see if...' He nodded to a closed bedroom door and Mikah nodded, his nerves returning.

'Okay. Cool.'

'I'M DECENT, COME ON IN,' Harpa called when Arlo knocked at her door. She was toweling her long dark hair, wrapped in a robe and she smiled at him. What's up?'

'There's someone here to see you. A very nervous someone.'

Harpa looked confused, and Arlo smiled. 'It's Mikah,' he said gently then put up his hands as she looked first shocked then panicked. 'Relax, he just wants five minutes to talk.'

Harpa sat down heavily on her bed, staring at him. 'I don't know... all of this...I just...'

Arlo sat down next to her. 'Maybe it's good...closure at the very least. You should talk to him; he's invested, Harp, he deserves five minutes. And can I tell you something?'

'Of course.' Her voice was soft, trembling. Arlo nudged his shoulder to hers.

'Don't waste love, not even for one second. There's no good reason for you not to be with the man you're crazy about. Cosima would kick your ass.' His mouth hitched up in a grin, and she couldn't help but join in.

'Okay...but five minutes – and I'm not promising anything.'

'You don't owe me any promises, nor Mikah neither. Go with your heart, Harp.'

She swallowed and nodded. 'Okay. Let me throw some clothes on.'

'I'll send him in a minute or two.'

. . .

HARPA TOOK a deep breath in and opened the door. *Oh God*, she'd forgotten just how beautiful he was, his dark skin shining, his eyes big and soulful, and his cute way of wearing his porkpie hat on the back of his head.

'Hey,' he said. Even his voice was rich and made her stomach warm.

'Hey. Come in.' She stepped out of the way to let him in and closed the door behind him.

For a long moment, they stared at each other, drinking the other in. Then he smiled – making her stomach flutter.

'I want you to know...that I have superpowers.'

That she didn't expect. 'Huh?'

Mikah chuckled. 'Go with it. Yeah, I have this power...to transform into anything you need right now. A rock, a punching bag, a friend, a lover, hell, even a unicorn – if that's what you need right now. Anything, Harpa. You say you didn't want me messed up in your family's crap...too late, Bedi, I'm already in deep.'

She gazed at him then closed her eyes before she spoke. 'My sister is probably dead.'

'Yes.'

His honesty stung but she liked he didn't bullshit her. 'It hurts like all hell. If it's true, then I don't know how to be in a world without her.'

'Who would? This situation is so fucked up but, as Arlo must have found, some things really are out of our control. The only control we have is how to react to the situation – and even that's tenuous. No one is expecting you to hold it together if Cosima's been murdered. No one. I'm offering to be the person you can go absolutely batshit crazy on if that's what you need.'

He stepped closer and when she didn't back away, he put his hands on the tops of her arms. 'I know we haven't known each other for that long, but I'm all in, Harpa. All in.'

Harpa gave a sob, and he took her in his arms, holding her tightly. 'I don't pretend to know what you're going through, baby, just know you're not alone in this.'

. . .

ARLO STEPPED out onto the balcony of the penthouse and looked down at the crowds of tourists below, milling around the Quarter. He was curious to know what Mikah was saying to Harpa, and he hoped that the young woman would be responsive to her former lover. Mikah Ray was a good guy and if the worst had happened, well, Harpa would need him. Because if Cosima was dead, then Arlo didn't know how he could go on. All he could think of was the first night they'd met, or the look on her face when he'd walked into that restaurant after all those months apart, or the first night they'd spent together here, in her hotel. That's how he thought of this place; her signature, her taste, her brilliance was all over this hotel.

A squeal of tires made him look down. A black S.U.V. weaving a wild path down the street below suddenly screeched to a halt outside the LaBelle. He heard shouting, and then he saw Steve and Roger burst out from the hotel below, scattering the people, as the door of the S.U.V. was pushed open and a small figure almost fell out of the vehicle.

Arlo's heart began to pound as he watched Steve and Roger run to the driver...the driver who had long dark hair and was obviously in some distress....*oh god....oh god.....*

'Cosima!' His scream made everyone below look up, and Harpa and Mikah burst out from her bedroom as Arlo darted for the elevator.

'Arlo, what the...'

He was wild-eyed and breathless as the other two crowded into the elevator with him. 'It's her, it's Cosima...'

He was babbling, press the down button again and again until Harpa took his hand away.

'Stop. Breathe. What about Cosima?'

Arlo looked at her, his mania calming. 'She's downstairs...'

. . .

THEY BURST out of the elevator doors as soon as they opened onto the hotel lobby and saw her, their Cosima, alive, breathing, as Steve and Roger carried her inside. Harpa screamed her sister's name and ran to the wilting woman as she began to sob. She hugged her sister, reaching out to Arlo as he wrapped his arms around them both, shaking his head in disbelief, saying her name over and over and over...

SABINE HISSED in frustration as the news reporter, standing outside the LaBelle, brought the viewers the news of Cosima Malhotra Bedi's miraculous escape. *God damn it.* She wondered what Naveen had been thinking, keeping the princess alive.

To Sabine's dismay, Arlo hadn't risen to her offer of help, just thanked her in a dead voice and ended the call.

And now Cosima was home, safe in Arlo's arms again. Sabine sighed. Maybe it was time to let it go after all. Sabine simply didn't have the energy to break them up. Maybe she should concentrate on Naveen; a man of means certainly, the ease with which he moved around the world constantly, never staying in one place too long.

Yes, she could get used to a life like that...

'Okay, Arlo, you win,' she said aloud to the picture of her former lover that flashed up on the screen. 'You keep your princess. I have bigger plans.'

If only she knew how to get a hold of Naveen.

ARLO WAITED until the doctor had finished his examination then stepped back into Cosima's room. He still couldn't believe that she was here, in front of him. In the melee that had followed her arrival at the hotel, the emergency services were called, and it wasn't until the police insisted that Cosima go straight to the emergency room to be checked out that Arlo had time to gather his thoughts. The doctors and hospital staff had been kind and thorough; Cosima didn't appear to have any significant injuries, apart from cuts and bruises, but mentally, Arlo could see the pain, fear, and confusion in her eyes. After being locked away for so long, Cosima got quickly overwhelmed by all the people around her. When the doctor had told her, gently, he needed to do a rape kit, Arlo had been heartbroken when Cosima looked ashamed and nodded slowly. *God, what she must have been through...*

The doctor smiled at him. 'She's exhausted and dehydrated, and we'll keep her in for a couple of days. She'll need to talk to the psychiatrist and of course, the police, but for tonight, she should rest.'

They both went back into the room, and Cosima's delighted smile made Arlo's heart soar. He kissed her forehead. 'I love you,' he whispered.

She leaned into him as the doctor wrote some notes. 'Can I shower now, Doctor?'

He looked and smiled. 'You can, then I'm going to order some hot food for you. I want that drip to stay in overnight; you're dehydrated so drink plenty of water. I'll be back in couple of hours to give you a sedative to help you sleep.'

Cosima sighed. 'Sounds good.'

'Can I stay with her, doc?'

'Of course, I'll have a cot brought in for you.' He patted Cosima's hand gently. 'Rest as much as you can, Cosima. You deserve it.'

'Thank you, Doctor Arno, you've been very kind.'

WHEN THEY WERE ALONE, Arlo tipped her face up to his and kissed her softly. 'God, I missed you, every second, Cos. Thank God you're okay.'

She smiled, but her eyes were troubled. 'Arlo...there was one day...he drugged me and I was hallucinating that it was you...'

'I want to kill him for doing that, but it wasn't your fault, Cos, you realize that, I hope? I'll make him pay, I promise you. Are you sure you didn't recognize him?

Cosima shook her head. 'Maybe Jack will have something in one of his files but, to be honest, I'm just relieved to be away from him. Did the police find anything at the house?'

Arlo shook his head. 'Jack said he was going to find out what they knew, what the crime scene people could find.'

'Is he okay?'

'Jack? I think like the rest of us, he's overwhelmed you're safe. He said he'll come see you as soon as he can.'

'Good.' Cosima leaned against him and sighed. Then her eyebrows shot up. 'Oh, right, I was going to ask...who was that guy with Harpa at the hotel?'

Arlo grinned. 'That, my darling, is Mikah Ray. They met in Seattle and were hot and heavy until you disappeared and Jack made Harpa come to New Orleans.'

Cosima chuckled. 'Arlo Forrester, you sound like an old gossip. Wow, so that's Mikah? Nice work, sis.' She grinned at Arlo but then her smile faded. 'I keep waiting to wake up and find out I'm still trapped in that house.'

Arlo stroked her face tenderly. 'Cos...you'll never have to go through that again, understand? Look, we've got a lot to talk about but for now, please, you need to rest.'

LATER, when Cosima had bathed, eaten and was finally asleep, Arlo stepped out into the hallway to call Jack again. The FBI agent sounded harassed. 'Hey, sorry for not calling you back, Arlo. Got dragged into another sting and got clobbered by the perp.'

'You okay?'

'Oh yeah, just had the wind knocked out of my sails. How's our girl doing?' Jack's voice warmed considerably, Arlo noticed, but he pushed any jealousy aside. Now was not the time for that.

'She's doing okay, I think. They've treated her so well here, but I think we need to wait a few days for it to fully hit her. She seems dazed.'

'Not surprising, really.'

'Jack?'

'Yeah.'

Arlo sighed heavily. 'Jack, he raped her.'

'*God.*'

'Yeah.'

Arlo heard Jack curse softly under his breath. 'Is it wrong to say that as horrific as it is, I'm not surprised? That it was kind of inevitable?'

'Terrible thing to say but, yeah, in the world we live in.'

'Arlo...I've never brought up the money thing, your wealth, I mean, because it's none of my business and I know Cosima always shies away from any mention of it but just this one time, can I make a plea?'

'Go ahead, whatever you want.'

'Get the best psychologists, psychiatrists, and hypnotists, whatever. For her, for Cosima. She shouldn't have to have this on her plate for the rest of her life.'

'Oh don't worry, I'm going to insist,' Arlo's voice was firm, 'there's no price I won't pay to make this right, Jack, you can be assured of that.'

'Good. Thank you. Arlo...cutting all bull here, you know how I feel about Cosima...and I want you to know I think you are the best thing that has ever happened to her. I wouldn't be able to give her half what you have, even with the best will in the world and despite my family money. I just ask...don't shut me out. I promise I'll keep my feelings to myself.'

Arlo was touched and nodded. 'Of course, Jack, you will always be a part of the Malhotra's lives.'

'Thanks. Now, I may be gone for a few more days, we want to follow every lead, every suspect. I still think this has nothing to do with the Malhotra family, but we have to check.'

HARPA SAT down by her sister's bedside. Mikah pulled up a chair across the room. 'Are you sure it's okay for me to be in here?'

Harpa smiled at him and nodded. 'Of course. I want Cos to meet you properly at least once before you go back to Seattle.'

He smiled. 'I'm here for as long as you need me, Harpa.'

Really?'

He rolled his eyes. 'Of course. Besides, when your sister's better, I need to take you out on a proper date.'

Harpa pretended to consider. 'I'll think about it.'

'Don't be a tease,' Cosima's voice was wooly and thick, but she smiled sleepily at her sister as she opened her eyes. Harpa smoothed her hair from her forehead.

'I'm sorry, Cos, did we wake you?'

Cosima shook her head as she pulled herself into a sitting position. 'Nope, I've just been pretending, waiting for you two to talk dirty or something.'

Harpa and Mikah both laughed. 'Sneaky,' Harpa stuck her tongue out at her sister then beckoned Mikah closer. 'So, Cosima, this is Mikah, Mikah, Cosima.'

The two shook hands and Cosima grinned at him. 'So, I'll just say that the sedative they gave is making my brain a bit squirrely so I apologize if my filter doesn't work.'

'Fair enough. How are you feeling?'

'Glad to be back.'

Harpa squeezed her sister's hand. Arlo told us you went ninja on the asshole...did he tell you they found the place?'

Cosima nodded. 'Yep but not Goaty.'

Harpa looked bemused. 'Goaty?'

'He had a goat's mask, he wore it over a balaclava. I called him Goaty – not showing that much imagination,' Cosima tried to laugh it off but her breath caught in her chest. 'He's still out there.'

'But he will never get close to you again, Cosima, I won't permit it. Arlo's already hired extra security...'

Cosima sighed. 'I don't want to be a prisoner again, though, Harp.'

Harpa nodded, her eyes full of understanding. 'I'm sorry, Cos, but until we catch the guy...'

Mikah sat forward again. 'Look, I just had an idea...some friends of mine have an island just off the coast of Hawaii. They're always telling me to make the most of it, go down there, and take whoever I want. How about the four of us go away – when you're out of here, obviously?'

Cosima smiled at him warmly. 'That does sound tempting, but it might have to wait for a while. Arlo's lined me up some pretty hard-core counseling for the next month.'

'Well, the offer stands. Just say the word.'

Cosima looked at Harp and nodded at Mikah. 'This one's a keeper,' she pronounced as Harpa rolled her eyes.

'And with that, you need more rest. Come on, Mikah, before she has us picking out china patterns.'

COSIMA WENT BACK to sleep after her sister and Mikah had left but this time, her dreams were terrifying; Goaty in her hospital room, her loved ones on their knees as he pressed the muzzle of a gun to her and fired more bullets than a gun could possible hold into her...she felt the pain of each burning piece of metal slamming into her, but all she could feel was fear for Arlo and Harpa as they begged Goaty to stop killing her. He swung the gun around and shot Arlo between the eyes as Cosima screamed; Arlo dropped to the floor, eyes staring, lifeless as Goaty dragged Harpa to her feet by her hair then shot her through the heart. Cosima screamed....then realized she was being shaken awake, but she couldn't stop screaming, a panic attack in full flood.

'Cosima! Cosima, darling, calm down!'

Oh. God.

Her mother.

NAVEEN SHOWED up on the Friday following Cosima's escape. Sabine opened the door to him, smirking. He looked amused as he took in her expression. 'Something funny?'

She shut the door and leaned back against it. 'Couldn't quite keep a grasp on the little princess then?'

His face shut down. 'No idea what you're talking about.'

She chuckled and cupped his face in her hands, pressing her lips to his. 'Yes, you have. Cosima...all of a sudden she reappears, bedraggled, tormented and yet still beautiful – and still very much alive.'

Naveen nodded. 'So I hear.' He shrugged out of his jacket – dark blue today which highlighted the salt and pepper hair at his temples – and pulled his tie loose.

Sabine waited. 'Well?'

He shrugged, his expression insolent. 'So what? I told you before, Sabine, what I do or don't do to Cosima Malhotra is my business. Now, I came here to fuck – I assume that's what you want too?'

Sabine flushed but reached for the zipper on her dress. Naveen smiled, his tone warming. 'Allow me.'

As always with him, Sabine forgot everything else as soon as he touched her, his strong hands working her body like no one ever had, and she was panting and gasping his name. As his cock drove her toward heaven, she realized she didn't care about Arlo or Cosima and anything else in this world apart from this dark, dangerous man in her arms. When she came, she looked at him with tears in her eyes and, forgetting her nature, forgetting that she wanted to remain aloof, told him she loved him.

NAVEEN WAITED until Sabine fell asleep then got up and swiftly dressed. He wasn't good at this despite his outward coolness. When Sabine told him she loved him, just for a second, he had seen a future with this blonde ice queen – kids, a mansion, and family dinners. He had dreamed of that all of his life – had envied his childhood friends who had that – the Malhotras. He'd fallen in love with the elder sister the moment he had seen her, and both the girls and their father were more than generous with all they had. But his own father was a proud man, and had hated the Prince and his 'whore' daughters and had eventually instilled that hatred in Naveen, who'd built up so much resentment towards Cosima that all his adult life, he'd been trying to find a way to get to her.

But someone else had beaten him to it. Someone had taken her and he didn't have a clue who it was. That pissed him off – and at the same time, he was astonished to find he felt some relief – that his burden had been taken from him, that he had a choice about the life he led.

Because he had watched the news reports and seen Cosima looking exhausted, worn down, hunted – and he had felt sympathy... and, unbelievably, fondness. He saw again the young girl he had played with, had adored, and he felt ashamed. His hatred – for so many years, a burning, raging thing inside of him, dissipated. The realization hit him like a sledgehammer. She was just a young woman trying to live her life and he – as well as her father's enemies and clearly now this new threat – had made her life a living hell. For years.

For no good reason except petty revenge and childish jealousy.

Last month the order had come down from the families; the threat to the Malhotra children was no longer acceptable. Naveen had called his father who had railed against the order, of course – impotently as it turned out, as the order came through again, stronger: Cosima and Harpa were *not* to be harmed under any circumstances.

And then Cosima had disappeared, and the in-fighting had begun. Naveen flew to India to make sure his father didn't have anything to do with it; that he wouldn't be censured or worse by the powers that be. But no one knew anything – or at least that they would admit to.

Which meant there was a new threat, and Naveen, in an about-face that staggered him, wanted to know who it was and how to stop him coming after her again. He'd thought hard about what he should do, and now he was contemplating going to the one man who he knew would desperately want the same thing as he.

The ex-lover of the woman he had just fucked.

Arlo Forrester.

. . .

AFTER DAYS and days of other people, finally, on the fifth day after Cosima escaped, they were alone – really alone – in their apartment in the hotel. Cosima walked slowly around, acclimating herself to it again.

'It's weird, it feels brand new,' she smiled at Arlo, who was watching her. He laughed.

'Well, if you think about it, it is. Come here, beautiful.'

She went into his arms, and he kissed her. 'God, I missed you.'

Me too, baby,' she rubbed her nose against his, All the time, I just thought of you and every day we'd been together, what we've done or haven't yet done. I came up with so many ideas for things to us to do together or new projects...and of course now I've forgotten them all.'

They both laughed. 'We can make new lists,' he said softly, and she touched his face.

'There's only one thing I want right now.'

He looked surprised then stepped back. 'Cosima...with what you've through...'

She was stung. 'You don't want me?'

'God, of course, I do, every second but Cos...you were raped. You need time.'

'Rape is not sex, Arlo, it's violence. I was subjected to a violent act. It had nothing to do with you and me making love...unless of course...' She didn't finish the sentence, but her meaning was clear.

Arlo shook his head. 'No, Cos, no...'

'I'm soiled goods.' Her voice was flat and dead. 'Okay. then.'

'No, hang on a minute, you are putting words in my mouth, Cos, that's not what I meant at all.'

'It's okay, Arlo, I don't want to fight.'

'Me either, baby. I just think you need time...god, Cos, there is nothing I want more than to take you back to our bed right now, but one of us has to be...'

'...if you say responsible, I'll scream.' But she smiled when she said it. 'Like I said, I don't want to fight. Look, okay. I'll see the psychologists or whoever, I'll work through what I have to. But don't keep me waiting too long, Forrester.'

Arlo, relieved, chuckled. 'I promise. Now, in lieu of our favorite activity, how about you join me in our second favorite pastime?'

She looked excited. 'If you mean *'eating'* then bring it on, Julia Child.'

HARPA AND MIKAH were at a restaurant in the Quarter. To give Arlo and Cosima some privacy, Mikah had offered Harpa the suite next to his in his hotel, but she had waved it off.

'Baby, if this has taught us anything, it's to not waste time being 'polite.' We both know what will happen if we go out on a date – why pretend?'

She had been all big talk but now, as they lingered over coffee, she was nervous. He was so beautiful, so present and vital that she felt awkward and kiddish, like a lovesick teenager.

Mikah grinned at her. 'You okay, babe?'

She smiled. 'Of course. I never said thank you, for coming out here, for roundly ignoring my wishes...' and she laughed as he looked guilty, '...and for being a friend. A really good friend.'

'Well now, you're welcome. After all, what else are friends for?' But his smile was so wicked that she shook her head, laughing.

'You make everything sound so filthy.'

'But you like that?'

'Oh yes.' She sipped her now cold coffee. 'So...'

'So...' Mikah smiled at her, 'Is this the right time to ask what you plan to do next? I mean, I wouldn't blame you if you wanted to be with your sister, if you moved back here. I know Stan would understand.'

Harpa sighed. 'I can't answer that question right now, it's too soon. I mean, it's not that I don't want to go back to Seattle; I love the city, my job, being near you. I just need time to trust myself to be away from Cosima again.'

'I get it and listen...it's a plane ride. Obviously, my business is there, but I can come back here as often as you like. That is, if you want to try and make something of this, us.'

Harpa smiled. 'I would, I really would...'

Mikah signaled for the check. 'Then, Miss Bedi...Miss Malhotra... would you do me the honor of escorting me to my hotel suite?' He held out his hand and, giggling, she took it and stood.

'I do hope,' she said in an undertone, 'that you won't be so polite when we get to your room, Mr. Ray.'

Mikah kissed her. 'You can count on that, sweetcheeks...'

HE WAS NEITHER GENTLEMANLY nor polite as he pushed her against the wall of the elevator, but she loved it as his hands slid under her skirt and he dropped to his knees, pushing the fabric of her skirt over her knees and burying his face in her sex. Harpa gasped as he snagged the delicate material of her panties in his teeth and drew them down her thighs, but then as she started giggling, the effect was ruined when the elevator stopped and Mikah toppled backward. Harpa shrieked with laughter and by the time they got to his suite, they were breathless.

'God, I am so crazy about you, Harpa Malhotra,' he said, cupping her face and she grinned.

'Shut up and fuck me, Ray.'

He lifted her into his arms and carried her to the bed. She was already wriggling out of her top as he set her down and as he pulled his own t-shirt off, she was attacking his fly.

'Greedy girl...' But he let out a rush of breath as she freed his cock from his underwear and took him in her mouth. She teased the tip with her tongue before tracing the blue vein that ran down the long length of him.

Mikah stroked her hair gently, but as he grew harder and thicker under her touch, he moaned. 'Harpa...I have to be inside you.'

She grinned, laying back on the bed and spreading her legs wide. 'Come on in...' she whispered, and Mikah dropped on top of her, growling and making her giggle.

· · ·

SOMEHOW, Cosima had fallen asleep in the middle of the movie they were watching, and now she was sprawled across the couch, her head in his lap. Arlo stroked her hair, still not quite believing she was home. It had been weeks but still every day, waking up with her, sent his soul into the stratosphere. He had meant what he said all those weeks ago; he wanted Cosima to be absolutely certain she was okay before they made love again, but it was driving him crazy too.

His cell phone rang. 'Hey, Jack.'

'Hey buddy, how is she?'

Arlo looked down at his love, all stress erased from her lovely face in sleep. 'She's good...well, getting there. We're just doing our usual thing; watching trashy t.v. and eating enough calories to feed a small country.'

Jack chuckled. 'Good move, sounds blissful.'

'Where are you at? Cosima's been asking after you, wondering when you're going to come see her – you haven't seen her at all since she got back and she's worried.'

Jack sighed. 'Dude, I wish I was there too, but I'm calling with good news.'

Arlo was immediately wide awake. 'Really?'

'We've had a communication come through from India. Sources close to Arjun Malhotra's enemies. The threat is lifted. The orders have come down from the highest authorities. Arjun's children are not to be harmed.'

Arlo's breath caught in his chest. 'Are you serious? Oh, my God....Cos...Cos wake up...shit, Jack is this true? That's un-fucking-believable! Cos...'

Cosima sat up, blinking at him, faintly annoyed, but he grinned at her and handed her the phone. 'Talk to Jack, Cos...

Cosima took the phone from him. 'This better be good, Hampton, I was having a really good dream.'

Arlo watched her face as Jack relayed the news. For almost a minute she said nothing...then dropped the phone and burst into tears.

Arlo laughed and picked up the phone. 'Jack...I think she's happy!'

'I hear crying.'

'Yep, that too, but she's smiling like an idiot.'

'Will she call Harpa? I have to get off the phone.'

'Of course, we'll tell Harpa...and thank you, Jack.'

Cosima was still sobbing and laughing. 'I don't believe it...I don't believe it.'

He gathered her into his arms, feeling the weight of years of stress falling from her. 'You're free, baby, you're free.'

'*Oh god...oh god...*'

WHEN SHE HAD CALMED down she wanted to tell Harpa immediately, but the call went to voicemail and she didn't want to tell Harpa the biggest news of their lives with a message. 'Just call me back, please, Harpa, I have huge news. Whatever time of the night, it's okay, just call me.'

Then she got up from the couch and yelled with joy, leaping around the room like she was on drugs. Arlo watched her, laughing, and when she yanked him to his feet and started to dance with him, he couldn't resist. 'God, I love you, Cosima Malhotra.'

'And I love you, Arlo, and guess what, I can love you wherever I want now...'

'Damn right you can, beautiful...'

Cosima kissed him, her hands moving down to cup his cock through his jeans. 'Take me to bed, Arlo Forrester...tonight, I need to celebrate.'

He swept her into his arms. 'God, yes...'

They tore each other's clothes off and tumbled onto the bed. Cosima climbed on top of him, grinning down as he cupped her breasts in his big, warm hands. She leaned down to kiss him, running her hands over his hard chest. 'I missed this body,' she whispered, reaching down to take his cock in her hands, stroking along the length of him, massaging his balls in her palm. Arlo groaned and, with one movement, flipped her onto her back.

'I can't wait, I'm sorry...'

Cosima grinned wrapped her legs around his waist, arching her back. 'Don't apologize, just do it.' She guided him to the entrance of her cunt and then gasped with delight as, with one strong thrust, he plunged into her. 'Oh...god...yes...'

Arlo pinned her hands to the bed with his own, locked eyes with her as they moved, their need for each other desperate now, after all those weeks apart. Arlo slammed into her, his cock thickening with each movement, her vagina muscles gripping him tightly, driving each other insane with excitement and desire. They came together, and Arlo didn't give her time to recover before he turned her onto her stomach and took her again, pushing into her ass and making her scream with pleasure.

THE NIGHT WAS LOST as they took each other again and again, tumbling from the bed in their frenzy, Cosima straddling him, riding him so hard her body undulated above him, and he couldn't take his eyes from her breasts moving with her thrusts. The muscles in her stomach rippled as she moved and when he was close, he pulled out and came on her belly. Collapsing back on the bed next to him, Cosima kissed him, smiling. 'We get to do that forever now, my darling.'

'You bet that sweet ass of yours we do. Cos...now that you're a free woman, where do you want to live? Here? Or would you want to be in Seattle, nearer to Harpa?'

She propped herself up on her elbow. 'No, Seattle is Harpa's thing; I wouldn't want to cramp her style now that we don't have to live in each other's pockets. To be honest, Arlo, I love New Orleans, despite everything that's happened here and in fact, in spite of every-thing. This is where we built your hotel, where our first home together is. What about you, though? Are you missing San Francisco?'

Arlo nodded. 'A little, I must admit. I really want you to see it, meet Margaret, my assistant and the closest thing to a mother I have. She'll love you.'

'That sounds great....' Then she groaned. 'Talking of mothers...'

Monica had stayed in New Orleans since Cosima's homecoming, and both Arlo and Cosima had had their fill of the woman. Constantly needy, constantly whining that her daughters were ignoring her, despite their visiting her almost every day. Cosima had been trying to persuade her to go back to London for weeks.

'Mom, I'll be going back to work in a couple of weeks, Harpa's going back to Seattle. What will you do all day? All your friends are back in the UK.'

'I'll be fine, besides I want to get to know my son-in-law better.'

Cosima rolled her eyes. 'Mom, Arlo isn't your son-in-law, we're not even engaged.'

Monica waved her hand. 'Semantics. It's inevitable.

'WELL, SHE IS RIGHT ABOUT THAT,' Arlo grinned at Cosima, 'but Lord help me if I want to discuss my intentions for you with Monica.'

Cosima wriggled with pleasure. 'Is that because your intentions are purely filthy?'

'Indeed. Look, sweetheart, let's go to Frisco for a couple of weeks before you go back to work.'

'That, sir, is a wonderful idea.'

UNFORTUNATELY, Monica thought so too when Cosima went to her hotel to tell her they were leaving for a while. Monica clapped her hands together.

'Oh, I love San Francisco, it's been years...lord and I shall have to have a new wardrobe.'

Cosima was dismayed. 'Mom...Arlo and I are going on a vacation.

Together. Alone.' She let a warning tone creep into her voice, and Monica flushed.

'Really, Cosima, I don't think you've ever learned the importance of family, especially at times like this.'

Cosima sighed, used to the passive-aggressive machinations of her mother. *Not this time, Mom.* 'Whatever you say, Mom. But Arlo and I are leaving tomorrow so....have a safe flight back to London.'

Monica huffed. 'Well, then...shall I send the hotel bill to Arlo?'

Cosima had been walking towards to the door, but she turned, disbelieving. 'Excuse me?'

Monica waved her hand around her. 'For this. I assume he's picking up the tab for all of this?'

Cosima blinked. 'Why on earth would you think that?'

'Well, he's bankrolling you, isn't he? How else would you be able to afford to live in such opulence, take so much time off work?

Her words hit Cosima like a wrecking ball. For a moment, she was speechless. 'For your information, Mother, no, Arlo isn't bankrolling me. Yes, I live in his home with him – at his request – but everything else *I* pay for.'

Monica's smile was cruel. 'By spreading your legs?'

Cosima made a disgusted noise. 'No, Mom, I'm not you.'

Monica cackled loudly and moving swiftly, she pinched Cosima's face between her fingers. 'Don't think you've got any more currency than this, Cosima. You got your beauty from me, don't forget that.'

Cosima jerked her head free, her eyes cold. 'But, luckily, my moral compass from Dad. Goodbye, Mother, I can't imagine we'll ever have anything else to say to each other.'

Cosima slammed the door on her way out and went down to the hotel's reception, seething. Her mom always seemed to make her feel worthless, like damaged goods. Bitch. Cosima knew she would never see her mother again if she could help it. *Mom, you've insulted me for the last time.*

But some of her mother's barbs had hit home. Was she Arlo's kept woman? Cosima tried to push the thought away. No, her mom wasn't going to destroy her happiness out of spite.

She was so lost in her thought that she didn't see him at first, and it wasn't until he stepped directly in front of her and spoke that she stopped.

'Hello, Cosima.'

Out of the corner of her eye, she saw Steve and Roger dart towards them as she recognized the man in front of her. He smiled.

'It's so lovely to see you again.'

Finally, she found her voice. 'Naveen...what are you doing here?'

He smiled. 'I'm here for you, of course, Cosima...'

END OF PART Three

4

TORN IN TWO

A Billionaire, Bad Boy, Romance

❧

Steve and Roger slammed Naveen into the wall before Cosima could say another word. She watched as Naveen put forth no resistance as her two burly bodyguards searched him for weapons.

'He's clean.' They let him go and Naveen, with a slight smile on his face, straightened himself up.

'Cosima, I mean you no harm, on my mother's honor I don't. I just wanted to talk to you, resolve our...issues.'

Cosima looked at him coldly. 'The only issue is you threatening to kill my sister and me for years, Naveen. Other than that, I do not see any reason why we should talk.'

Naveen nodded. 'I know, I understand that. But, Cosima, I swear, that is behind me, and I'm here to ask your forgiveness. May we talk?'

Cosima hesitated then nodded. 'Not here, not in public. Steve, Roger, we're going to the penthouse.'

The two security men exchanged a look but Cosima was determined. She wanted to show this man that she was protected, that she wouldn't back down or be cowed by him.

As they drove back to the LaBelle, Cosima tried not to stare at Naveen. He was as handsome as she remembered: dark hair, longish, curling around the collar of his shirt; black-as-night eyes, framed with long thick lashes, the swarthy skin clear. He had a beard now, which suited him, and the hair at his temples was graying. Growing up he had been her teenage idol, and she had adored him – until the terrible day when she and Harpa were ripped away from everything they'd ever known and sent to London. She'd never forgotten the horrible day when her father had told her that Naveen was one of the people who now hated their family and wanted to see them dead.

At the LaBelle, Steve stood between Cosima and Naveen in the elevator on the way up, and Cosima had to smother a smile. At first aloof and polite, her two bodyguards had become more than just Arlo's employees to her, and she knew they were fond of her too. *Probably because I don't treat them like the staff,* she thought to herself. They would tease her like a little sister, and she would give them back as good as she got. *I know what you're doing, Malhotra,* she said to herself, *you're distracting yourself from the fact that Naveen Chowdry, the man who wanted to kill you for so long – and who was your first love – is less than a foot from you.*

So many conflicted feelings.

Once they were back in the penthouse, Naveen admired the apartment and made all the right noises as Cosima poured them both a drink. They sat opposite each other on the couches and Naveen studied her as he sipped his scotch.

'You've grown ever more beautiful,' he said softly.

Cosima rankled a little. 'I like to think my intellect has become sharper, my skills at my work more refined. My appearance is of little matter to me – it does not define who I am.'

'Touché, I meant no offense. I've followed your career, Cosima, you're a star.'

'I bet you have,' she muttered then fixed him with a cold look.

'Was it you, in New York? Was it your threats that were the reason for us being exiled from there?'

He shook his head. 'No, that was not me or in fact, as far as I can tell, was there *ever* any threat to you in New York. The death sentence may have still been in place then, but as far as I know, no one acted on it – or was planning too.'

Cosima was confused. 'I don't understand. For years, Harpa and I have been shifted from place to place by the FBI because of...'

'I'm sure you were, but I'm saying, New York wasn't us.'

Cosima sighed, rubbed her eye. After a beat, she took a deep breath. 'Naveen...was it you? This time? Did you have me abducted?'

He sat forward, his gaze steady. 'No, Cosima, that wasn't me, I swear. While I had come to New Orleans to kill you, had I done so, it would have been quick, not torturous.'

She blanched at his words and he held up his hands. 'But you should not be concerned about that, about me, I mean what I say: you are safe from me. But, Sima, you should know, neither was it the families – which means you have a new enemy.'

For a moment, Cosima looked away. 'You haven't called me 'Sima' for years...Nav.' She gave him a half smile and Naveen's body relaxed.

'I'm so sorry, Sima, for everything I put you through. I don't know what I was thinking, what was wrong with me. Hell, yes I do. Jealousy, pure and simple. When you left India, the pain of you going away...' He trailed off and sighed. 'Please, Cosima, forgive me. I have been a fool.'

She nodded but didn't say anything. Naveen drained his scotch. 'There is one thing I do know that may help you,' he said. 'I know who instigated the attack on you at the market. Sabine Karlsson.'

Cosima rolled her eyes. 'Well, that's not the biggest surprise but how do you know?'

Naveen grinned, his face suddenly boyish. 'Because I've been entertaining her.'

Cosima wrinkled her nose. 'Gross.'

Naveen laughed loudly, and she couldn't help but join in. 'I agree,

Sabine is not the most pleasant of people,' he said, 'Did you know she lost out on a big job to your mother?'

'Oh, so I've screwed her over twice in her reckoning? Well...good,' Cosima felt satisfied then sobered up. 'Do you think she had anything to do with my abduction?'

'Hard to say...she asked me if I was behind it so that could either mean she genuinely isn't involved or that she's bluffing.'

Cosima chewed this over for a few moments. 'For what it's worth, as much as I dislike the woman, the man who kidnapped me was twisted. Psychopathic. It felt...personal.'

'I swear again, Sima, it wasn't me.'

'I believe you.'

Naveen smiled at her. 'Thank you.'

'What's this?'

They both looked up as Arlo, his face set and grim, his eyes never leaving Naveen, entered the room. Naveen stood and offered Arlo his hand. 'Naveen Chowdry, good to meet you.'

Arlo ignored the proffered hand and went to Cosima's side, wrapping a protective arm around her shoulders. Naveen let his hand drop but kept the friendly smile on his face. Cosima looked up at Arlo.

'Arlo, this is Naveen...an old friend.'

Arlo nodded. 'The old friend who wants to kill you?'

Cosima sighed, but Naveen spoke up. 'Mr. Forrester, I have just been apologizing to Sima – Cosima – for my previous behavior. I swear to you, I mean neither her nor you any harm.'

'Naveen was just informing me that the delectable Sabine was behind the attack in the market. Seems she has major beef with me and not just because I'm with you.'

Arlo was taken aback. 'Sabine?' His brow creased in annoyance. 'God *damn* that woman...'

Cosima put her hand on his chest. 'Calm down. She's just a spiteful bitch, not worthy of our attention.'

He ran a hand through his hair in annoyance. 'A vindictive, violent one. Well, we'll see how she likes it when I cut her off.'

There was an awkward pause. 'You've been supporting her?' Cosima's voice was soft, but there was hurt in her tone. Arlo kissed her forehead.

'It was only supposed to be temporary until she found her next job. I thought it was the right thing to do.'

'You're a better person than I then.' Cosima looked irked.

Arlo looked at Naveen. 'You've been fucking Sabine?'

Cosima winced, but Naveen merely nodded, unfazed. 'Yes. It was a casual thing, nothing heavy.'

'So, what do you want from Cos and me? Congratulations?'

'Arlo.' Cosima's voice was warning, but he ignored her. Naveen shook his head.

'I don't want anything from you, except Cosima's forgiveness and she has been gracious enough to bestow that on me. I will tell you what I told Sima; you have a new enemy. The man who took her won't be satisfied until either he or Cosima is dead.'

Arlo cursed, and Cosima sighed, looking at him. 'Well, not fearing for my life was good while it lasted.'

Arlo pressed his lips to her temple. No one's getting near you, I swear it.'

Cosima nodded, even if she was unconvinced. Whatever this was, she knew it had to play out to its natural conclusion.

She just hoped that she would be alive at the end of it all.

WHEN NAVEEN HAD LEFT, Cosima followed Arlo into the bathroom and sat on the toilet seat while he showered. Arlo's body had been rigid with annoyance while Naveen was there and now, as the hot water hit his tired muscles, he couldn't help but be annoyed with Cosima's ready acceptance of her former enemy.

'What possessed you to let him into our home?'

'Steve and Roger were with me, it was fine.'

'He could have done anything.'

'But he didn't. For what it's worth, I believe him. He was the

Naveen I grew up with, not the angry fundamentalist he was for a while.'

Arlo turned and stared at her. 'And you think a man can change just like that? *I've seen the light!* I don't buy it.'

Cosima looked upset. 'Arlo, for once...can't I just believe in something good? I'm so sick of being suspicious of everyone *and* of you being suspicious of every other man in my life.'

Arlo was stung. He cranked off the water. 'Cosima...that's not true.'

'Really? What about Jack?'

Arlo grabbed a towel. 'Jack and I have sorted out our differences.'

'Which is why he feels so comfortable coming here,' she snapped, looking exhausted. 'Why hasn't he been here, Arlo? I haven't seen him since I came home.'

Arlo suddenly felt sorry for her. 'Sweetheart, I don't know. He's been trying to find the man who took you.' He sat on the edge of the bath and took her hands. 'I'm serious, I have no problem with Jack, but Naveen Chowdry spent years wanting to kill you. Give me a minute to get used to the fact you want to be his friend now.'

Cosima nodded but didn't say anything. Arlo cupped her face in his big hands. 'I love you, Cosima Malhotra. You and me, that's all we need.'

He brushed her lips gently with his then kissed her properly, his tongue massaging hers, becoming more aroused as they touched. Soon, he stood and led her into their bedroom, his towel falling away, his cock standing proud against his belly as he undressed her while they kissed. Cosima stroked her fingertips down the length of it and, groaning, he picked her up, pressing her back against the wall as his cock slid into her welcoming sex. At first tender, their fucking became rougher, intense until they couldn't stand up any longer and they tumbled to the floor, Arlo driving himself deeper into her with every thrust, pushing her legs as far apart as they would go to sink into her balls deep. Cosima raked her fingernails down his back, moaning blissfully, her breath coming in short, ragged gasps. Arlo grinned down at her.

'You have no idea how beautiful you look when I'm fucking you,' he growled, his thrusts becoming harder, deeper until she cried out, her skin flushing scarlet as she came. She tightened her legs around him, clenched her vaginal muscles around his cock, and Arlo came with a long groan, his hips spasming as he shot hot cum deep into her.

Afterward, they lay entwined, panting, grinning at each other. 'Do you think,' Cosima said, breathlessly, 'that we'll ever get tired of doing that?'

Arlo laughed. 'Not a chance. Not ever.'

Cosima rolled on top of him. 'Good, because when your cock is inside me, that's when I feel most alive.'

He grinned. 'How the hell am I ever going to get any work done when you say things like that?'

Cosima chuckled. 'That's my evil plan. Talking of work, I think it's time I went back to the office – Tal's been more than patient. Besides, don't we have a grand opening to arrange?'

Arlo stroked his hands down her smooth back. 'All done, my love, all set for this Friday. Once that is over, we can talk about our next project.'

Cosima's eyebrows shot up. 'Our next project? You want to work with me again?'

'Of course, we're a team. Besides, I think that will make up for lost time in Tal's case, yes? He's a good man.'

'He is that.' She sighed happily and laid her head on his chest. 'There's only one problem with going back to work that I can see.'

'What's that?'

She grinned. 'I have to move from this spot to do it.'

HARPA HAD BEEN early to work every day since she'd returned to Seattle from New Orleans and today, when her boss, Stan, arrived, he chuckled at her as she scrubbed the worktops clean. 'Sweetheart, you're making me feel lazy. You don't have to keep doing this.'

'Just trying to make up for lost time, boss.'

Stan reached over and took the wet cloth from her hand. 'You, sit,' he ordered. Harpa did as she was told, perching on one of the stools. She watched as Stan flicked the coffee pot on.

'Now,' he said a while later as he handed her a steaming cup of coffee. 'Why are you acting like a toddler on a sugar high?'

She grinned. 'I am not, I just feel bad about being away for so long. I wouldn't have been surprised if you canned me.'

'For taking time off because your sister was missing? What kind of tosser do you think I am?' Stan rolled his eyes. 'You ain't done anything wrong, love, so relax. Look, you've done brilliantly since you've been here so I'm taking you off pot washing and making you our new sauté-chef. Your palette is exquisite, so there's no question; Sandy will be leaving us soon to have her baby so she's agreed to train you. Do well at that for a few months, you'll be my sous chef.'

Harpa was stunned. Yes, she knew food was her talent, her passion, but in her wildest dreams she'd never expected to progress so quickly. 'I don't know what to say....thank you, Stan.'

He smiled. 'Don't thank me yet; you won't believe how much of a bastard I am to my sous chefs.'

Harpa giggled. 'Yeah, right.'

'You'll be busy; the hours are longer, the pay's still shite, plus I'll be on your back about your schoolwork. I expect you to graduate with honors, Harpa.'

She hopped off the stool and threw her arms around his neck. 'You are the freakin' best.'

'Yeah, yeah, gerroff me, you nutter, people will talk.'

THAT DAY'S shift was grueling and long, and by the time Mikah showed up to pick her up, Harpa was wilting. She smiled at her lover. 'You look even more delicious this evening.'

He grinned. 'You drunk?'

'On you.'

'Sweet talker. Have you eaten?'

She shook her head. 'Nope, we haven't had a minute's rest.'

'Come on then, I know a good place open past midnight.'

He took her to a small café in the center of the city, Mexican food, and Harpa fell on a plate of nachos, scooping up gobs of guacamole and sour cream and moaning with delight. Mikah, chuckling at her enjoyment, helped himself to a chip.

'So, I was thinking...'

'Does your head hurt?'

'Oh, *burn*...I thought maybe you might want to move in with me?'

Harpa swallowed her food and took a slug of coke. 'Huh.'

Mikah looked amused. 'That's all I get? A 'huh?''

'Maybe it's a *little* soon,' Harpa said gently. 'We just got Cos back, you and I are still in the honeymoon period. Don't get me wrong, I love every moment I spend with you, I do. But after being under... how can I put this...surveillance, for years and years, having my every move scrutinized I need time to experience the adult world for myself, live alone, sometimes be alone.'

Mikah nodded slowly. 'I think I get it...it just kills me when I wake up alone now, you know? Because, although it is soon, I'm falling...'

Harpa held up her hand, looking panicked. 'Don't say it yet, not like this, not when I've just turned your offer of co-habitation down. Because, yes, I feel *that* way too but call me sentimental, I want to say it and hear it at the perfect moment.'

Mikah sighed. 'You got it.'

She chewed another chip and studied him. 'I don't want to hurt you, Mikah, I'm crazy about you. Please understand, I just need...'

'Space?'

'Time.'

'There's a joke about a continuum in there somewhere, but I don't feel like making it.'

'Please don't be sad.'

'I'm not sad. I'm disappointed, but, okay, I get it. I have no earthly way of knowing what it must have been like for you.'

Harpa squeezed his hand and smiled. 'Let's talk about something else. What's going on with you?'

'Well, just so happens there're a few pieces up for auction on Friday in New Orleans so I thought we could swing by that before the hotel opening. You've still got that night off, right?'

'Damn straight. I'd love to see what you do, Mikah, I've never been to an auction before.'

'Grady Mallory will be there, so you can meet him, maybe Flori if she's with him.'

'We could double-date like grown-ups do.' She looked excited, and he laughed.

'Hey, has Cosima got any idea about the surprise Arlo is arranging?'

Harpa grinned. 'None. God, I am so looking forward to Friday night. Let's hope nothing spoils it.'

Hours later, in San Francisco, Monica Lascelles smiled benevolently at the reporter. 'Do you think you have everything?'

The young blonde woman smiled nervously. 'Ms. Lascelles, while your story is certainly...explosive, are you sure that you're ready for the fallout from it? I mean, your relationship with your daughters...'

'Has been strained for years. It's about time they paid attention to the woman who nurtured and shaped them. I had hoped Cosima's ordeal would soften her heart, but it seems not.'

'But it's not Cosima who you'll hurt the most with this story, is it?'

Monica smiled mockingly. 'Believe me, when you cut one sister, the other bleeds.'

The reporter, Bree, left the older woman in her hotel suite and headed back to her magazine's office. *God, what a hateful woman Monica Lascelles was* but Bree couldn't deny her story would be manna from heaven for her editor. She went straight to her boss's office and knocked on the door. Her editor, Lisa, looked up.

'What did you get from the raddled old witch then?' Lisa, it turns out, had worked with Monica in the good old days and had despised her even then.

Bree handed her notebook to Lisa. 'The headlines.'

Lisa read down the notes Bree had taken. As with most of the magazine's interviews, they took minimal notes, just bullet points really, and then built whatever story they could around them – slanting the interview depending on whether Lisa liked the interviewee, or how much groveling they would do to the magazine. Needless to say, the magazine Bree earned her money from wasn't one she'd proudly put on her resume, but it paid the bills.

Lisa whistled. 'Wow, she really gave you the goods, huh? Hell, approved, just go with it and try to get Simon to squeeze it into the next issue. Front page. It comes out Thursday, which should ruin that fancy hotel opening.'

Bree hesitated. 'You know, the daughters haven't actually done anything wrong. This is the rambling of a bitter middle–aged woman who hates that her daughters are still gorgeous and courting atten-tion when her star is fading. Ridiculous to be jealous rather than proud of your children. Monica Lascelles is still stunning – if only on the outside.'

Lisa was looking at her agog. 'Bree, are we in the business of wrapping people in cotton wool? It's a story, a good one. Run it.'

Bree went back to her desk to write up the story, but it bothered her. Surely an anonymous heads-up to the daughters wouldn't ruin the story? Checking no one could hear her, she pulled out her cell phone and called her friend, Vivien.

'Viv, hi, listen, I can only be a sec...are you still friends with Arlo Forrester's assistant? I need to get a message to him.'

COSIMA YANKED open the door and threw her arms around Jack. He laughed as he hugged her then, pulling away, she batted him.

'Jack Hampton, you have been away too long. How dare you put work before me?' she grinned at him. 'Come on in, Arlo's getting the wine ready. Even though you absolutely don't deserve it, I've made you one of my specialties. You like lamb pasanda, yes?'

Jack groaned. 'God, I dream about it. You're looking good, Cos.'

Pulling him by the hand into the kitchen, she grinned back at him. 'If you mean I've put on some weight, then yes. Being a lady of leisure will do that. Thankfully it's coming off now I'm back at work.'

'Is she still whining about her non-existent pot-belly? Again, Cos?' Arlo, grinning, shook Jack's hand. 'Hey, Jack, good to see you. Ignore her moaning. Wine or beer?'

'Beer, please.'

Cosima batted Arlo's butt as she went to the refrigerator. 'I've been looking forward to this all day. Damn, Jack, it has been too long. What gives?'

She handed him the cold bottle of beer. 'Chasing ghosts, I'm afraid,' he said. 'The trail went cold on me.'

Cosima's smile faded a little. 'Well,' she said finally, 'at least we know who it's *not*.'

Arlo rolled his eyes. 'Wait until she tells you who she's best buddies with now.'

'Who?'

Cosima flushed. 'Not best buddies, we've just reached a détente, is all.' She looked at Jack. 'Naveen Chowdry.'

Jack gulped a mouthful wine awkwardly. 'What the actual *hell?*' He looked at Arlo, who shrugged.

Cosima looked annoyed. 'Why do you look at Arlo as if he 'allowed' it to happen? I choose who I talk to, both of you. And it was nice. We talked, he apologized, and he's trying to make amends.'

'Trying?' Arlo spoke up, 'as in you're still talking to him?'

'I refer to my earlier comments,' Cosima said snippily but then sighed. 'Look, this was supposed to be a happy occasion so let's forget Nav, and concentrate on getting the gossip from Jack.'

The men nodded in agreement and Cosima relaxed. The lamb pasanda was a big hit and even though they all tried, they couldn't finish it all. Jack and Arlo sat back in their seats and groaned. Cosima looked at the leftovers. 'You think I made too much?'

Arlo chuckled and kissed her cheek. 'Maybe, baby. I'll clear it up.'

She waved her hands. 'Later, later. Jack, come let's go crash on the couch and chat. Will you stay, we have the room?'

Jack smiled. 'No, thanks, I have a room at a pretty swanky hotel downtown. Managed to get the agency to pay for it too.'

'Nicely done.'

THEY SAT in the living room talking, Cosima curled into the crook of Arlo's arm.

'So, what's next for you two now this place has finished?' Jack smiled at the both of them, gesturing around the beautiful apartment.

Cosima grinned up at Arlo, who nodded. 'We're thinking of going to San Francisco for a while, to find a new build there.'

'You're working together again?'

Cosima nodded. 'Through my company, of course, Arlo has very generously negotiated a contract with Tal, which means I get to work exclusively with Arlo, wherever he wants. So we decided to go to Frisco, as Arlo's friends and family are there.'

'Wow...that's great.' But Jack didn't look happy, and Cosima frowned.

'What is it, Jack?'

He shook his head. 'No, nothing. I just...you're safe here; this place is like a fortress now. But look, ignore me, I'm too used to policing where you go, I'm sorry, it's a hard habit to break. Seriously, that does sound great.'

LATER, when Jack had left, promising not be late for the opening the next night, Cosima was wrapping the leftovers in tin foil and stacking the dishes in the washer when Arlo, finishing a business call, came back into the kitchen.

'Jack wasn't keen on us moving, huh?'

Cosima hid a smile. She knew this tone of his – he wanted to know what *she* really thought about the move, not Jack. She kissed Arlo's cheek. 'It's no longer any of his concern. I can't wait to see the Golden Gate Bridge, Alcatraz...but most importantly, I want to meet Margaret.'

'I just spoke to her actually.' His tone had changed, and she looked up to see him studying her, his brow furrowed.

'What? What is it?'

Arlo sighed. 'A reporter called Margaret. Apparently your mother – '

'Oh god, what has that viper done now?' Cosima's whole body wilted in defeat, and Arlo put his arms around her.

'Apparently, she's been giving interviews to some tabloid rag – and said some pretty inflammatory things. At least that's what the reporter said. Seems this journalist has some morals and wants to talk to us about them before the story goes to print. In the morning.'

Cosima glanced at the clock. It was past ten at night. 'She didn't leave us much time, did she? Does she want you to call her tonight?'

Arlo hesitated. 'Not me. You.'

Cosima stared at him. 'What?'

'She says she'll only talk to you.'

Cosima sighed and reached for her phone.

NAVEEN CHOWDRY WALKED SLOWLY BACK to his hotel. It was time to leave New Orleans, he figured. His relationship with Cosima was – if not mended – then resolved enough that he could leave now. Except...he felt responsible. Whoever had taken Cosima was still out there.

And then there was Sabine Karlsson. Despite himself, despite seeing her for the gold-digging Machiavellian creature she was, he still felt drawn to her. When they were in bed together, after her usual, initial wildcat thing was done, he saw the real woman underneath, vulnerable and soft.

Who are you kidding? Sabine hired someone to attack Cosima with a knife – soft? Vulnerable? Still...he pulled out his phone and called her. She was surprised and nonplussed to hear from him but invited him to her hotel room.

'You just caught me,' she purred, 'tomorrow I leave for Geneva.'

Naveen grinned to himself. A likely story if Arlo had cut her off. 'I'll be there in five minutes.'

～

IN THE CAR across the street, he watched the handsome Indian change direction and walk back down to the Quarter. Now the news had been reporting that the Malhotra girls were safe from their father's enemies, was this dude still a threat? *No way.* But he could be a useful scapegoat...

The watcher started the car and moved off. *Soon,* he thought, *soon...*

～

COSIMA SAID GOODBYE TO BREE, the journalist, and slowly put her phone down on the table. She was trembling and wide-eyed. Arlo waited patiently.

'That evil, fucking bitch,' Cosima said, slowly, 'that low-life, dirty, bottom-dwelling *whore...*'

Arlo looked alarmed as Cosima stood, obviously looking for something to throw. 'Hey, hey, hey...'

He locked his arms around her, but she shook them off. 'Don't touch me right now, Arlo, I'm too angry.'

He let her go, half concerned, half-amused. 'Just tell me.'

Cosima paced some more then sat down. 'That venal bitch who calls herself our mother? Did an interview where she basically told the world I'm a cold-hearted bitch who deserved what she got. That's not the bad stuff.'

'It isn't?' Arlo felt his temper flare. 'Cos, I gotta tell you, that sounds bad.'

Suddenly Cosima looked bleak and her eyes filled with tears. 'Arlo...she said Harpa isn't my father's daughter. She told that interviewer that she had an affair after I was born, when I was about eighteen months, and she found she was pregnant. My father knew and decided to raise Harpa as his own. *Jesus*...this could all be bullshit, of course, except...'

'Except?'

'There was something, once, my dad said to Harpa and I overheard and thought it was a weird thing to say to a kid.'

'What was it?' He reached for her as tears dropped down her cheeks.

'He said, *Blood isn't a bond, love is a bond*. Oh, God, Arlo, what the hell am I going to tell Harpa?'

HARPA WOKE to hear Mikah talking on the phone in the living room. Throwing his t-shirt over her body, she padded into see him standing at the window, talking on his cell phone in a low voice. His body was taut, racked with tension. Harpa glanced at the clock – just after one a.m. Who the hell was he talking to this late? A little jolt of jealousy flashed through her, but she swatted the thought away.

She was about to go back to bed when he turned and caught sight of her. His eyes were wary, but he beckoned her over.

'Yeah, she's awake now. Talk to her.'

He handed his phone to Harpa. 'It's Cosima.'

Harpa was shocked. What was going on? She took the phone. 'Cos?'

'Hey, Bubba.' Her sister sounded tired and upset.

'Are you okay, Cos? Is Arlo okay?'

'Yeah we're both fine, Harp, don't worry. Listen...I have something to tell you and ordinarily I would want to tell you this in person, but we don't have any time left.'

Harpa's heart began to thud uncomfortably, and her legs trembled. She sat down on the couch with a bump. Mikah put his arm around her. 'Just say it, Cos, please, you're scaring me.'

Cosima drew in a long breath. 'Harp, Mom's done an interview, trashing me. Now, that I can deal with. It's what she said about you... Harp...she said that...oh *god*.' Her sister's voice cracked and Harpa's eyes filled with tears.

'What?'

'She says that Dad....wasn't your biological father.' Cosima rushed the end of the sentence then gave a sob. Harpa, numb, heard Arlo's voice, comforting her sister then taking the phone. 'Harpa?'

'Arlo, what the fuck...?' Her voice was barely a whisper.

'I'm so sorry, Harpa. We had to tell you because the magazine will be out in the morning and we didn't want you to find out like that.'

'But she's lying, Mom's lying, right?' Bewilderment had set in, and Harpa couldn't stop shaking her head. *No. No. It wasn't true.*

Cosima came back on the line. 'I'm so sorry, Harp.'

'Tell me it isn't true.'

There was a long silence then, in a broken whisper, her sister said, 'I can't. I just don't know for sure, Harpa. All I know is you're my sister, and I love you. We'll get to the bottom of this, I promise.'

Not knowing what to say, Harpa ended the call abruptly and walked out of the living room.

Mikah followed her and watched her pulling her clothes on. 'What are you doing?'

She didn't look up. 'Mikah, I need to ask you a favor.'

'Anything, baby, just ask.'

She looked up then, and her eyes were hard, cold, and broken-hearted. 'I need to get to San Francisco. Now.'

COSIMA AWOKE HOLLOW-EYED AND DRAINED. When Harpa had hung up on her, she had cried in Arlo's arms, tried to call her sister back. When eventually they got through to Mikah, he told them he was taking Harpa to San Francisco to confront her mother. Harpa didn't want to talk to Cosima.

'I shouldn't have told her,' she had fretted, but Arlo shook his head.

'You didn't have a choice, darling.'

Cosima hoped her relationship with her sister wasn't irreparable; that Harpa wouldn't blame her for not being able to reassure her. But she couldn't lie – inside she had held that secret with her for a lifetime. She had even, at age eleven, asked her father what he had meant by the 'Blood isn't a bond' statement and he'd told her that she would understand one day.

She had hoped never to find out what it meant but when the reporter – Bree – who had been kind and apologetic – had told her, she knew, for once, her mother wasn't lying. That she'd been saving this particular piece of information for when it could hurt her daughters the most. A piece of Cosima's heart turned dark at that moment, with loathing for the narcissist in her mother, the selfish being.

The best revenge is to live well – wasn't that the saying? *Then fuck you, Monica...*

Cosima got up and went to find Arlo. He was at his desk and looked up as she came in. He raised his arms, holding them out to her and she went into them, settling on his lap and kissing him.

'Good morning lover.'

'Morning, gorgeous,' he swept a hand over her hair and smiled, his eyes alert and concerned. 'Are you okay?'

She nodded. 'Yes. We will get through this.'

His arms tightened around her. 'At this point, Cos, I don't think there's anything you couldn't get through.'

'Thank you for saying that, honey. What's this?'

She glanced down at his desk, frowned when she saw a to-do list for the Grand Opening with '*Cancel?*' written on it. 'Absolutely not,' she said firmly. 'Today, we are opening our hotel. Nothing more is getting in the way of it. Nothing, Arlo.'

He smiled at her. 'I agree, honey. Why let your mother win? There *will* be journalists there.'

'And I'll answer any questions they have about the interview honestly.' She looked at the clock. 'I'm going to grab a shower then go downstairs to check everything is ready.'

Arlo nodded. 'Good idea. I'm meeting the shareholders at Tal's office, and then we'll bring them here before the ceremony starts.'

Cosima half-smiled. 'Come join me in the shower first.'

'Right behind you, sweetheart.'

ARLO WAITED until Cosima had left the room and quickly dialed Jack's number. Voicemail. 'Hey, Jack; hope you're still coming tonight. Listen, we need to talk, but I don't want Cos overhearing me so can you call me back in about an hour? Thanks.'

He ended the call then went to join Cosima in the bathroom.

HARPA ASKED for her mother's room as soon as they reached the hotel. The smug receptionist told her that Monica was expecting her, and giving the simpering woman a death stare, Harpa went to the elevators. She had asked Mikah to stay away from the hotel until she called him and he had graciously acquiesced albeit with a concerned expression on his face.

Monica opened the door without a trace of remorse on her face. 'Harpa, darling.'

Harpa stalked in, and Monica had barely closed the door when Harpa started talking in a low, angry voice. 'Is it true?'

Now Monica wore a regretful expression. 'I'm sorry, darling, yes.'

Harpa knew it, had readied herself for it but it still hurt like hell. After a moment, she spoke again. 'Then who is my father?'

Monica didn't answer for a time, settling herself down into her chair, arranging her dress carefully. 'Iqbal Chowdry.'

Harpa's knees collapsed, and she sank to the floor. 'Iqbal Chowdry? Naveen's father...Naveen, the man, who up until recently, had planned to murder Cosima? Naveen is...'

'Your half-brother. As Cosima is your half-sister.'

Harpa shook her head. 'No, Cos is my sister...*my sister*. You can't take that away from me, I don't give a fuck who the sperm donor was, you filthy whore.'

Monica bristled. 'How dare you...?'

Harpa was incensed. 'How dare I? How dare *I*? Who the *fuck* tells their daughter that her dad isn't her dad in a god damned tabloid interview? What's the matter, Mom, running low on cash? Your dealer getting antsy? Your plastic surgeon getting tired of ramming poison into your face? What am I saying? You have enough poison inside you anyway. I hate you, Monica, I hate you for this, I hate you for making Cos's life a misery because she's a billion times more loving and beautiful than you've ever been. I hate you for cuckolding my Dad. Because Arjun Malhotra *was* my father, whether he provided the sperm or not.'

Monica's smile was chilly. 'Have you finished?'

Harpa shook her head. 'No. There's one last thing, and you better listen. I never want to see you or speak to you or even think about you again. *Ever*. And I'm speaking for Cosima now too. You go for her again, and I'll be standing right in front of her. I wish it had been the other way around, that Dad had cheated on you, that I had a real mother, someone with an ounce of empathy in her. Actually, I guess I did; I had Cosima. Thank God. And don't think I won't use Mikah or Arlo to close *major* doors on your career. Because I will, God help me, and I know they'll do it.'

Monica smirked. 'And you accuse me of being a whore? Do you open your legs for every rich man that crosses your path?'

Harpa's smile was humorless. 'People in glass houses, Monica. I mean it...don't get in contact with either of us ever again and leave our names out of your pathetic interviews. Or I'll make you sorry.'

She turned and left the room, slamming the door behind her. In the elevator, she sucked in deep breaths. Her anger was a wild, burning thing that would not abate and even when she saw Mikah, she almost growled at him until he put his arms around her and would not let go. They stayed locked together, out in the middle of the sidewalk, people eyeing them curiously as they moved around them.

Harpa closed her eyes and leaned against Mikah's solid, warm chest. He stroked her back gently, rhythmically until she felt calmness descend on her. She looked up into his eyes.

'It's over, it's all done. Monica confirmed what she said. I'm not a Malhotra, it seems, I'm a Chowdry.'

Mikah frowned. 'Isn't that the name of...?'

'Yep. Naveen Chowdry is my half-brother.' She looked at her watch. 'We have to get on a plane to New Orleans.'

Mikah nodded. 'Although I think Cos wouldn't mind if you wanted to give the opening a miss.'

Harpa looked away, and when she spoke, her voice was gravelly. 'I'm not going to see Cosima. I'm going to see Naveen.'

NAVEEN SLOWLY PUT down the phone, confused and unsettled. Sabine, naked, fresh from the shower, wandered into the bedroom, towel-drying her hair. She caught his awkward posture, the way he was staring at the screen of his phone. 'What's up?'

He looked at her unseeing for a moment then focused. 'I'm not sure. Mikah Ray just called me and asked me to meet him before the opening.'

Sabine stopped. 'Who is Mikah Ray?'

'Harpa Malhotra's boyfriend. An art dealer from Seattle. I've met him a few times – that was before he knew Harpa though.'

'Did he say what he wants?'

'Just that he needs to talk to me today. He's flying into New Orleans in a couple of hours.'

Sabine lost interest and shrugged. She began to dress then stopped. 'Wait...before the opening? You're going to the opening of the LaBelle?'

Naveen met her gaze steadily. 'Yes. I was invited.'

'Oh.'

Naveen smothered a smile. 'I would ask you to accompany me but, in light of your history with Arlo Forrester...'

Sabine gave him a weak smile. 'Plus I had his girlfriend attacked. Probably not the most popular girl with those two.'

'Probably not.' Naveen touched her face. 'Do I detect a hint of remorse?'

Sabine rolled her eyes but then grinned shyly. 'You know what? Yes. I was jealous. Crazy jealous...I mean...look at her. Gorgeous, brilliant and sweet. Ugh.' But she laughed. 'I honestly don't know what I was thinking because now I get why Arlo just fell for her. That utter and complete feeling when you're wiped out by love. *You* make *me* feel like that.'

Naveen pulled her to him. 'You are a viper, Ms. Karlsson, a conniving, slippery pit viper but I have to admit...you're intoxicating. Both of us have done things or planned things that are the worst that people can do. How about we try and make amends for that – together?'

She studied him, and he saw mistrust in her eyes. 'Sabine...are you really that damaged that you cannot trust a man telling you he loves you?'

Sabine's eye filled with tears. 'I guess I am...but I don't want to be, Nav. I want to trust myself that this is different, that I don't care how much money you have, or status or connections. This is new for me, wanting to be with a man for him...even with Arlo, although I did love him, without everything he had, I doubt I would have felt this strongly.' She pressed her lips to his. 'Darling, can you trust that I love you for *you*?'

Naveen smiled, cradling her face in his. 'Why don't we both try and see?'

'WHERE'S COS?'

Jack was sitting in the small diner where Arlo had suggested they meet, a half-empty glass of soda in front of him. Arlo, his tie pulled open, his jacket off, sipped his coffee. 'Back at the hotel. She's distracting herself with work...she's hoping Harpa will call her or turn up tonight.'

'It's not Cosima's fault, any of this.'

Arlo shrugged. 'I know...and I'm sure Harpa knows that but I can imagine what's going through her head right now. Cosima is Arjun's daughter, Harpa loved her Dad as much as Cos did but now she finds out...Mikah called me earlier. Harpa went down to Frisco to confront her mother. He was waiting outside Monica's hotel for them to finish when I last spoke to him. God, that woman...'

'Piece of work, isn't she? You know, she never once got in touch when the girls were being threatened, asked how they were, if enough was being done to protect them. She just didn't give a crap.'

Arlo made a disgusted noise. 'God, just when I think we're getting back on track, something else happens.'

Jack nodded but was silent. 'Changing the subject...you two made any firm plans for the Frisco move?'

Arlo shook his head. 'All I know is that we definitely won't be going while Monica's in town. Cosima is contacting a lawyer to see if she can get a restraining order on her mother ever contacting her again. She knows it's a long shot because there's no physical threat but she says it's worth a try.'

'Unless there's money in it, I doubt Monica will be in touch again. Not that that's any consolation in this case. Any idea who Harpa's real dad is?'

'None.' Arlo shook his head. 'Damn it, I feel so useless. If she were coming after me, I'd throw every legal thing at her but when it's not my call...anyway. You'll still come tonight?'

'Of course. After that, though, I'm probably being reassigned... now the international and political threat to the girls has gone, it's unlikely they'll fund any more protection. But you've got it from here, right?'

'You have my word. Until we find Cos's abductor, I won't rest. I already have people out looking for him...it would help if you could spare any information?'

Jack smiled. 'All I know, that I can tell you, you know already. The guys didn't find anything at the house where Cosima was held – dude wiped the place clean and the ownership was buried so deep in false papers we'll never know. I promise, though, anything I think of, I'll let you know.'

'I appreciate it.' Arlo glanced at his watch. 'Look, I have to get going – see you tonight?'

'Count on it.'

It was late afternoon and as Arlo got home, he heard the shower running. Smiling, he walked towards the bathroom, pulling his clothes off and leaving them where they fell.

Cosima jumped slightly as he pulled open the shower door and stepped into the cubicle with her. She grinned at him, her hair soapy with shampoo. 'Hey, gorgeous.'

He kissed her mouth then let his lips trail down to her throat. 'Hey yourself, beautiful.' He cupped her full breasts in his hands and then smoothed his hands down over her curves. 'Everything all set for this evening?'

Cosima's hands were in his hair, her fingers knotting in the dark strands. She nuzzled her nose to his. 'All set. All done. It's going to be great...I tried to take a peek at the new signage and was batted away by Mac.'

Arlo grinned. 'You're so impatient. I told you I wanted one thing to surprise you with...'

Cosima was ignoring him, tilting her head up for a kiss. 'We have a few hours left...what *shall* we do?'

He grinned and pulled her against him, sliding his hands down to cup her butt. 'Well, if I remember rightly, there's a basket of toys in our closet which haven't seen the light of day for a while...wanna play?'

Cosima grinned. 'Oh hell, yes I do...'

They finished showering and then Arlo was lifting her into his arms and carrying her to their bed...she protested as he dropped her onto the bed, still wet. Arlo dropped on top of her, pinning her hands to the bed.

'I love it when your skin is wet, it glows...in fact, let me get the basket because I remember some special oil...'

He found the basket and took out the small bottle of monoi oil. He dripped some into her navel then smoothed it over the rest of her belly and her breasts with his warm palms. Cosima sighed happily as his hand dipped between her legs and he began to massage the oil into her sex, feeling her dampen, her labia swell and redden at his touch.

'Sweet, sweet Cosima...I'm going to fuck you so hard right now... first with my tongue on your clit, as I fuck you with that big dildo that we have yet to use...then I would like you to suck me until I come....then my cock is going to nail you to this bed, and this floor...'

Cosima moaned with arousal and excitement as he dropped to his knees between her legs. 'You have the prettiest little cunt, my darling,' Arlo smiled lazily up at her before his tongue found her clit, already sensitive and trembling. His tongue lashed around it, his teeth grazing the small bud. His fingers dug into the flesh of her inner thighs, pushing them apart.

Cosima gasped as Arlo slowly inserted the dildo into her vagina, the friction of his tongue working her into a frenzy as the toy filled her. Arlo slammed it in hard and Cosima cried out as he worked the toy, teasing her with it before plunging the length of it in. Her back arched as she came and he quickly moved to grab the silken rope from the basket and used it to tie her hands in front of her. Her eyes were alive with passion, almost delirious with pleasure. She cupped his cock in her hands; it was already engorged and throbbing and jerked when she gently ran her fingertips down the long shaft. Before she took him in her mouth, she looked up at him.

'Tell me what you want to do, Mr. Forrester...' Then her warm, wet lips enveloped him, taking him deep, the gentle sucking motion enhanced by her tongue teasing the tip, licking the salty pre-cum from the head, her hands fisting the root of his cock. Her other hand massaged his balls and Arlo sighed at her touch.

'The things I want to do with you, to you, Cosima Malhotra...I want to fuck your perfect cunt until you scream, kiss and taste every delicious part of you, suck your delicate nipples, bite the soft mound of your belly, wrap your thighs around my head. I want to put that rope tighter and have you completely at my mercy as I fuck your perfect ass.'

Cosima moaned at the thought, and her mouth grew quicker on his cock, her pull harder, drawing him close. He tangled his fingers in her long dark hair. 'I want us to fuck like animals, hard, dirty, fast then slow and sensual like lovers. I want to spill my seed onto your belly and massage it into your skin. I want to fuck you against the cold glass of the big windows in the living room, taking you from behind, pressing your breasts and belly to the cool glass so everyone can see your breathtaking loveliness.'

He felt his cock thicken to a painful extreme and knew he was close. 'Cosima...my love...my life...' He came, and she swallowed his seed down as it shot onto her tongue. He couldn't wait any longer and pushed her back onto the bed, pushing her knees to her chest so her swollen, red, wet cunt was laid bare to him. He plunged into her, as deep as was possible, and his balls were hard against her butt as his cock slammed into the center of her. God, the way her muscles tightened around his cock made him almost frenzied. Her hands still tied stroked his stomach, her mouth sought his hungrily. Her legs curled around his chest as he slammed into her, her back bending with the effort. He felt her vagina contracted around his cock, become warm and she shuddered and whimpered with an overwhelming orgasm. It was the perfect sound to his ears and he felt himself peak again, shooting hot, sticky cum deep into her womb.

As they recovered, he pulled her on top of him, released her hands then tied them again behind her back. She grinned down at him. 'You like tying me up, don't you?'

He nodded, still breathless, his fingertips tracing patterns on her belly. 'As much as it sounds caveman-like, I like that you're entirely mine when we make love. When we fuck...'

Cosima smiled. 'That's better...I do love you but damn it, Forrester, we *fuck*, and we fuck *hard*...that's us, that's what we do. You nail me to the freakin' bed and I love every moment of being yours when we're in bed.'

Arlo grinned. 'Good. Now be a good little girl and sit on my cock, would you?'

Cosima laughed. 'My pleasure, sir...would you be so kind as to help guide you in...my hands are a little tied up.'

As he spread her labia with his big fingers, she lowered herself back onto his already hard cock and sighed happily. 'Consider this hotel duly christened....*oh god, Arlo....that's so good...*'

NAVEEN CHOWDRY MADE his way down to the hotel bar where he had agreed to meet Mikah Ray. When he got there, however, he was surprised to see not Mikah, but Harpa Malhotra waiting for him. The young woman stood, and he could see she was trembling. She didn't look much older than when he'd last seen her, nearly twenty years previously. He had been so preoccupied with Cosima then, and had dismissed her younger sister, but he could see now she had grown into a beauty: dark hair, dark eyes, slim but curvy figure. He held out his hand, and she shook it.

'You remember me then,' she said in a soft voice.

'Of course, Harpa, it's very nice to see you. Shall we sit and you can tell me what you needed to see me for. Can I get you a drink?'

When their drinks were brought to the table, Harpa took a big gulp of her cocktail then winced as the tequila hit the back of her throat. She glanced at the patiently waiting man with a half-smile. 'Thanks for not killing my sister.'

Nav inclined his head. 'It would have been a tragedy and one brought about by petty jealousy and age-old grudges that are no longer relevant to my or your lives.'

'Yes.'

A long silence then Harpa, in a half-broken voice, spoke. 'So, I don't know if you've heard...my mother – ' she spat the word ' – gave an interview in which she said that I am not the biological daughter of Arjun Malhotra. My dad is not my dad.'

Nav shook his head. 'I hadn't heard, no.

Harpa shrugged. 'That's not surprising unless you were an involved party or a reader of some of the gutter press.'

Nav smiled. 'Not really.'

Harpa took another slug of her margarita. 'The thing is...you *are* involved. At least, that's what my mother says.'

Nav laughed. 'Harpa, I may be older than you, but I assure you, I am not your father.'

Harpa gazed steadily at him. 'Not you. *Your* father. Iqbal.'

The smile faded from Nav's face. 'No, that isn't possible.'

'According, to my mom, it is. We're brother and sister, Nav.'

Nav shook his head. 'No. Look, my father worshiped my mother, there's no way...'

He trailed off, and Harpa looked sympathetic. 'I know how you feel. Look, the quickest way to settle this is a DNA test.'

'No,' said Nav shortly, 'the quickest way to settle this is to go to the source. We're going to see my father.'

COSIMA GRABBED Jack as he arrived, a relieved look on her face as she handed him a flute of champagne. 'Thank God, Jack, I'm surrounded by Arlo's business associates who either ignore me or can't stop staring at the ladies.' She indicated her chest and rolled her eyes. 'How Arlo puts up with them, I do not know.'

'Do they stare at his breasts too?' Jack said with a mockingly inno-cent look on his face. He grinned and she laughed.

'I hope so, and then he'd know how I feel. Thanks for coming, though, I mean it, it's good to see you.'

'Anytime, sweetheart, you know that.' He held her gaze for a beat too long, and she colored and changed the subject. They were in the reception room of the hotel, a room now filled with businessmen, journalists, local celebrities.

'Lord knows if Harpa is going to turn up, or Mikah or Nav. Tal's coming later with the others.'

'Naveen Chowdry's coming?'

She nodded, searching his face. 'Yes. I invited him. Problem?'

Jack shook his head. 'I do not trust that guy. Who spends years fixated on killing someone then changes his mind, just like that? It doesn't make sense.'

Cosima sighed. 'That's what Arlo thinks too, but I've had enough of this unpleasantness for a lifetime. I'm choosing to believe he's changed, that he's my childhood friend again.'

Jack again shook his head, taking a sip of his champagne. 'Don't blame me if you end with a bullet in your gut.'

Cosima flinched, and he regretted his harsh words. 'Sorry, Cos, I didn't mean that. Just...for me, for Arlo...be vigilant, okay? I couldn't bear it for anyone else to hurt you, I just couldn't.'

She touched his face briefly. 'Jack...'

'Hello, hello.' Tal appeared behind Jack, grinning widely. 'Cosima, this place is a triumph.' He kissed her on both cheeks then stuck his hand out to Jack, and they shook as Cosima introduced them. Jack excused himself then wandered around the room, out into the lobby. Although he'd now been here many times, he never stopped marveling at the renovation Cosima had masterminded. The hotel, full of Orleans flavor, was finely balanced with a classic, elegant French atmosphere while incorporating state of the art technology. Talmidge Hunt was right; this place was a triumph.

Jack finished his champagne and went to grab another, looking for Arlo or Cosima, but finding the place full of strangers instead. He turned and stopped when he saw a blonde woman slide silently into the room. Jack's mouth popped open in amazement. What the hell was *she* doing here? He stood back, never taking his eyes of the newcomer, waiting to see the next move she would make.

Sabine Karlsson told herself again, and it would be okay. Naveen had called her, told her he had to suddenly leave town on business. It had taken her no more than a few minutes to decide to come to the opening, use Naveen's invite. The doorman hadn't blinked.

The hotel was gorgeous; she had to begrudgingly admit, as she wandered around. She kept her eye out for Arlo...she was really here for Cosima. She reckoned the younger woman would be more receptive to her. *Ha, you're kidding, right? You had her* stabbed*, you psycho.* Sabine grabbed a glass of champagne from a passing waiter and took a big swig.

There was Cosima, all elegant, a dark red dress that fell halfway down her thigh and that clung to every curve, her dark hair piled up on her head, minimal make-up except for a deep red lipstick. As jealous as she was, Sabine could appreciate true beauty, and it shone from every cell in Cosima's body. *She would have been a fantastic model if she'd been taller,* Sabine, thought, critically. She could see a little of Monica Lascelles in Cosima's face, but Cosima's face was softer, kinder, sweeter than Monica's had ever been.

Draining her glass for courage, Sabine moved slowly to Cosima's side. The other woman didn't see her at first, but as she turned to Sabine, her smile faded.

'Sabine.'

Sabine gave a slight smile. 'Hello, Cosima.'

Cosima's face hardened. 'I don't remember inviting you.' She took a deep breath. 'But seeing as you are here, welcome.'

She started to move away, but Sabine caught her arm. 'Cosima, please, please just give me a moment.'

Sabine let go of Cosima's arm; then noticed the jagged scar on her forearm. She touched it with a finger. 'For this, I am truly sorry. I mean it. For years, I have been behaving badly, with no one to check me, no one to reel me in. I take full responsibility; however, I don't know what possessed me. I'm sorry.'

Cosima studied her, her eyes wary then she gave a brief nod.

Sabine smiled. 'Thank you. That's all I came here to say, I won't keep you. It's just now that I am seeing Naveen – and I know you have reached a peace between you – we may run into each other from time to time. I don't want it to be awkward.'

Cosima sighed. 'Fine.' She chewed her lip. 'You modeled with my mother on some shoots, didn't you?'

Sabine nodded and Cosima half-smiled. 'Utter bitch, isn't she?'

Sabine wasn't expecting that and burst out laughing; Cosima had to join in eventually. Sabine wiped her eyes. 'Sadly, yes. The apple fell a long way from the tree, though.'

'Thank you. Look, there's food later, after the official sign...disrobing, is that what it's called? Anyway, the ceremonial bit – Arlo's so excited, he's like a kid. Stay, have some food, meet some people.'

'Maybe we can meet for coffee sometime?'

Cosima smiled. 'Maybe. Look, I need to find Arlo, we're about to start.'

After Cosima had gone, Sabine felt a satisfaction settle inside of her. *Yes. A new life. A new woman, that's what I'll be.* She considered Cosima's offer and decided to take her up on it. She wandered around, trying to see anyone she knew; a blonde man she faintly recognized was talking to a short man who looked like he didn't belong there – maybe one of the construction workers. She saw Arlo the other side of the room but didn't feel like dealing with him tonight. He might ruin her buzz. Instead, she aimed for a group of businessmen who looked bored and turned on every last bit of the Sabine Karlsson charm.

MIKAH HAD TRIED to convince Harpa not to go with Naveen, but when she refused, he gave up and told her – 'I'm coming with you.' Now they were on a flight that took them from Los Angeles to Mumbai, a grueling nearly twenty-four-hour journey. Harpa also refused to call Cosima to tell her where she was going. Mikah reasoned with her.

'None of this is Cos's fault,' he said again and again, but Harpa merely shook her head.

'This has nothing to do with Cos – and I'm not blaming her for anything, it's just something I have to resolve on my own. If I told Cos, she would go into Mother Hen mode, and I'm old enough to sort this out myself. Cos's had to deal with enough. I *will* call her when things are settled.'

She also banned him from texting Arlo, whipping his phone out of his hand. 'For the next few days we are incommunicado,' she said firmly, 'or I don't want you to come.'

He'd reluctantly agreed to that too. Now she was curled up asleep on one of the airline's business class beds – Naveen had insisted on paying for all three of them despite Mikah's protestations. The other man sat reading a book across from Mikah, and he took the time to really observe him.

The truth was he could see similarities between Naveen and Harpa. The shape of their eyes, the quick smile, the chin dimple. It had never even occurred to Mikah when he'd seen photos of Arjun and Monica that neither of them shared the same trait.

Naveen felt his scrutiny and looked up. 'Something the matter?'

'Not at all. Forgive me, I was comparing and contrasting. Naveen...' Mikah leaned forward. 'Deep down...you know this is true, right?'

Naveen sighed. 'I do...but I need to hear it from my father's lips.'

Mikah raised his eyebrows. 'What if he didn't know?'

Naveen closed his book and set it aside. 'I don't that is possible. I think he knew all along but couldn't say anything. I think that's the reason he hated Arjun so much, why he wanted Cosima killed. Revenge. Now that I think about it, he never once said anything about Harpa – his wrath was for Arjun and his offspring. My father was directly involved with Arjun's murder. He must have known.'

Mikah rubbed a hand over his eyes. 'Naveen...will Harpa be safe in Mumbai?'

'I guarantee it, Mikah. No one will touch her.'

Mikah glanced over to his sleeping girlfriend. 'If anything ever happened to her...'

Naveen nodded. 'Regardless of whether she is my sister or not, and I think she is, she will be well protected.' He glanced over at her. 'It'll take some time to get used to.'

Mikah noticed how warm Naveen's tone was when he spoke about Harpa. 'I worry what it'll do to Harpa and Cosima's relationship. Your father being involved with murdering Arjun is bound to have some effect.'

'Yes. But I cannot do anything about that, I'm afraid. What's done is done.'

Naveen went back to his book then, and Mikah decided to try and grab some sleep. Boy, if he had known what he was getting involved with when he agreed to have dinner with his friend that day in Harpa's restaurant...

Wouldn't change a thing. Not a thing. Because when it came down to it, he was in love with the young woman asleep across the aisle from him. One day soon, he hoped that she would allow him to tell her just how much she meant to him. Something told him she would need him in the next few days, and he couldn't imagine being anywhere else than by her side.

ARLO CALLED for the attention of the gathered guests and led them outside to the front of the hotel where the hotel's new sign was draped with a curtain. He made a speech, thanking them for coming, praising the efforts and professionalism of the contractors (most of which were listening and cheered when he mentioned them). Smiling, he congratulated Tal and his company and raised a glass to the elderly architect.

'Finally, the most important person on this project. The most important person in my life. Cosima Malhotra had led this project from the beginning, finding the old LaBelle and seeing its potential. You see her masterful touch in every painting, every fixture, and fitting, every fabric. She is the reason that we are booked solid for the next year. She is the reason I breathe in and out every day. Cosima, come up here, darling, and take your due.' He held out a hand to the furiously blushing Cosima and led her to the front.

Cheers and applause – the loudest from her co-workers and the workmen she had supervised over all those months. Arlo leaned to kiss her cheek, murmuring, 'I love you, baby. I hope you enjoy the surprise...'

He grinned at her bemusement and then grabbed the rope of the curtain. 'Ladies and gentlemen, without further ado, we say goodbye to the old *LaBelle*...and welcome you all to the *L'Atelier Cosima*...'

He pulled the rope sharply and the curtain fell, revealing the new name, scrolled on a beautiful sign above the main entrance. The crowd burst into loud applause.

L'Atelier Cosima.

Cosima's hands flew to her mouth, stunned, overwhelmed. Arlo laughed at her shock. 'Gotcha,' he said and kissed her thoroughly to the delight of the crowd.

AFTERWARD, people came up to them both and congratulated them, and Cosima didn't have time to let the surprise sink in. It wasn't until Tal hugged her and said, 'Well, I've never had a colleague have their project named after them before.'

Cosima shook her head, laughing. 'I'm so shocked, Tal. He didn't give an inkling that he was planning this, not a clue.'

She finally managed to get Arlo alone, pulling him around the corner of the hotel into the alleyway. She kissed him then looked up at him with shining eyes. 'Thank you, my love, for the sweetest thing anyone has ever done for me. I can't believe it.'

Arlo tightened his arms around her. 'You're welcome, my love, my Cosima. It was only fitting that your masterpiece should bear your name. I should say, your *first* masterpiece. Notwithstanding this fine body of yours,' he grinned, and kissing her, ran his hands down her body. 'This dress is something else, but I can't wait to take it off you.'

Cosima chuckled. 'You have a one-track mind.' She smiled, but her eyes were suddenly sad. 'I wish Harpa were here.'

'I know, baby, but she has to do what she has to do.'

Cosima nodded. 'I just hope she forgives me.'

'For what? Your mother being an adulterer?'

Cosima shook her head. 'It doesn't matter. I don't want to spoil our night. Come on, let's get back to the party.'

As they made their way back to the lobby of the hotel, a journalist stopped Cosima and asked her if she had any comment on the interview her mother had given. Arlo started to protest, but Cosima stopped him and smiled at the young woman.

'Actually,' she said, 'I do. Come and have a drink and we'll talk.'

HARPA STOOD under the cold shower, trying to shake off the jetlag. Mumbai was even more beautiful than she remembered – the little she saw of it in the cab ride to the hotel. She was so tired, her eyes kept closing, and her head would fall onto Mikah's shoulder. In the end, he'd chuckled and said, 'Sleep, baby. We have plenty of time.'

She'd woken up in a sumptuous, thankfully air-conditioned hotel bedroom, Mikah beside her, reading. She'd forgotten how hot the city was at this time of year, and now she felt gross and dirty from the heat and the plane journey.

Walking back into the bedroom, naked, the air-conditioning cooled her skin. She pulled on panties and a cotton dress. Mikah was working on his laptop. He looked and smiled at her. 'There are pictures of the opening on the news sites if you want to look at them?'

Harpa hesitated then shook her head. 'After.'

Mikah nodded, understanding. 'Of course. Let's go get some breakfast, Nav's already down there.'

Nav. My brother. She had been thinking about that the whole time she was awake on the plane. She'd even pretended to be asleep so she could study the man from beneath half closed eyes. She still couldn't believe they shared some DNA.

Nav met them with a smile. 'The breakfast buffet here is out of this world,' he said, steering them toward tables laid out with every kind of food: Indian, American, European. 'Caters for every taste.'

Harpa fell on the food, but Mikah looked a little lost. Harpa grinned at him. 'Try that one,' she pointed at a curry dish. Nav laughed loudly.

'Don't listen to her; that's *Misal* – for the uninitiated, it can be intense. Try the *Sali Par Edu*, it's like a potato chip omelet with chili.'

Mikah grinned. 'Thanks for the tip. I'll remember that, munchkin,' he murmured to a giggling Harpa.

The coffee was hot and strong, but Harpa went for the chai. The men laughed at her blissed-out face. 'There's nothing like Indian food in India,' she said, 'the spices are more intense, fruitier, hotter, the sweetness is intense...god, I have missed this place.'

'How old were you the last time you came here?' Nav was digging into a fiery looking curry, scooping it up with roti.

'Ten,' she said, and swallowed, looking at him. 'About two months later, my father was blown to pieces. The man I thought was my father.'

'I know.' Nav put down his fork. 'Harpa, if I could turn back time...'

'We'll get answers later. I assume you've called your...*our*...father, set up the meeting.'

'Yes,' Nav resumed eating, 'Although he thinks it's just me. We're more likely to get the truth out of him if he's caught off guard.'

Harpa concentrated on her food for a moment. Mikah finished his breakfast and sat back, sipping his coffee. 'What's your read on what he'll do?'

Nav shrugged. 'I honestly don't know...my father doesn't have the power or the position he thinks he does in his own mind. There was a time when his word was almost law in certain circles. Now he's just an old, angry man.'

'Impotent rage,' Harpa muttered, and Nav smiled.

'Quite.'

Harpa glanced at her watch. 'What time is he expecting you?'

'Eleven a.m.

Harpa blew out a long breath. 'Well, then. I guess we'll soon know how this pans out.'

HARPA FOUND herself trembling violently as they drove towards Iqbal Chowdry's home. The man lived in an affluent suburb in South Mumbai and on the short journey, Harpa's hands began to sweat. The fact Nav didn't know how his father would react made her nervous. She began to imagine the worst scenarios...Iqbal, outraged, gunning them all down in his anger. She glanced at Mikah and wished she'd insisted he stay at the hotel, safe, out of reach.

Nav squeezed her hand as they got out of the car at the apartment complex. 'Remember, he's just an old man now. Don't be scared. If he gets nasty, we're out of here, and he will have lost a son as well as a daughter.'

She smiled gratefully at him as they walked into the plush lobby of the luxury building. Mikah whistled as he looked around the interior.

'This is something else...'

Harpa half-smiled. 'Cos would love it here.' She realized how much she missed her sister being part of this...but even though the threat had been lifted, she knew Cosima would be in danger here, still, the anger still raw among the older generation.

Iqbal's maid opened the door, and her eyes popped when she saw all three of them but led them into the living room. Iqbal was sitting at his desk, writing, and he too looked surprised to see them all. He stood and greeted his son. Nav took care to introduce Mikah first then Harpa saw him take a deep breath.

'Father...this is Harpa Malhotra.'

Iqbal blinked, and Harpa saw the battle in his mind – was it because he knew she was his daughter or was it the fact a hated Malhotra was in his home? Finally, he nodded, gave her the hint of a smile. 'Welcome, Harpa. It has been a long time.'

Neutral. She couldn't read his mood. *Damn...*

'Thank you, Mr. Chowdry. It has been a long time since I was back home.' She kept all recrimination out of her voice.

Iqbal recovered himself. 'Please sit, we'll have some tea.'

Harpa felt Mikah take her hand and was grateful for it. Nav glanced at him then turned to his father.

'Dad...we've come because we have to ask you something. Something important and I would ask you, as your only son, for you to be honest with us.'

The wary look was back in his father's eyes, but he nodded. 'If I can.'

Nav took a deep breath. 'Here it is....Monica Lascelles has claimed that you, and not Arjun Malhotra, are Harpa's biological father. Are you aware of her claims?'

'I am.'

Harpa couldn't bear the tension. 'Is it true?' Her voice was soft but heavy with emotion. Iqbal gazed at her, and a small smile played on his lips.

'Yes.'

Harpa let out the breath she was holding in and with the rush of air, tears popped into her eyes and she crumbled. Mikah hugged her to him. Iqbal got up and walked to her side, Nav getting up so he could sit next to his daughter.

'Harpa,' Iqbal said softly, 'Your mother told me at the time that she had fallen pregnant. We argued. I was afraid the affair would become common knowledge, that my position in the community would become untenable. My wife....my beloved wife...was the one with the family connections, not me, and if it became known, then she would leave me. But I wanted to be part of your life. Your father... I mean, Arjun, would not permit it. As far as he was concerned, you were *his* daughter. At first, I was resigned, but as you grew, I became resentful, angry. When my wife died suddenly, I went to him, told him I wanted my daughter back. He refused. Then the families started warring and I was on the opposite side to your grandfather and your father. When he was exiled, he sent you away, and I knew I would never see you again.'

Harpa studied him. His old eyes were full of remorse – and of hope. Hope that she would be part of his life. Harpa looked away from him.

'Did you kill my dad?'

'I did not. But neither was I ignorant that it was going to happen.'

Harpa swallowed and closed her eyes. 'And my sister? Why was she targeted for so long?' She glanced at Nav who nodded.

'Yes, Dad, and I was as much to blame for that.... I just got caught up in the frenzy of anti-Malhotra feeling. But I too would like to know why Cosima was such a threat.'

Iqbal hesitated. 'Because she was Arjun's daughter and he had taken my own daughter from me. So...if I couldn't have my daughter, then neither should he.'

Harpa felt sick. 'And her kidnapping earlier this year? Was that your people?'

Iqbal shook his head. 'No, and I have made extensive investigations within our circle but no one is admitting anything, and I think the threat must have come from outside.'

They all sat in silence for a time. 'Did you love my mom?'

'I was enchanted for a time. To my great regret, I was not strong enough to resist her charms.'

Harpa gave a humorless laugh. 'She has that effect.'

'I take it you are not close.'

'No, we are not. In fact, I don't plan on ever being the same room as her ever again.' Harpa's voice was getting higher now, angry, the rush of emotions an unstoppable torrent. She stood up and paced.

The three men in the room were silent as she stalked about the room. When finally she stood still, she looked at Iqbal. 'Arjun was my dad, even if he wasn't my father.'

Iqbal nodded. 'Understood. Look, Harpa, I do not expect anything from you except perhaps we can be friends.'

Harpa gazed at him, still conflicted. 'I don't know, Iqbal. I really don't.'

He smiled gently. 'Shall we try?'

She hesitated and then nodded. Iqbal's shoulders relaxed. 'Thank you. Now, as my guests, you will stay for lunch, yes?'

ON SATURDAY MORNING Cosima woke up late with the faintest hangover banging around her head. She wasn't a big drinker, but last night had been such a triumph, such a landmark day in her personal and professional life, that she threw caution to the wind. Of course, most of the drinking had occurred later, alone with Arlo, most of the champagne being sprayed all over her body and then licked off by him slowly until she was screaming his name. Then his huge, pumping cock had sent her into heaven, again and again, late into the night.

She slipped out of bed and into the shower, feeling the relief of being clean again after the hot night. Throwing on some shorts and a t-shirt, she wandered out into the living room to find Arlo had left her a message. *Going out to get fresh bagels, be back soon. I love you, A.*

She wondered how the rest of the hotel was coping with the sudden influx of customers. Today was the first day that the whole hotel was open for business and Cosima suddenly wondered at the wisdom of living above it; she hoped the manager they had hired was proficient and didn't keep bothering them with problems. The woman, Ellie, had been their first pick; college degree, experience, and a warm, efficient manner. Her references had been glowing, and Cosima liked her immensely.

Five minutes later, Arlo came through the door, grinning. 'Good morning, beauty.' He kissed her then showed her the bags. 'I got pre-filled ones because I was feeling lazy.'

'Good idea.' She slipped her arms around his waist. 'Today should be all about lazy.'

'I agree.'

They ate at the table next to the vast window that looked out over New Orleans, and Cosima told him about her concerns they might be living too close to work. She grinned while she was telling him but he nodded. 'Hey, I've been wondering about that too. Sweetheart, we talked about San Francisco a while back…what are your feelings on it now?'

Cosima took a bite of her bagel as she considered. 'As long as my wretched mother isn't still there,' she joked but then nodded. 'I like the idea that we can go anywhere, anytime now and I really would like to see where you grew up. And meet Margaret of course. Do you have any real family left?'

'A couple of cousins. One's in the music business; the other lives in Lima. You might meet Dash, though, he's a riot.'

'And you've already met all of my family. I wish you could have met my dad.'

'And I wish you could have met Mason. My brother would have adored you.'

She nudged his shoulder with her own. 'I guess if we want a bigger family, we're going to have to make our own.' She realized what she said and colored. 'Not that I mean…'

'It's something we should talk about,' Arlo said evenly. 'There's nothing I'd like better than to have kids with you but I get the sense your career comes first.'

She nodded. 'I'm not ready for them yet, that's a definite. But yeah, maybe, eventually.'

'And of course, there's the little matter of you marrying me.'

She grinned. 'I remember what you said to me the day you came to New Orleans.'

'That I was one hundred percent sure I was going to marry you?'

She nodded and laughed. 'So cocky.'

Arlo grinned. 'And yet so right. So, tell me, Cosima Malhotra, would you do me the honor of becoming my wife?'

HARPA WAS LOST in thought as they drove back to the hotel that afternoon. Lunch had been a pleasant affair, but the conversation was mostly led by Mikah talking to Iqbal about the art that hung on his walls. Harpa was grateful – yet again – for her lover's understanding and patience. Really there wasn't anything he wouldn't do for her, she realized. *Oh, how much I love you,* she thought now, looking at his handsome face, his ear-splitting smile as he chatted easily to Naveen. Her brother. She giggled, and the two men looked at her.

'I'm sorry,' she said, 'I think it just hit me. I have a brother as well as a sister.'

Naveen checked her cheek with his finger. 'You do. It's weird for me too, given our mutual family histories. So much blood and anger.'

Harpa nodded. 'But we can start to make up for it.'

'I'll drink to that.'

Back at the hotel, Harpa and Mikah arranged to meet Nav later for drinks, but as they headed back up to the room, Mikah turned to her. 'When we get back to the room, there's something I want you to do before we take a nap...or whatever we decide to do. He grinned wickedly, but his eyes were serious.

'What's that?'

'Your mother isn't the only one who can give interviews. Last night, at the opening, your sister gave a pretty lengthy interview to a journalist, and it's something else. Something special. You need to read it.'

In the room, he handed her his iPad, and she sat, a lump already forming in her throat. First, she looked at the pictures; Cosima looking radiant, her dark red dress hugging her curves, and the look of surprise when the new hotel name was unveiled. Harpa smiled; it had been so hard not to reveal the secret that Arlo had confided in her. She remembered that conversation clearly.

'I'm worried she'll think it's cheesy,' he had told her, and Harpa had laughed.

'It *is* cheesy, but the good kind. *You,* Arlo, are not cheesy and so Cos won't suspect a thing. And it is a beautiful name and a lovely tribute.'

Harpa flicked to the interview – at first, it was just about the hotel, but then the interviewer got personal...

· · ·

'So, obviously, we have to talk about your mother's interview...did you have any idea she would say the things she did?'

Cosima smiles at me, and I'm struck by the friendly manner with which she approaches a difficult subject. 'To be honest,' she says, without a hint of malice, 'I'm kind of used to my mother being vitriolic. The things she said about me? I could not care less. The people who know me, the people I love know who I am. No one else's opinion matters to me. What I cannot forgive is what she did to my beloved sister. What decent person does that?

'Have you spoken to your sister about it?'

She looks away from me and hesitates. 'Yes. She's hurt. Upset. Wouldn't you be?'

'What would you say to her if she was here, right now?'

Cosima Malhotra looks me steadily in the eye. 'I would tell her: Blood isn't a bond, love is a bond.'

HARPA'S EYES spilled over with tears, and she began to sob, all the tension of the past days flooding out. Mikah said nothing, just took the iPad from her and wrapped his arms around her.

'Is now an appropriate time, Harpa Malhotra, to tell you that I love you?'

Laughing and crying, she looked up into his eyes. 'Yes...I love you, Mikah Ray, so, so much.'

He kissed her, wiped his big thumbs over her cheeks to catch the tears. 'Well, good then,' he grinned. 'Now, go call your sister.'

COSIMA BLINKED AND SUDDENLY FLUSHED. 'Oh...you're really asking?'

Arlo laughed. 'I never wanted to do the one-knee thing; it's so dated. I thought I might just ask and catch you off guard. The odds are in my favor that way.'

She laughed. 'Well, in that case...I'll think about it.' Arlo groaned, going along with her joke. She leaned in and kissed him. 'Oh, alright, if I must.'

He grabbed her and started to tickle her mercilessly. 'I'm going to buy you the biggest, tackiest gumball ring in the world.'

Cosima giggled. 'Is there such a thing as an engagement cock-ring? Because I think you should have one of those.'

Arlo laughed and pulled her onto the floor, and they rolled around play-wrestling. Finally, laughing too hard to continue, he looked down at her. 'We're engaged.'

Cosima grinned. 'Yes, we are. How grown-up of us.'

He caught her mouth with his, tasting her sweet lips, caressing her tongue with his own. 'I think we need to celebrate.'

'I wonder how?'

'I wonder...' He got to his feet and pulled her up. 'Have we fucked in every room yet?'

'I think we have, but maybe we should start another circuit.'

'Good idea. *Oh darn it*,' Arlo sulked as her cell phone buzzed. Cosima looked at the i.d. then up at him.

'It's Harpa,' she suddenly looked nervous but answered the call anyway. 'Hey, Bubba, how are you?'

She listened as Harpa spoke, her eyes widening. 'Really? That's....I'm not sure how to feel about that, but it's not my....no....no, of course not. When are you...? Okay. Okay. No, of course, we'll come to you, I'll check with Arlo, but I'm sure...yeah.' She smiled suddenly, a bright beam of light on her face. 'Okay, honey. I love you. See you soon.'

She ended the call and put her phone down, sighing. 'So, Harpa... is in India.'

Arlo goggled at her. 'What?'

Cosima laughed, shaking her head. 'You are never going to believe what I have to tell you.'

A MONTH LATER...

. . .

'SO THE QUESTION REMAINS,' Harpa said, spooning the last of her gelato into her mouth as she and Cosima sat at the little table on the terrace. 'To meringue or not meringue.'

Cosima grinned. She and Arlo had been here in San Francisco for two weeks and she'd finally been able to spend some time with a vacationing Harpa. The two of them were having a ball, hitting every tourist trap in the city.

'Definitely not meringue and it's way too early to think about that. We haven't set a date yet.'

Harpa shrugged. 'Why wait? You and Arlo are practically married already.'

Cosima rolled her eyes. 'Cool your boots, Harp. Let's talk about what you're wearing tonight.'

Harpa smiled shyly. 'I have a beautiful sari that Iqbal sent me. Orange and gold. I think I might wear that.'

Cosima sighed. 'Lovely...you know, I think it's great you're communicating with him. It makes me hopeful for the future.'

'Our dad will always be our dad,' Harpa said hurriedly, and Cosima patted her hand.

'I know. But it can't hurt.'

Harpa studied her sister. 'You're a very forgiving person, Cos. I wish I were more like that. Like that woman Arlo used to date – she has you attacked, and you *go for coffee* with her.' She pulled a face and Cosima laughed.

'Once, Harp, I went for coffee with her once and only because she's with Nav now and I know it makes him happy. Anyway, I do have news...we're going to stay in Frisco a little longer than we said. Tal and Arlo have been talking; we're opening a West Coast office of the company.'

Harpa's eyes grew wide. 'Wow. Will you be the boss?'

Cosima grinned. 'Hell, no, it's still Tal's company and can you imagine me, a junior architect, being suddenly promoted above the colleagues who had been with him for years, just because I'm boning the major investor? Instant credibility destruction, no thanks.'

'So...' and Harpa grinned wickedly, 'Arlo's just your boss in the bedroom?'

'Hey, you better believe *I'm* the boss, sis.'

They both laughed then Cosima sighed. 'Can you believe this year? All that's happened?'

'Even for us, it's been a real doozy.' Harpa looked out over the Bay and shook her head. 'Incredible highs and seemingly bottomless lows. The worst was when you were gone. I'll take Mom being a fucking bitch over and over rather than that again.'

Cosima clinked her glass against her sister's. 'Cheers to that.' She checked her wristwatch. 'What time do we need to pick up Mikah?'

'Three...listen, I can do that then take him to our hotel. You go home and get ready, it's your engagement dinner after all. What are you wearing?'

'Very pale pink tunic dress. Skirt's way too short but what the hell?'

That's what I like to hear. The Malhotra girls slutting it up.' Harpa chuckled. They both got up and started back towards the car then, abruptly, Harpa stopped her sister and threw her arms around her.

'Thank you for being so understanding about Iqbal, and Nav, I know he's delighted that you're friends again. Not just that, thank you for bringing me up, for making me the person I am.'

Cosima hugged her fiercely. 'You made you the person you are, Harp.'

Arlo had been feeling antsy all day. It wasn't the party that evening; it wasn't even the pile of work on his desk. It was just...a feeling. It had started this morning after Cosima had gone to meet Harpa, a sense of, *God*, just dread. Was it because everything in their lives suddenly seemed settled and happy and right? Was he just being cynical, waiting for the other shoe to drop?

'Get your head out of your ass,' he muttered to himself. There was so much to do here, back in his office in San Francisco – it had seemed strange to him to come back here after all those months in

New Orleans. Margaret was delighted to have him back, and she and Cosima had immediately gotten along – so much so they would gang up to tease Arlo whenever they could.

He looked up as Margaret came to the door. 'Just to let you know, Jack Hampton's plane was delayed so he'll meet you at the restaurant this evening. Naveen is coming alone – thank God – and Cole and his new wife send their apologies.'

Arlo shrugged. 'I thought they may not come.' He'd invited his old friend as a way of beginning to rebuild their friendship after Sabine – he and Cole had met for drinks after work and said their peace to each other.

'I wouldn't take it personally; the baby is due any day,' Margaret said, sanguine. 'How's Cos, is she excited?'

Arlo smiled, his whole body relaxing at her name. 'Very.'

'Have you bought that girl a ring yet?'

Arlo chuckled. 'Believe it or not, she says she doesn't want one – doesn't want the appearance of being 'owned'. God, I love that girl.'

Margaret rolled her eyes. 'She's definitely *not* Sabine.'

'That she's not – although she tells me Sabine is a changed woman.'

'I'll reserve judgment on that if you don't mind. Anyway, everything that's urgent is done...why don't you go home and enjoy the afternoon?'

He smiled at his friend. 'You throwing me out?'

'Yes – and not just because I want to go home and get dressed.'

ON THE DRIVE back to his apartment, the feeling of dread seeped back into his bones, but he pushed it away. *Nothing was wrong, everything was fine.*

He forgot all his fears when he saw Cosima, wrapped in a towel, fresh from the shower, her long dark hair hanging in wet strands around her face. Scrubbed clean of make-up, she looked five years younger.

'What a shame you showered,' he murmured as he slid his arms around her waist, 'because I'm about to get you very, very dirty...'

Cosima chuckled as he pulled her towel from her then ran his tongue down her spine. 'Well, now, that's a nice idea...*oh dear god, Arlo...*'

He tumbled her to the carpet and kissed from her throat to her belly. Cosima wriggled with pleasure as he stripped quickly and hitched her legs around his hips and before long, they were moving together in a slow, leisurely motion. Arlo's thick cock drove into her rhythmically as they kissed, drinking each other in.

Afterward, they showered again and dressed. Arlo wore a dark gray suit that highlighted the salt and pepper hair at his temples, his dark green eyes. Cosima slipped into the pink dress she had bought. It was a loose fit and clouded around her body as she moved. Her caramel-colored legs were shown off by the pale color, and she strapped leather sandals on to complete the look.

'Gorgeous,' Arlo approved, and she twirled for him, before kissing him again. 'You kiss me like that, and we're going to get all mussed up again.'

Chuckling, Cosima steered him out of the bedroom. 'Come on, Don Juan, let's get going.'

AT THE RESTAURANT, they were greeted by their friends and family and Cosima hugged Jack and Mikah, kissed Harpa. 'Thank you for being here, it means the world.'

Naveen joined them a little while later. Seated next to Cosima, he leaned over to kiss her cheek.

'You look radiant, Sima, I'm very happy for you both.'

When Margaret and Tal and Jennifer from her office got there, they ordered wine and food and sat talking. Cosima looked around the table. *Everyone I love is here,* she thought and sighed happily. Arlo, at the opposite end of the table to her, grinned and mouthed *I love you* to her. She blew him a kiss and giggled. Jack, on her other side, was talking to Nav and Cosima could see the mistrust still in his eyes. *Old habits die hard,* she thought.

The food was extraordinary, the wine vintage and flowing and after dinner, Arlo stood to make a toast as the champagne was being poured into flutes and handed around.

'Friends, thanks for coming tonight to help celebrate with us. It means a great deal to both of us.' He paused and looked at Cosima. 'It's now just over a year that I sat in a restaurant on a tropical island in the Indian Ocean and looked up to see the most beautiful woman I had ever laid eyes on. Not just her obvious physical beauty, something shone – and still shines – from her – warmth, love, brilliance. I was lost the moment I saw her.'

'Cosima, my life began when I met you. Throughout this year you have been through so much, things that a lesser person would not have survived. You are my heroine, for all time, and I love you with every cell in my body, every breath in my lungs. Thank you for the honor you bestow upon me by promising to be my wife. I cannot begin to repay your gift, but I'll happily spend my whole life trying. Friends, please raise a glass to my beautiful fiancé. To Cosima.'

Everyone smiling raised their glasses towards a furiously blushing and tearful Cosima. 'To Cosima.'

She couldn't speak, couldn't express how she felt at that moment. Instead, she got up and went into Arlo's arms, and they kissed passionately, not caring who was watching. Their friends cheered and laughed.

During coffee, they all switched seats and Cos finally got to sit next to her sister. 'That sari is heavenly,' she said, nodding approvingly at the orange silk, decorated with a hand-stitched gold paisley design.

'Isn't it? I forgot how much I loved to wear a sari, so comfortable.' Harpa's dark hair was piled on her head and decorated with a *Matha Patti,* a head chain. Cosima smiled.

'You've inspired me...no meringue, I think I want to get married in traditional dress.'

'Perfect,' Harpa looked excited. 'Wow, can I help choose your sari?'

'Of course, you're my maid of honor. Listen...I was thinking...do you think if I asked Nav to give me away, he would?'

Harpa's smile faded. 'I think he would...but, Cos,' she lowered her voice, 'with the history....don't you think you should ask Jack? After all, he's been with us for years; he is part of our family.'

Cosima blinked. 'I hadn't even thought of that. Gosh, I feel bad now...perhaps that would be better.'

'Don't worry about it tonight,' her sister said, 'let's just enjoy this wonderful evening.'

AT ELEVEN P.M., they stood to leave. Walking out, Arlo and Cosima linked hands. 'Did you have a good time, baby?' She gazed up at him adoringly, and he grinned, brushing his lips against hers.

'A great time, sweetheart. We should get engaged more often.'

The restaurant led out onto the sidewalk and the night air was cool. Arlo had arranged limousines to take everyone back to their hotels, and as they said their goodbyes, Cosima hugged Jack.

'Thank you for coming, honey, it means so much to me.'

Jack smiled, his gaze intent on hers. 'My pleasure, Cos...always.'

The trash can across the street exploded. The noise shattered windows and caused everyone to panic.

Then the shooting started. A man, a pistol in his hand, fired rapidly at the group. The smoke from the trash can blinded them all as they tried to duck. Jack grabbed Cosima and pushed her into a limo; Mikah threw himself in front of Harpa. Arlo, shocked, watched from the ground as the limo with Cos and Jack inside screeched away from the scene. He felt relief – Cos was safe – but the shooting continued. Suddenly, Naveen, on the ground beside him, swore violently, and Arlo looked to where Mikah, on the ground, had been hit in the shoulder. Naveen was up then, ripping his concealed gun from his hip and shooting back at the attacker. Three pops then the shooting abruptly stopped.

Arlo scrambled to his feet to see the gunman lying in the road, his chest a mess of bloody holes, sucking air in. Arlo dropped to his feet. 'Who are you? Why have you done this?'

The gunman breathed in one last rattling breath and then his chest stopped moving, his eyes stared unseeingly.

'Fuck!' Arlo shouted then scooted back to his friends. Mikah sat against the building, his shoulder pouring blood. Harpa was beside herself, trying to call the emergency services.

Arlo took her phone from her and calmly dialed 911. After he had finished, he crouched down. 'Let me see, Mikah?'

Mikah moved his hand, and Arlo could see his blood pumping from the wound. 'Jesus.'

'It's not too bad,' Mikah said calmly, 'Could be a lot worse. Everyone else okay?'

Arlo checked everyone. Tal, Jennifer, and Margaret were shaken but physically okay, Nav had a cut on his forehead from dropping so quickly to the sidewalk, but he nodded when Arlo asked him if he was alright. 'Fine, Arlo. Harpa...sweetheart, it's okay now, he's dead.'

Harpa, by Mikah's side, looked shell-shocked. 'Where's Cos?'

'Jack got her into a car and got her away.'

Harpa sighed with relief. 'Thank God. Let's call him, tell him the danger's over.'

Arlo nodded and pulled out his cellphone. Jack didn't answer for a while, and Arlo began to get anxious. Finally, the call was picked up.

'Arlo! God, man...'

'Do you have Cos? I saw you get her in the car...tell me she's okay.'

Jack hesitated and in the second pause, Arlo knew. His heart dropped to the floor. He went back inside the restaurant so the others couldn't see his face. 'Jack...'

'She was hit, Arlo. She took a slug to the gut...I drove straight to the hospital but, man, it's bad...she's lost so much blood...'

'She's not dead,' Arlo almost screamed it down the phone, 'Cosima is *not* dead...'

'No. she's not dead, but it doesn't look good. Come to the hospital, now, Arlo, right *now*...' He gave Arlo the address and Arlo was out of the door. He grabbed Harpa on the street.

'We have to go to the hospital...Cos was hit.' He couldn't say any more; his terror making him numb.

Harpa shook her head wildly. 'No, no, Arlo...that's wrong, it's wrong, Jack got her in the car.'

'Not soon enough...'

Naveen stepped forward, his own face drawn. 'I'll drive you.'

Harpa went to find Mikah, the paramedics still attending to his shoulder. 'I really do advise that you let us take you to hospital, sir.'

Harpa took his hand. 'Yes, that's a good idea.' Mikah stared at her.

'What is it, what's wrong, baby?'

She looked at him, her eyes full of the deepest sorry.

'Cosima was hit. She was shot. *Oh my god,* Mikah...'

ARLO MET Jack at the reception and almost threw up when he saw Jack's shirt covered in blood. 'Is that?'

'It's not mine,' Jack said gently. He hugged Harpa. 'She's in surgery. Come; let's go to the relatives' room.'

Once there, Arlo let out a shaky breath. 'Right, from the beginning, what happened?'

'It must have happened as we got into the car. One minute she was okay then when we were in the car, I tried to talk to her, but then I noticed she was breathing hard. That's when I saw the blood. She got hit in the abdomen and Jesus, there was so much blood, and I think the bullet must have hit an artery. There was no exit wound. There's blood all over the car. I got her here as soon as possible, and they took her straight down to surgery. Arlo, Harpa...it doesn't look good. If that bullet tore her abdominal artery, she doesn't stand a chance.'

Harpa gave a strangled cry of anguish and Arlo sucked in a sharp breath. Jack grabbed his shoulder. 'I'm so sorry, man. What happened to the shooter?'

'Nav took him down.'

Jack looked up at the silent Indian standing in the doorway, noticing he looked wan and devastated. Nav nodded. 'I have a concealed weapons license. As soon as the shooting started...'

'You probably saved everyone else. The downside is we don't know who the killer...sorry, I mean, the *shooter* was targeting. Obviously one of you.'

'Of course we know,' Harpa exploded. 'It's him! It's the fucking psycho who took her....I knew he'd kill her in the end, *that cocksucking motherfucker*...' She was screaming now, raging in her grief.

'She's not dead,' Arlo said quietly, his voice cracking and broken, 'she's *not* dead.'

'The surgeon will come see us when he can,' Jack stood. 'I have to go brief the police on what happened.'

'Where's your driver?'

'With the police, he's pretty shaken up as you imagine. Stay strong, folks.' And he left the room.

Harpa and Arlo stared at each other. 'She'll come through, she has to.'

But they both knew it would take a miracle.

THE SURGEON PULLED his gloves off and went to scrub out. He hated cases like this when he couldn't give the family a definitive answer. The bullet had nicked Cosima Malhotra's abdominal artery, and it was weakened, possibly in danger of rupturing. A graft to help strengthen it had been applied – but if it ruptured, the young woman would bleed out in seconds.

God, the things we humans do to each other. The bullet had smashed into the young woman's belly but had not exited, bouncing around, causing major damage. He'd already had to remove her spleen, a kidney, and her liver was damaged. It would take a strong person to come through that.

The nurse came to see him, and he gave her aftercare instructions. 'I want her monitored closely, blood and saline in. Pain meds… because *if* she wakes, she's going to be in agony. I'll go see the family.'

WHEN THE SURGEON ENTERED, Arlo stood, his whole body feeling like ice. Harpa had gone with Mikah to get his wound looked at. Arlo was glad she wasn't able to see the doctor's solemn expression.

'She's stable for now. We removed the bullet and repaired what we could, but she is in a delicate situation. We'll monitor her closely, of course, but I'm sorry I can't give you better news.'

'Can we see her?'

'Later. She's in the ICU. I'll come back when we have more news, but there isn't much you can do here. I suggest only immediate family stay.'

Naveen told Arlo he would drive the others back to their hotels. 'I'll wait until you have news but if you, any of you, need me, just call. Tell Mikah I hope he's not in too much pain. I mean it, if you need anything…'

Arlo saw Jack's eyes following Naveen out of the room. Jack noticed his scrutiny and nodded. 'I don't trust that guy,' he said in a low voice to Arlo. 'Who knew we were going to be at that restaurant tonight?'

Arlo was silent for a moment. 'I won't believe it until there's proof, Jack. I don't think Naveen would do that to Cosima…certainly not to Harpa.'

'Don't be fooled. Once a killer, always a killer. I hear he didn't blink taking that shooter down…covering his tracks?'

'Jesus,' Arlo rubbed his eyes. 'Can we talk about that later? I just want to focus on Cos's recovery.'

'*If* she recovers.'

'Jack, Jesus…'

Jack sighed. 'Look, I'm going to check in with the investigation. Call me when things…change.'

And he was gone, and Arlo was alone. He sat down and dropped his head into his hands, feeling utterly bereft, and powerless. He didn't think it possible to feel worse than he had when Cos was abducted, but this was actual hell. She was dying, and he could not do a thing. He could pay the best surgeons in the world to come, that might be something, but the surgeons here were already amongst the best of them. When Mason, his brother, had been stabbed to death, the doctors here had worked on him for hours – even though Mason was already dead by the time he had reached the emergency room.

That was a scintilla, a glimmer of hope. While she was alive, she could breathe, she would fight. *Fight, Cos, fight.*

He sucked in a deep breath and got up, meaning to go find Harpa, but she came through the door at the same moment, followed by Mikah, his arm in a sling. He patted Arlo on the back with his good hand.

'Just a flesh wound, no biggie. How's Cos?'

'No more news yet.'

Harpa clenched her hands into fists. 'I can't bear this,' she said, her voice breaking. 'I thought we were good now, I thought everything would be fine. After everything we've been through...'

Arlo hesitated before he spoke. 'Harpa, I think you should know... Jack thinks Naveen might have had something to do with this.'

Both Harpa and Mikah, with some force, spoke up. 'No.'

'No way.'

'I agree. I think Jack, like the rest of us, is just reaching. He's hurting, looking for any explanation.'

It was Mikah who spoke next. 'Arlo, what you didn't see, while we were in India, something was forged then. Between Harpa and her father, but also between Harpa and Naveen. They found each other, truly. Naveen would never do anything to hurt Harpa, and I think he's very, very fond of Cosima. He really would not do this.'

Harpa smiled at her boyfriend gratefully and nodded in agreement.

Arlo sat back down. 'At the moment, all we know is that asshole on the street shot Cos. Keeping her alive is all that matters right now.'

· · ·

THEY SAT IN THE RELATIVES' room for hours. The night turned into day turned into evening. Naveen came back just as they returned from grabbing something to eat in the cafeteria. When Arlo told him there was no news, Naveen's body slumped. Harpa slipped her hand into his.

'Where have you been all day?'

Naveen smiled ruefully. 'Talking to the police. I went in to see them as no one had contacted me about shooting the guy...which I thought was weird. I asked about Jack's driver, if he'd made a statement, but no one knew anything. So I went in and talked to them for hours, handed in my gun and went through some formalities. They're not charging me with anything, so that's something, not that I wouldn't do it again. First time I've had my fingerprints taken.' He held up his hand to show her the ink on his fingertips and smiled.

'Have you been there all day?' she asked, her eyes widening. 'Did you come straight from the police station?'

He nodded. 'I wanted to do anything to help, I would have stayed longer. I asked around...Arlo, apparently the shooter was from New Orleans – and get this – he was in construction. Maybe he worked on the *L'Atelier Cosima*? If he did, he could have fixated on Cosima during construction. I tried to find out more, but they clammed up so I came straight here.'

Arlo looked at him gratefully. 'That means a lot, man. Thank for the information...I guess we'll find out about this guy over the next few days.'

Naveen nodded his thanks as the door opened and the surgeon, looking as exhausted as they did, came in. He nodded to them politely then turned to Arlo. 'We had to go in again and stabilize her artery, prevent further blood loss. She has a fever which is not unusual in gunshot wounds to the abdomen, but we think she's picked up slightly this afternoon. You can go sit with her if you'd like, but please, not too much physical contact. She's very susceptible to any infection or virus so use the antibacterial gel on your hands beforehand.'

'Doctor? Will she live? I hate to be blunt, but we all need to know.'

Harpa's voice wavered but didn't falter as she locked her gaze on the surgeon's face.

'I don't want to give you false hope, but I think she has a very good chance of recovery. She's young and healthy. Listen, gunshot wounds, especially close range, are nasty but survivable if they don't destroy organs or shred arteries. Cosima was lucky the bullet only nicked her abdominal artery and that she can live happily with one kidney and no spleen. It could have been a lot, lot worse.'

'Can we go see her now?' Harpa said before anyone else could speak.

The doctor smiled. 'Of course.'

COSIMA DRIFTED BACK INTO CONSCIOUSNESS, but the fog in her mind would not lift. She could remember nothing – only that a trash can had exploded, some firecrackers – had it been firecrackers? – something making a *pop pop* sound anyway then after that...

God, her whole body hurt. Where the hell was she and why was this tube in his mouth? She opened her eyes.

'Cos? Darling?'

Arlo. She tried to smile, but any movement was agony. She moved her eyes around to focus on him. He looked so tired. She tried to raise a hand to touch his face, but she was so weak. She felt his fingers interlink with his. *Try to squeeze them.* She watched his face as she tried to move her fingers and saw him smile. *Good.*

'Sweetheart, just fight, okay, just keep fighting. We're all here, and we love you so, so much.'

She managed to nod her head a little then winced as pain shot through her body.

'Cos?'

Harpa. A small hand was placed on her other arm. 'I love you, sis. Please be better.'

I'll try, I promise. But she couldn't say anything. A wave of weariness passed over her, and she closed her eyes again. She felt someone come into the room, murmur something then a needle was pushed into her arm, followed by a wave of cold medication being pumped into her. The morphine spread quickly, and she drifted back down into blackness, glad of the relief from the pain.

THREE A.M. COSIMA SLEPT, Arlo at her side, stroking the hair back from her forehead. Harpa and Mikah were asleep on the cot at the other end of the room, Naveen stood at the window, gazing out into the night.

'She looks a little better, don't you think?' Arlo said softly. 'There's more color in her cheeks.'

Naveen came over to the bed and studied her. He smiled at Arlo. 'I think so.' He reached down to squeeze her fingers then glanced back at Harpa and Mikah. 'Listen, Arlo, I don't know how to put this, but something struck me earlier when the doctor was talking – '

'Hey.'

They both turned at the sound of Jack's voice. He stood in the doorway, not taking his eyes from the young woman in the bed. 'How is she?'

They told him what the doctor had said. 'Good, that's good.' But Arlo found the expression in his eyes hard to read.

'What is it, Jack?'

Jack shook his head. 'Just...we have no leads. No one – ' and he glanced quickly at Nav – 'no one knows who could be behind this.'

'Perhaps,' Nav said, his voice cold; he hadn't missed the accusatory glance that Jack had thrown his way. 'Perhaps the shooter was working alone. Perhaps he was aiming for someone else but hit Cosima by mistake.'

'Who else would he be aiming for?' Jack retorted. 'He's clearly the man who abducted her, planned to kill her. He was just finishing the job.'

'How the hell did he know we'd be there tonight?'

'Maybe he followed Arlo or Cos or anyone of us.'

Arlo stopped them. 'Enough. You'll wake Cos again.'

Jack look startled. 'Again? She's been awake? That's great.'

Arlo nodded. 'But she needs to rest so if you two are going to argue, take it outside.'

'SORRY, ARLO,' said Naveen and turned away from them. As he did, he saw the Mikah was awake and looking at him. Almost imperceptibly, he nodded then looked at Jack then back to Naveen. Naveen's heart began to thump. Mikah was thinking the same thing as he was. There was someone else who had been close to Cosima, who had been in love with her, who'd had a knowledge of practically every move she had made in the last twenty years. Someone who might be driven to madness by the fact she was head over heels in love with Arlo. Someone who would kill her rather than lose her to another.

Mikah got up, making sure Harpa was still sleeping and nodded to Naveen. 'Let's go grab some coffee for these guys, Nav.'

They walked down three corridors before Mikah stopped Nav and stared at him. 'Close-range gunshot,' he said simply, and Nav nodded.

'Yeah.'

'Jesus Christ.'

Nav could not think of anything else to say. Nothing. Because it was unthinkable; it was disgusting that they even considered the worst. But both of the men knew in that instant that it must be true. There was only one possibility.

Jack had shot Cosima.

❧

JACK GRABBED *Cosima and wrenching open the door of the limo, pushed her into it, diving in behind her. 'Get going,' he shouted at the driver who pulled away immediately.*

Cosima whirled around. 'We have to go back...Arlo might be hurt, Harpa...'

'They're fine.' Jack's voice was cold and Cosima gaped at him.

'How do you know?'

She watched him throw his agency pistol to one side then reach inside his jacket pocket.

'Because the shooter wasn't aiming at anyone, he was just there to provide cover.I paid him to be there.'

Cosima shook her head. 'What are you talking about? Cover for what?'

Smiling now, he pulled out a pistol, with a long slim silencer attached to the muzzle. 'I'll tell Arlo that I got you in the car, that we drove away, but you were hit. So I rushed you to the hospital but you bled out, and they couldn't save you.'

Cosima went cold. 'No...no...what...Jack?'

He aimed the gun at her. 'You shouldn't have chosen him, Cosima.'

Cosima shook her head. 'No...no, Jack, please, don't...'

He moved quickly, pressing her back against the car seat, shoving the muzzle against her belly.

'I'm sorry, Cos, it has to be this way. I meant this to be over a long time ago, but I underestimated you. You were meant to die in my house, slowly, painfully. But I'll settle for killing you now.'

Cosima stared at him in horror. 'Your house? Oh god...it was you...you kidnapped me...you raped me...'

'Of course, it was, Cosima, my beautiful darling. Of course, it was. Don't you know I've loved forever...protected you, worshiped and yet you spread your legs for the nearest billionaire' He ground his mouth down on her, and she cried out, struggling. He smiled. 'I have been looking forward to this moment for a long time, Cos...' The muzzle of the gun was cold on her skin, her thin dress no barrier. Jack flicked off the safety and looked deep into her eyes.

'Goodbye, my beautiful Cosima...'

'No...please...'

But he shot her anyway, and the bullet slammed into her belly – lava-hot metal punching through her flesh. Cosima could only gasp – all the air was pushed from her lungs, and her ears rang from the gunshot. But nothing could compare to the indescribable pain. As her consciousness began to shut down, her muscles failed, and she slid down the seat.

The last thing she saw was Jack's face, smiling down on her bloody body as if it were the most beautiful thing he'd ever seen...

SHE HAD WOKEN UP. *Yes, the breathing tube was preventing her from speaking, from pointing her finger, telling the world that he, F.B.I. Agent Jack Hampton, son of New England billionaire, Ronald Hampton, had kidnapped, held captive and raped her and just when she thought she was safe, had shot her in cold blood at point-blank range.*

He would have to finish the job before she could say anything.

He stood in the doorway, watching Arlo stroke her lovely face. Getting her alone was the problem. He could offer to watch her, but then they would know it was him. He needed a window where they didn't know he was there. *Take out the security camera, that was no problem. Creep in and switch off the machines that monitored her, then pull the dressing from her wound and stab her repeatedly in and around the original wound. That way, it might delay them finding out how she died...*

No, that was ridiculous. He should have shot her in the heart, made sure she was dead. He had dismissed putting a bullet into her head; no way would he want to spoil the beauty of that face, even in death. *But to press the gun below her left breast...it would have ended her life instantly.*

You fucking idiot, he said to himself, *all because you wanted to see her suffer, see her bleed, see the understanding that he was the one ending her life, watch her in agonizing pain. Your fetish could bring about your downfall.*

Make a plan. Get your passport and cash ready. Kill her and flee the country. It wasn't as if you don't have enough money to disappear forever. But not without seeing Cosima die. She had to die; it wasn't acceptable that she live...

THE DOCTOR REMOVED the breathing tube the fourth day after the shooting. 'Now, this doesn't mean you can get up and start partying.

Take it very, very slowly. But, good work, Cosima. You have a lion heart.'

She smiled at him. 'Thank you, doctor.' Her voice was croaky, dry and Arlo held a cup of water to her lips.

'Drink. Baby.'

After a moment, after the doctor had gone, Arlo sat down next to her, kissing her lips gently. 'I love you. Thank you for fighting.'

She smiled, stroked the hair over his ears. 'I had a lot to fight for, the best reason to stay alive. I love you so much, Arlo, you didn't think a little thing like a bullet was going to keep me from you, did you?'

He chuckled, but his eyes were sorrowful. 'No way. There's way too much sex still to be had.'

She laughed, wincing slightly as the motion pulled on her tender muscles. 'Of course.' She sighed and pulled his lips down to hers.

After a while, after they'd stared at each other, not quite believing they'd made it through another crisis then Arlo, his eyes serious, spoke softly.

'Sweetheart...do you remember anything about the shooting at all?'

Cosima's face hardened 'Oh Arlo...I remember everything. *Everything.*'

JACK'S CHANCE came sooner than expected. He'd had the idea as he spent the previous evening drinking beer in his hotel room. He'd laughed out loud. Of course. So simple. A hypodermic syringe full of nothing but air. Stick it into one of Cosima's veins, cause an air embolism to her heart. *Boom. Dead.* Less bloody than he would have liked but he'd already had that pleasure.

He could be in South America before they discovered what killed her.

. . .

WHEN HE ARRIVED at the hospital, he went straight to her room. Arlo was there, but the others were M.I.A.

'Where is everyone?' Jack looked at Arlo, who looked worn out.

'Gone home for now. They're exhausted.'

'You look all done in, too. Look, man, I can sit with her for a couple of hours. Go grab some sleep.'

Arlo nodded slowly. 'That would be great.' He got up and smiled at the other man, but Jack noticed something in his eyes – wariness, doubt.

'Everything okay?'

Arlo nodded. 'Everything is fine. I'll be back before six.' He leaned over the sleeping Cosima and kissed her lips. 'I love you, chicken.'

Chicken? Jack worked to hide the sneer; could this dude be more of a sap? When Arlo had left, he went to work. Pulling the syringe from his pocket, he drew the plunger back, filling it with air.

He reached for her arm – and Cosima moved, quickly, her left arm coming up and he felt a sharp pain across his arm. Blood welled, and with a yelp, he dropped the syring, realizing she was holding a scalpel.

'You son of a bitch,' she hissed at him, 'did you think I wouldn't remember?'

Jack lunged for her – then felt something pressing against the back of his head, heard the click of a safety catch being flicked off.

'Don't even think about moving, motherfucker.' Arlo's voice was granite hard. 'Give me one reason to pull this trigger and I will.'

Jack, trained in combat, swerved around to try and knock the gun from Arlo's hand but the bigger man was ready. He brought his fist up under Jack's chin as Jack managed to knock the gun from his hand, and Jack screamed as he bit through his own tongue. The others were there then, Harpa darting in front of Cosima to protect her sister; Naveen, sleek and dangerous, his own gun back in his hand. Jack skittered to the far side of the room as Naveen took a shot, the bullet wide, smashing the large window behind him. Jack flinched down, outnumbered.

Arlo sneered at him. 'Did you think we wouldn't find out about the contractor? The one you bribed to shoot at us? Believe it or not, it was Sabine who saw you talking to him at the opening.'

Jack sneered at him and his gaze switched to Cosima, shielded by Harpa and Mikah. 'I loved you, Cosima, for years. I *worshiped* you. When I fired that bullet into your belly, you were finally mine, do you understand? I would do it again and again…'

Arlo, enraged, struck him savagely across the jaw with the butt of his gun. 'Shut your damn mouth, motherfucker.'

Jack laughed, spitting teeth and blood. 'Fuck you, Forrester, she was mine, and you took her away from me.'

Arlo roared at him. 'Cosima is not a possession for you to lay claim to, you asshole.' He stepped forward and pressed the muzzle of the gun against Jack's forehead.

'Stop!' Cosima screamed, and they all froze. Both Naveen and Arlo kept their guns trained on the cowering man. 'Look at him,' Cosima said, 'look at him cower. Harpa, help me up.'

Harpa looked concerned but then as Cosima began to get up, Arlo rushed to help her too.

On unsteady legs, Cosima walked to Jack and looked down at him. 'You bastard,' she began quietly. 'You filthy, despicable coward. Did you think you had any right to decide who I loved? That it would have made any difference? Even if I didn't love Arlo as much as I do, I could *never* love a coward like you. You're pathetic.'

Jack, smirking, got to his feet. 'I should have cut your throat the day I fucked you, little girl.'

Arlo growled, but Cosima stopped him. 'You're mistaken, Jack. Fucking is a wonderful, magical, thing between two people who love each other. You raped me, Jack. *Rape*. After you drugged me because that would mean I couldn't fight you off. You were scared *I* would fight you because that's the filthy coward you are.'

He lunged for her again but this time, Arlo was ready. With an almighty shove, he knocked Jack backward, jabbing him again and again, hard until Jack was backed against the open window.

With just one mighty push, Arlo could end this now…forever. He stepped towards Jack, who gave him a bloody grin.

'Do it, Forrester. Kill me. Because if you don't, I'll keep coming back and I swear, she *will* die.'

Arlo lunged but Naveen pulled him back.

'Arlo,' said Naveen, 'Let the police have him. He does not deserve a quick punishment. Let him rot in jail.'

Arlo, quivering with rage, didn't move, staring Jack down. It wasn't until he heard the police behind them, moving into the room, and felt Cosima's hand on his arm.

'Arlo, come to me. Leave this scum to get what he deserves.'

He turned and saw she was struggling to stand up; all the adrenaline had left her body. In one swift movement, he swept her into his arms and carried her out of the room and took her to the new room they'd arranged for her.

They had all set it up, of course. After Naveen and Mikah had talked to Arlo, he hadn't needed much persuasion to believe that Jack was Cosima's shooter. When she woke, after the tube was taken out, she'd confirmed it, telling him exactly what had happened. The horrific truth shocked him with its cruelty.

So cold blooded, so merciless. But Arlo finally felt there was something he could do – he'd arranged the police guard but used his influence to delay their arrival until they had dealt with Jack themselves. He wanted to kill Jack, rip him limb from limb, but knew they would never allow that.

But now, as they saw Jack being dragged past her room by the police, Arlo knew Cosima had been right to stop him pushing Jack out that window.

'You're not a killer,' she said, as if she could read his mind, 'There was no need to change who we are to beat him. It's over, Arlo.'

She winced as she shifted on the bed, and now the horror and trauma were over, she looked exhausted. Arlo sat on the side of the bed and touched her cheek.

'The minute,' he smiled at her, 'the minute you get out of here, we're getting married.'

Cosima smiled. 'That sounds good to me.'

He leaned in to kiss her, brushing his lips against hers 'Now I can believe you're safe at last.'

She wound her arms around his neck. 'You and me, Arlo Forrester, that's the only thing that matters. You, me, and our children...Turner and Hooch.'

Arlo burst out laughing and gathered her to him. 'To our family,' he said, kissing her passionately.

'To us, forever,' she whispered back, and they kissed until they could no longer breathe...

ABOUT THE AUTHOR

Mrs. Love writes about smart, sexy women and the hot alpha billionaires who love them. She has found her own happily ever after with her dream husband and adorable 6 and 2 year old kids. Currently, Michelle is hard at work on the next book in the series, and trying to stay off the Internet.

"Thank you for supporting an indie author. Anything you can do, whether it be writing a review, or even simply telling a fellow reader that you enjoyed this. Thanks

✸ Created with Vellum

Lightning Source UK Ltd.
Milton Keynes UK
UKHW021848231222
414411UK00005B/179